John Conroy Hutcheson

Bob Strong's Holidays

Third Edition

John Conroy Hutcheson

Bob Strong's Holidays
Third Edition

ISBN/EAN: 9783337320096

Printed in Europe, USA, Canada, Australia, Japan

Cover: Foto ©Andreas Hilbeck / pixelio.de

More available books at **www.hansebooks.com**

Bob Strong's Holidays

OR

ADRIFT IN THE CHANNEL

BY

JOHN C. HUTCHESON

Author of " The Wreck of the Nancy Bell, " "On Board the Esmeralda," etc., etc.

ILLUSTRATED BY JOHN B. GREENE

THIRD EDITION

LONDON

JARROLD & SONS, 10 AND 11, WARWICK LANE, E.C.

CONTENTS

CONTENTS.

LIST OF ILLUSTRATIONS

UNINVITED.—f. 20.

DICK TO THE RESCUE.—*p.* 42.

IN THE LION'S DEN.—*p.* 117.

BLOWN UP.—p. 194.

DRIFTING. — p. 258

GOOD SAMARITANS.—*p.* 270.

Bob Strong's Holidays;

OR

ADRIFT IN THE CHANNEL.

CHAPTER I.

DOWN THE LINE.

" Bob ! "

The noise of the train, however, drowned Nellie's voice ; besides which Master Bob was further prevented from hearing this appeal to him by reason of his head and shoulders being at that precise instant projected out of the window of the railway carriage, in utter defiance of the Company's byelaws to the contrary and of his sister's solicitous entreaties to the same effect poor Nellie, fearing, in her feminine anxiety, that the door would fly open unexpectedly, from the pressure of Bob's person, and precipitate her brother as suddenly out on the line.

"Bob!" she therefore repeated on finding her first summons disregarded, speaking in a louder key and giving a tug to his jacket the better to attract his attention "I say, Bob!"

"Hullo! What's the row?" shouted back the delinquent, hearing her at last, and wriggling himself in from the window like a snail withdrawing itself into its shell, turning round the while his face, slightly flushed with the exertion, to hers "Anything wrong, eh?"

Little Miss Nellie had not expected her timid and tentative conversational advances to be taken up in this downright fashion. Really she was only anxious for some one to sympathize with her and talk about the various objects of interest which came across her notice as they went along; so, Bob's abrupt address, coupled with his gruff tone of voice, fell on her enthusiasm like a wet blanket!

"Nothing's the matter," she replied timidly. "I only wanted to say how nice it is travelling like this."

"You don't mean to say you only called me in to tell me that?" said Bob, almost angrily. "I do think girls are the greatest geese in the world!"

With this dogmatic assertion, Master Bob shoved himself head and shoulders out of the window again, utterly ignoring poor Nellie's existence, much to her chagrin and dismay.

He was very rude, it must be confessed; but, some allowance should be made for him, all things considered.

In the first place, he was a boy just fresh from the rougher associations of school life; and, secondly, his inquiring mind was intently occupied in endeavouring to solve a series of mathematical problems that set all Euclid's laws at defiance, as the train whizzed on its way with a 'piff paff! pant pant!' of the great Juggernaut engine, the carriages rattling and jolting as they were dragged along at the tail of the mighty steam demon, swaying to and fro with a rhythmical movement of the wheels, in measured cadence of spondees and dactyls, as if singing to themselves the song of 'The Iron Road.'

Strange to say, this was a song of which, Bob noticed, the involuntary musicians never completed the second bar.

They re commenced all over again from the beginning, when they reached some particularly crucial point, where the 'click' or the 'clack' of the ever echoing 'click clacking' chorus proved too much for their overworked axles!

Bob, though, was not thinking of this music of the rail, or paying any attention to it, albeit it was distinct and plain to him; as, indeed, it is to all with ears attuned in harmony with this mystery of motion, and who choose to listen to it, just as there are 'sermons in stones' for those who care to read them!

No, all his energies were bent on finding out how it was that the straight hedgerows and square fields became round, while curving outlines grow straight in a moment, as if ruled with a measure, at the instant of their speeding by them; and, it occurred to him, or probably would have done so if he had given himself time for reflection, that the question of squaring the circle, which has perplexed the philosophers of all ages, was not so very difficult of solution after all looking at the matter out of the window of a railway carriage, that is!

Yes, so it really appeared; for, everything seemed 'at sixes and sevens,' the landscape having its middle distances and foreground irretrievably mixed up and its perspective gone mad, the country through which they passed resembling in this respect the land of topsyturveydom!

Bob's surprise, and wonder and delight, at all he saw became presently too great for him to remain silent any longer or to keep his thoughts to himself; so, affably forgetting his previous 'snub' to his sister when *she* had wished to express her feelings, he jerked in his head as suddenly as he had popped it out the moment before.

"I say, Nell, isn't it jolly?" he exclaimed in eager accents. "Just look out with me and see how funny everything seems!"

"Why, that was what I wanted to speak of a little while ago, only you wouldn't listen to me," replied Nellie, more good humouredly than Bob would have answered under the circumstances. "It is nice, though, I must say!"

"'Nice' indeed!" replied he indignantly. "It is just like a girl to say that. I call it 'jolly,' nothing more nor less. There's no other word to express what a fellow feels; and I do wonder, Nell, at your putting it so tamely!"

The girl laughed out merrily at this; and her smiling face,

wreathed in dimples, expressed as much animation as her brother could have wished.

"Do forgive me, Bob," she cried. "You are quite right. It is 'jolly,' the fields flying by, the trees all jumping up when you least expect them, the hills coming close, and everything! I have noticed them all; for, I've been looking out, too, Master Observer, and have eyes like you, old chappie!"

"Ah, but you haven't seen all that I have," said Bob, mollified by Nellie's sympathetic accord. "Look at those little woolly lambs, there, frisking about, with their sedate old mothers standing by, watching the train with wondering eyes "

"Yes, I see, I see," said she, interrupting him. "What great big eyes they have, to be sure! I declare, too, I can hear them 'baa' above all the noise of the railway!"

Just at that moment, the engine gave a shriek of its steam-whistle, which startled the sheep and lambkins, sending them scuttling over to the other end of the field, in company with a number of skittish heifers and young colts, which kicked up their heels in such a funny way that Bob and Nellie both burst out laughing together in concert, in one burst as it were.

"Hullo, Nellie, look!" presently exclaimed Bob, who was the first to recover himself. ' All the horses have not run away. There is one old fellow there, close to the line, who hasn't budged an inch."

"Perhaps he's the veteran of the field?" said Miss Nellie, rather poetically. "He's an old war horse, maybe, who has heard too many clanging trumpet calls and guns fired to be upset by the mere noise of an engine, which is only a bugbear to the ignorant."

"Bosh!" cried Bob, who did not believe much in senti-ment, 'flummery' he termed it. "Much more likely he's an old cart horse, and is as well accustomed to the row of the railroad as he is to the plough, and that's the reason he took no notice of us as we dashed by. See, he's only a little dot in the distance now."

They were running along at such a rate that every object which in turn presented itself, first ahead of the train, then alongside and then behind, became speedily but 'a dot in the distance,' to use Bob's words over again; the snugly secluded seats of the county gentry, the scattered villages and sparse red roofed farmhouses, with their outposts of hayricks and herds of cattle and other stock, that one moment appeared and the next disappeared from view behind masses of foliage, all dancing a wild Sir Roger de Coverley sort of country dance, 'down the valleys and over the hills,' until poor Nellie's eyes became quite dazed in watching them.

"Come over to the other window, Bob," she cried at length, turning round and getting up from her seat, suiting the action to the words, or at least trying to do so. " Let us cross over, Bob."

But, here a difficulty arose.

An old gentleman, who was the only other occupant of the carriage besides themselves, had dropped asleep over the newspaper which he had been reading, letting this slide down on his knees while he stretched out his legs right across the compartment, thus preventing Nellie from carrying out her intention.

"I can't get by," she whispered to Bob, who had also turned round from his window, and now giggled, grasping the situation. "I can't get by!"

"What, what?" ejaculated the old gentleman, suddenly waking up and clutching hold of his paper, as if afraid that some one was going to take it from him. "What, what did you say?"

Strangely enough, although Bob and his sister had been talking quite loudly before, nothing that they had said had roused their fellow passenger until now, when, probably, Nellie's hushed voice led to this very undesirable result just in the same way as a miller is said to sleep soundly amid all the clatter of the grinding wheels of his mill, his repose being only disturbed when the motion of the machinery stops. Poor Nellie hardly knew what to say now on the old gentleman, all at once, sitting bolt upright and addressing her so unexpectedly.

"I was only speaking to my brother," she managed to stammer out, after a little hesitating pause; "I am sorry to have awakened you, sir."

"Awakened me, eh?" snorted the old gentleman in a snappish tone. "Pooh, pooh, nonsense, girl! I wasn't a bit asleep. Heard every word you said. What was it you said, eh—what, what?"

Bob and Nellie exchanged a smile at this; for, the old gentleman had not merely nodded previously to their having determined to change windows, but his gold-rimmed spectacles had almost tumbled from his nose, the latter organ also having given audible vent to certain stentorian sounds uncommonly like snoring!

The old gentleman, however, did not appear conscious of all this evidence against his fancied wakefulness; and he blinked out so queerly from a pair of little black beady eyes, half hidden under a fringe of bushy white eyebrows, which made them look all the blacker from contrast, as he glared over his spectacles at the brother and sister, that Bob's giggle expanded into a fit of irrepressible merriment, although he endeavoured vainly to conceal his want of manners by burying his face in his pocket handkerchief.

Bob some time afterwards told Nellie in confidence that, just then, the old gentleman so comically resembled 'Blinkie,' a dissipated old tame jackdaw they had at home, in the way he cocked his head on one side, with his ruffled hair and all, that he couldn't have helped laughing, if he had died for it!

"Well?" said the old gentleman inquiringly, after a bit, tired apparently of waiting for an answer to his original question as to what Nellie had said as he woke up, gazing still fixedly at her, his beady black eyes twinkling and his bushy eyebrows bristling up like the whiskers of a cat when it is angry. "What did he say, eh?"

"He he was only speaking to me, sir," stammered poor Nellie, now trembling with fright. "He was only speaking to me, that's all."

"What, what?" jerked out her unappeased questioner. "Who is 'he'?"

"My brother Bob, sir," said she, still trembling and nervous; "my brother here, sir."

"Bob what?"

"Strong, sir," replied Nellie, a little less timidly, now that she saw the old gentleman was not going to eat her up quite "Robert Dugald Strong, sir."

"Humph!" he grunted out in reply to this. "He may be Strong by name and he looks strong by nature; but, really, he seems unusually weak in mind—he's a lunatic, I should think!"

But, there was a quaint, good humoured expression on his face that somewhat belied his abrupt manner and harsh, peremptory voice, which sounded like that of a bullying old barrister, cross examining a hesitating witness in court; so Nellie, therefore, gathered increased confidence as she caught his glance, to proceed with her explanation anent Master Bob.

"You're mistaken, sir, he isn't silly," she said. "He only wanted me to cross over to the other side of the carriage; and I told him I couldn't pass by you, sir. That was all, sir."

"Oh, indeed! Then I'm sure I beg your pardon," said the old gentleman very politely, drawing in his legs, so as to leave the road clear. "I don't see, though, what the young rascal has got to laugh at in that way, like a regular young yahoo!"

"Please, sir, pray excuse him," pleaded Nellie on behalf of Bob. "It is only a way he has got. He cannot help laughing for the life of him when the fit is on. He really does not mean to be rude, sir, I assure you."

"Doesn't he?" repeated the old gentleman, smiling in a knowing fashion as if he knew all about it. "Then, he's very unlike all the boys I have come across in my time; and they've been a goodish few, missy! But, there, get along with you both, and look out of the window to your heart's content. Take care, though, that neither you nor that young jackanapes don't manage to tumble out on the line, for I can't pick you up from here!"

Bob and Nellie took advantage at once of the permission granted them; but, soon, becoming tired of the monotonous sameness of the ever whirling landscape, turned back within the railway carriage, and, sitting down like ordinary and regular travellers accustomed by this time to all the sights and scenes of the road, the pair were presently engaged in earnest and confidential conversation with the now extremely affable old gentleman.

"Ah!" he exclaimed, breaking the ice on seeing the pair at last quiet. "So, your name is Strong, eh?"

"Yes, sir," answered Bob, acting as spokesman. "Father is a barrister, and he cannot get away from London yet for his holiday like us; and, of course, sir, my mother couldn't leave him alone, you know "

"No, of course not," agreed the old gentleman, "of course not."

"So, then," continued Bob, "they sent us on first; and we're going to the seaside, where we've never been before! Isn't it jolly?"

"Very jolly," responded the old gentleman smiling. "I wish I were as young as you are to enjoy it all over again, in spite of my having seen enough of the sea in my time."

"Are you a sailor, sir?" asked Nellie, chiming in. "I mean a sailor officer, sir, you know?"

"Yes, an old one, put on the shelf after fighting the battles of my country for many a long year!" said the old gentleman, with a deep sigh that almost made the carriage shake. He then extracted a silver snuff-box from his waistcoat pocket ; and taking a pinch, which seemed to relieve his feelings, added, as if to change the subject, " But, my young friends, you haven't told me where you are going "

" Why, to Portsmouth, to be sure, sir," said Bob promptly. " I thought you knew it ; and —"

" And we are to stop at aunt Polly's till papa and mamma come down," again interposed Miss Nellie, who had lost all her timidity and wanted to have her share in the talk. " Dear aunt Polly, how glad I shall be to see her again ! "

" Oh, indeed ! But, who is aunt Polly ? "

Really, he was a most inquisitive old gentleman !

The children, however, did not seem to notice this ; and went on to tell how their aunt Polly was the dearest aunt they believed any one ever had, and the nicest.

They informed the old gentleman, likewise, that this loved aunt of theirs came up to town every year regularly at Christmas-time to pay them a visit ; although they, on their part, had never been able to go down to see her until now, something or other having always happened to prevent their proceeding to the sea.

" Well, better late than never," said their fellow traveller, whom Bob and Nellie began to look upon now quite as an old acquaintance " I've no doubt you'll enjoy yourselves. But, my dears, you haven't mentioned your aunt's name her surname, I mean. Perhaps I might know her, for I'm an old resident of Portsmouth, or rather Southsea, which is just outside the lines and where all the best people live now."

" Mrs. Gilmour, sir," replied Nellie. " That's aunt Polly's name."

" What, Polly Gilmour, the widow of my old shipmate Ted Gilmour, who commanded the *Bucephalus* on the West Coast for two commissions and died of fever in the Bight of Benin ? Bless my soul, who'd have thought it ! "

" Yes, sir, Uncle Gilmour was in the Navy," put in Bob as

B

if to corroborate the surmise of the old gentleman. "He was Captain Gilmour, sir."

His questioner, though, appeared for the moment lost in thought, his mind evidently occupied with a flood of old memories connected with his lost friend and their life afloat together.

"Dear, dear, who'd have thought it!" he repeated, as if speaking to himself. Then, presently, recovering his composure with an effort, aided by another pinch of snuff, he said aloud "And so, you two children are poor Ted Gilmour's niece and nephew, eh?"

"Yes, sir," replied Bob and Nellie in one breath, answering the question. "You just ask auntie and see what she says, sir."

"I'm very glad to hear it," said the old gentleman, hastily pulling Nellie towards him and giving her a kiss, much to her astonishment, the action was so sudden; while he next proceeded to shake Bob by the hand until his arm ached. "I am very glad, very glad indeed to meet you; and, if it be any satisfaction to know, I may tell you that I go round to your aunt Polly's every evening to have a game of cribbage, summer and winter alike, except those three weeks when she goes to London to stop with your father, whose name, of course, I recollect now, although I did not think of that when you told it me awhile ago "

"Then, you're Captain Dresser?" interrupted Bob at this point, anxious to show that he had heard the old gentleman's name before and recognized it. "I'm sure you're Captain Dresser, sir."

"Yes, I'm Captain Dresser," replied that individual, smiling all over his face, his queer little beady black eyes twinkling more than ever with excitement, and his bushy eyebrows moving up and down. "Yes, I'm Captain Dresser—Jack Dresser, as your uncle and all my old shipmates in the service used to call me, much at *your* service, ha, ha, ha!"

Bob and Nellie could not help joining in with the old gentleman's laugh at his little joke, the Captain's "Ha, ha, ha!" was so cheery and catching.

It was a regular jolly "Ha, ha, ha!"

The trio, thereupon, got very confidential together, Bob telling how they had got their dog Rover with them, only he was travelling in the guard's van, being too big to be put in the box under the carriage, as he would have been if he'd been a little dog instead of a fine big black retriever, which he, Bob, was very glad to say he was, and 'not a mere lady's pet like a pug or a toy terrier;' while Nellie, in her turn, intimated her intention of making a collection of shells and seaweed when she got to the shore, which, she said, she longed to reach so as to 'see the sea,' that being the dearest wish of her heart.

The Captain, on his part, reciprocated these friendly advances in the heartiest way, expressing the strongest desire to make the acquaintance of Rover, as well as to take his fellow-travellers out in his yacht for a sail whenever the weather was fine enough; that is, if they promised to behave themselves properly, and always 'did what they were told and obeyed orders,' Captain Dresser saying, with an expressive wink that made him look more jackdaw-like than ever, that he invariably insisted, even in the presence of their 'dear aunt Polly,' on being 'captain of his own ship.'

They were in the midst of all these mutual confidences, the Captain chattering away like an old hen clucking round a pair of new found chicks, and Bob and Nellie full of glee and exuberant anticipations of all the coming fun they were going to have afloat and ashore; when, suddenly, the light of the further window of the railway carriage, opposite that near to which the trio were grouped in close confab, was obscured by a dark body pressing against it from without, as if some one was trying to gain admittance.

"Hallo!" cried the Captain. "What's that   who's there?"

But, before the old gentleman could rise from his seat, or

Bob and Nellie do anything save gape with astonishment, the window-sash was violently forced down; and, without a 'by your leave' or any word of warning, a strange uncouth figure, so it seemed to their startled gaze, came squeezing through the opening and fell on the floor of the carriage at their feet in a clumsy sprawl.

CHAPTER II.

A RUNAWAY.

NELLIE half sprang from her seat at this unexpected addition to their little party, uttering a scream of terror the while, as genuine as it was shrill and ear piercing.

She was a slight, delicate looking girl of twelve, with a shower of curls of the colour of light gold that rippled over her forehead and shoulders and down her back, reaching well nigh to her waist; and it seemed almost impossible that such a fairy like little creature could have uttered such a volume of sound.

However, she did it; and then, satisfied apparently with having exerted herself so far for the protection of all, Miss Nellie crouched down in the corner of the carriage behind Bob, who, two years her elder and a stoutly-built boy for his age, with short cropped hair of a tawnier tinge, stood up sturdily in front of his trembling little sister to defend her, if need be, as man fully as he could.

But, the gallant old Captain was first in the field, jump'ng forward with an agility of which neither Bob nor Nellie thought him capable; and, in an instant, he had clutched hold of the intruder.

"Who the dickens are you?" he cried, shaking him as a terrier would a rat. "What the dickens do you want here, confound you!"

"Please don't, ma aster," gasped out a half suffocated voice. "I be a'most shook to pieces!"

"Humph! 'when taken to be well shaken,' that's what doctors advise, eh?" said the Captain, somewhat sternly, although with a sly chuckle at his witty illustration of the phrase, as, with a strong muscular effort, he raised up the struggling figure he had clutched hold of and proceeded to inspect his capture a lanky woebegone lad, whose rugged garments and general appearance was by no means improved by the rough handling he had received in the grip of the old sailor, who, as he now put him on his feet and released him, repeated his original imperative inquiry, "Who the dickens are you and what do you want here?"

"Please, sir, I ain't a doing nothink," snivelled the lad, screwing his knuckles into his eyes, as if preparing to cry, each word being sandwiched between a sob and a sniff. "I ain't a doing nothink!"

"Doing nothing?" echoed the Captain indignantly, overcome apparently by the enormity of the culprit's offence. "Why, you young scoundrel, here you have been and gone and committed a burglary, breaking into a railway-carriage like this, besides nearly frightening the occupants to death; and, you call that nothing! Do you know, if I were on the Bench, I could sentence you to penal servitude?"

"Oh, pray don't, Captain Dresser, please!" cried out Bob and Nellie together, impressed with the terrible powers of the law as thus presented to their view and the extent of the Captain's authority. "He really did not mean any harm, poor fellow, I am sure he didn't!"

"Then what did he do it for?" asked the old gentleman snappishly, though both could see, from the merry twinkle in his eyes, that he was not in such a bad temper as he pretended to be. "What did he do it for? That's what I'd like to know!"

But, even the stranger lad, who had so unceremoniously intruded into the carriage, seemed to become aware as he confronted him that the Captain's 'bark was worse than his bite';

for, dropping his snivel and looking his questioner manfully in the face, he at once went on to tell who he was and explain the reasons for his unexpected appearance on the scene his earnest accents and honest outspokenness testifying to the truth of his statement in the opinion, not only of Bob and Nellie, but of the whilom grumpy old Captain as well.

The lad said that his name was Dick Allsop and that he belonged to Guildford, the last station the train had passed, and the only one at which it had stopped since leaving Waterloo. His father had died some years before, but his mother had lately got married again to a regular brute of a man, who behaved very badly to her and treated Dick, he averred, so cruelly, that he could not stand it any longer. That very morning, Dick stated, he had beaten him so unmercifully that he had suddenly determined to run away to sea; and this was the reason why he wanted to get to Portsmouth.

"But, you might have entered the carriage like a christian!" interposed the Captain at this point of the lad's story. "The train stopped long enough at Guildford for you to get in through the doorway, like any ordinary passenger, surely?"

"No, sir, I couldn't," answered the other. "I couldn't a done it."

"But why not?"

"Because, sir," snivelled the lad, "I didn't have no money, sir."

"Humph! you had no money, eh?"

"No, sir; nothing but thrippence a'penny, which mother gave me afore I started, when she wished me good bye. She was sorry as how she could give me nothing more; and so, I couldn't pay the fare, and had no ticket."

"So, my joker, you got on the train without one at all!" said the Captain, interrupting him. "Do you know that was really cheating the railway company?"

"I knows it, sir," replied Dick Allsop, who had better now be called by his own proper name, looking down as if ashamed of what he had done. "I knows it's wrong; but, sir, I couldn't help it, as there was no other way I seed of getting to Porchmouth."

"But, why didn't you jump into the carriage like a christian, as I said just now?" observed the Captain. "Eh?"

Dick seemed amused by this question.

"Does yer think, sir, the porters would ha' let me if they'd seed me a-trying it on?" said he, with a radiant grin that lit up his face, quite changing its expression. "Not if they knowed it!"

"Perhaps not," agreed the Captain, nonplussed by the lad's logic and knowledge of human nature. "No, I don't think they would."

"No, sir; that they wouldn't," exclaimed the runaway triumphantly, as if he knew all about that matter at any rate. "So, sir, I waits down by the side o' the line, where I lays hid, sir, without nobody a seeing me; and then, jist as the train was started and quite clear o' the station, a-going into the tunnel as ain't fur off, as yer know, sir——?"

"Yes, I know the line, my lad," said Captain Dresser. "I ought to!"

"Well, sir, there I climbs on by the buffers and coupling-chain of the guard's van to the step of the end carriage, and works myself along till I reaches this; when, drawing myself up and looking in through the wind y, I thought I would get in here, not seeing nobody but young ma aster and little missis in the corner "

"You didn't see me, eh?" questioned the Captain, with one of his quizzical chuckles. "You didn't see me, I'll wager."

"No, sir, or I wouldn't have tried it on," confessed Dick, with the most open candour. "I would a been afeard like."

"Lucky for you that you did, though," said Captain Dresser, his little black beady eyes blinking away furiously. "If you had got in anywhere and not come across such a good natured

old donkey as myself, you would have had the signal bell rung
to summon the guard, who would have stopped the train and
given you in custody at the next station for travelling without
a ticket! But what are you going to do now, eh?"

"Please, sir, I dunno," replied Dick, looking puzzled.

"Humph, that's a pretty state of things for an independent
young gentleman running away to sea!" said the Captain in a
quizzing tone. "Do you know you're not half out of the
scrape yet? You have got into the train all right; but, how are
you going to get out of it, eh tell me that, my lad?"

"I dunno, sir," again answered Dick laconically, still
seeming unmoved by the critical nature of his position "I
dunno, sir."

"Drat the boy!" exclaimed the Captain impatiently, stamp
ing his foot. "There you are again with your 'dunno!'
Why, when we arrive at Portsmouth, the collector will be ask
ing for your ticket; what will you say then, eh?"

"I thought, sir, of jumping cut afore the train got there,
sir," said Dick, scratching his head reflectively. "Aye, I did."

"Broke your neck, probably!" growled the old Captain.
"The best thing that could have happened to you, my lad."

Bob and Nellie meanwhile had been whispering together
and comparing notes apparently as to the state of their re
spective funds; for, Nellie had extracted a little leather purse
from some hidden receptacle in her dress, while Bob was
feeling in his pockets. Before either could speak, however,
Captain Dresser anticipated their evident intention.

"Suppose now I paid your fare for you?" he went on,
addressing Dick. "What would you say to that, eh?"

"Lor', sir, I'd be orful grateful, that I'd be, sir I would
indeed, sir," eagerly replied the lad in an outburst of thank
fulness; "and if, sir, I could work it out in any way so as to
repay the money, I'd be that glad yer wouldn't know me."

"Humph!" grunted the Captain again. "We'll see about
that."

Bob and Nelly, both of whom had been listening with intense interest to Dick's cross examination, were quite carried away with enthusiasm at this happy termination of the animated discussion that had gone on.

"Oh, you dear Captain," cried Nellie, hugging the old sailor rapturously. "You've just done what Bob and I wished."

"Have I?" said he smiling. "I don't see it, I'm sure."

"Yes, you have, you have," she replied impulsively. "Bob and I were just going to offer the same thing when you took the words out of our mouth."

"And the money out of my pocket, eh?" slyly added the Captain with a chuckle "eh, missy?"

"But we'd like to pay too," said Bob. "Let us go shares, sir."

"Not a bit of it," retorted the other, blinking away as he always appeared to do when excited. "That was only my joke. I will pay his fare for him when we get to Portsmouth; for, I like the pluck of the lad in climbing on to the train like that, and not being daunted by obstacles in carrying out a planned purpose. Can't say much for his looks though. He seems to me half starved."

The latter observation was uttered in an undertone, the Captain having too much delicacy to comment on Dick's appearance in his hearing. Miss Nellie, however, acted instantly on the suggestion, which gave it a practical turn.

"Are you hungry, poor boy," she asked Dick "very hungry?"

"No, miss," he answered humbly; "not pertick'ler, I be."

"But you could eat a sandwich, perhaps?" said she, opening a parcel which their mother had put up for the refreshment of Bob and herself during their journey. "Don't you think you could?"

Dick's eyes glistened.

"I'll try, miss," said he, trying to speak calmly; although

they could see that he was really almost ravenous at the sight of the food. "I thinks as how I could eat a mou'ful."

"Give him the lot, poor chap," cried the old Captain; but Nellie did not need this admonition, being in the very act of handing over the parcel of sandwiches to Dick even while the old sailor spoke. "There's no good in his making two bites of a cherry, as the saying goes."

"Eat these, my poor boy," cried Nellie. "Bob and I had buns at Waterloo before the train started, and we shan't want anything till we get to auntie's house."

"Fire away, old chap!" chimed in Bob, noticing that the lad hesitated a moment in accepting the proffered gift. "You needn't be afraid. Nellie and I are not hungry like you."

Bob's friendly tone, coupled with the sight of the tempting viands, at once removed any of Dick's lingering scruples; and, in another minute, he was gobbling up the sandwiches like a famished wolf his fellow travellers looking on with the utmost complacency and satisfaction at the rapidity with which he got rid of them, bolting the little squares of bread and meat one by one.

All this time, the engine was puffing and snorting away as if it had a bad attack of asthma, giving a fierce pull every now and then to the dragging carriages behind it; while, when the stalwart iron horse occasionally loitered in his paces or slackened speed in going round a sharp curve on the line, the coupling chains would rattle as they lost their tension and the buffers of the carriages behind, going faster for the moment than the engine, would come together with a bang that vibrated through the marrow bones of all!

The scenery altered, too, every instant along the route; the wooded heights around Guildford and Godalming and Hasle mere, which the poet Tennyson loved and where he lived and died, being succeeded by a stretch of level landscape, and this again by the steep bare hills encircling sleepy Peters-field.

Presently, a range of downs came in sight, curving away in
horse shoe fashion from right to left, on which were a series of
red-brick, detached structures, placed along the topmost ridge
at equal intervals apparently, until they were lost in the distance

As they approached these nearer, Miss Nellie's sharp eyes
noticed that on the landward side these brick piles were covered
with a slant of smoothly shaven green turf that contrasted
conspicuously with the chalky surface of the sloping ridge.

"What funny things those are!" said she, pointing these out
to Bob. "Are they houses, or tombs, or what?"

"Where, what do you mean?" asked the Captain, turning
round from his contemplation of Dick, who, having finished
the packet of sandwiches, was now carefully searching the
piece of newspaper in which they had been wrapped up on
the chance of there being a few stray crumbs left. "Why,
hullo, here we are close to our destination! Those 'funny
things,' as you style them, missy, are the Portsdown forts—
you are not far out though, in your estimate of their appearance, for they're called 'Palmerston's Follies' by the political
wags here."

"Are we near Portsmouth then?" said Nellie, peering out
anxiously. "I don't see anything!"

"Oh yes, missy, quite near," replied the Captain, also look
ing out of the window. "There s Havant just in front. Don't
you smell the sea?"

"Yes, Captain, yes, I do! Yes, I do!" cried Bob and Nellie
together, clapping their hands. "Isn't it nice! Isn't it jolly!"—
Bob, it may be taken for granted, using the latter term of
approbation; Nellie adding on her own private account
another "Ah, how nice!"

"Well, that's a matter of opinion," said Captain Dresser
dryly, his experiences of the fickle element not having, per
haps, always been pleasant ones; but, before he could explain
this, the train, with a piercing shriek of warning from the
steam whistle of the engine, glided into the station.

"Hav 'nt ! Hav—'nt !" shouted the porters with lungs of brass and voices of leather or gutta percha. "Hav 'nt ! Hav 'nt ! '

"That's just what this boy will say when the g 'ard asks him presently for his ticket, or the money for his fare," said the Captain, with his comical chuckle and merry twinkle of his bird like eyes, pointing to Dick as the ticket collector banged open the door of the carriage as if trying to wrench it off its hinges and held out his hand. " He haven't got his ticket. Hav n't, you see, my dears ! Ha ha ha."

CHAPTER III.

THE ticket collector appeared puzzled for the moment, espe cially on noticing a poor, ragged fellow like Dick travelling in a first class compartment 'in company with gentlefolks,' as he thought to himself; but, at the instant this reflection passed through his mind, he recognized the Captain as an old and regular passenger on the line, besides being one from whom he had received many a 'tip,' so he at once touched his cap, responding with a grin of sympathy to the Captain's cheery laugh, as if he thoroughly entered into the joke.

"Oh, haven't he, sir?" said he, the ungrammatical phrase dropping more naturally from his rustic tongue; "then he'll have to get 'un sharp, or pay the fare, sir."

"Never mind about that, my man, I'll pay for his ticket, for he's travelling with me," replied the old sailor as he fumbled in his pockets, shoving his hand first in one and then in the other; producing, at last, a number of gold and silver coins, mixed up with coppers, a bunch of keys, a clasp-knife, and his snuff box, which somehow or other he had put back in the wrong place. "How much is it?"

"Where from, sir?" inquired the man, reaching out his hand for Bob and Nellie's tickets. "Far up the line, sir?"

"No, only from Guildford," replied the Captain. "That's

only half way from London; but there's half a sovereign, and you may keep the change for yourself."

"Thank you, sir," said the collector, touching his cap again and taking the coin. He still lingered, however, as if wanting something more but hesitated to ask for it.

"Well?" ejaculated the Captain impatiently. "What is it, my man?"

"Your ticket, sir," said the man deferentially. "You forgot to give it me, sir."

"Zounds!" cried the other, blinking away furiously and moving his eyebrows up and down as he searched vainly in all his pockets, finally discovering that he held the missing ticket in his fist all the while! "I declare I forgot all about it. You see I was ready for you, though, eh?"

"All right, sir, good day," said the man; receiving the ticket and shutting the carriage door gently, with a bow and a smile and another touch of his cap; and, the next moment, with another sharp unearthly shriek of the steam whistle similar to that which had heralded its entrance into Havant station, the train, giving a joggle and a jerk as it got under way, was speeding along again, across the rattling bridges that spanned the moats of the fortifications and through the Portsea lines, to the terminus beyond at Landport.

"Here we are, children," exclaimed the Captain, on its pulling up at the journey's end. "Here we are at last!"

"And is this Portsmouth?" inquired Nellie. But, she need not have asked the question; for, as she looked down the platform she cried out excitedly in the same breath— "Why, there's aunt Polly! There's aunt Polly!"

"Let me look, let me look," said Bob, trying to squeeze in between Nellie and the Captain, who was fumbling at the handle of the door, endeavouring to open it. "I can't see her, Nell! Where is she?"

"Hold on, can't you!" grumbled the old sailor, angry with the door for not yielding at once to his efforts. "If you wait a moment you'll be able to see your 'aunt Polly' and everybody else to your heart's content; that is, as soon as we can get out on to the platform. Bother take the door, how it sticks!"

With this exclamation, muttered in a hoarse, stifled voice, by reason of his half stooping position, the Captain put his knee against the obnoxious door; and this, giving way to his shove, unexpectedly, nearly precipitated him into the arms of Mrs. Gilmour, the aunt of our hero and heroine, who had recognized little Nellie's face at the window and advanced to the side of the carriage, without his perceiving her approach.

"Dear me, Captain Dresser " she cried with a laugh, just catching him from falling on his face. "I've no doubt you are very glad to say me again, but you needn't be quite so demonstrative in public."

The Captain rose up, looking very red and confused.

"I'm sure I beg your pardon, ma'am," said he, bowing and laughing, too, as he recovered himself; "but those porters slam and jam the doors so, that they never will open properly when you want to get out quickly!"

His further excuses, however, were cut short by Nellie springing out of the carriage before he could utter another word.

"Oh, aunt Polly!" she exclaimed, hugging the smiling lady, who was a plump merry looking little body, with dark wavy hair and large, lustrous, almond shaped eyes, which, strange to say, were of an intense violet blue, presenting a curious contrast. "You dear auntie Polly! How glad I am to see you again ."

"So am I, me dearie, to say you," replied the other, with the slightest wee bit of a brogue, aunt Polly having been born in the North of Ireland, where blue eyes with black hair and brogues are common; "an' Bob, too, the darlint! How are you, me boy!"

"All right, auntie, right as a jiffy," said he brightly, greeting her with like effusion to his sister. "Really, I don't know

when I was so glad as I am to come down here to the sea
and see you. Hullo, though, I'm forgetting about Rover!"

With these words, Master Bob darted down the platform to
the guard's van at the end of the train, with Miss Nellie
cantering after him; both leaving their newly-met aunt as
unceremoniously as the Captain had tumbled against her on
emerging from the carriage the moment before!

However, Mrs. Gilmour did not appear to mind this, only
exchanging a smile with the old sailor, who of course
remained beside her; while Dick, as if anxious to make some
return for the kindness shown him, had started taking the
children's traps out of the train without waiting for any one's
orders.

As for the Captain, he had no luggage beyond the queer-
looking malacca walking-stick called a 'Penang lawyer' which
he held in his hand, never troubling himself with 'stray
dunnage,' as he said, when travelling by railway.

Bob and Nellie were presently seen in the distance, in close
colloquy with the guard, who, after a bit, lugged out from his
van, with much deliberation of movement and 'gingerliness'
of manner, a huge black retriever, who apparently did not wish
just then to issue forth from his retreat.

No sooner, however, had the imprisoned animal once more
touched the firm ground of the platform with his four paws,
than, carried away with delight at being able to stand again
on something that wasn't moving, he suddenly wrenched himself free from the guard and began plunging about in a mad
gambol around.

"Come here, Rover!" cried Bob. "Come here, Rover!"
echoed Nellie, alike in vain; for, although Rover approached
and jumped up on each in turn in expression of his pleasure
at seeing them, he would dart away the next instant out of
reach, evidently afraid lest the chain should be taken hold of
and he be boxed up again in purgatory. He would not attend
to any "Come here, sir!"

C

"He's too artful to be caught, sir," said the guard, laughing at the dog's antics. "He's too knowing by half."

"Oh, he'll come along fast enough after me," answered Bob with some reserve of manner, thinking it rather beneath his dignity, as well as unjust to Rover, to bandy words about the latter's disobedience of orders; and so, he walked on up the platform, whistling as he went and followed by Nellie, towards where aunt Polly and the Captain were chatting, the old sailor explaining to Mrs. Gilmour how Dick's acquaintance had been made, she having been much impressed by his civil and attentive demeanour, if not by his appearance.

"Come on!" shouted Bob between his whistles, as he got nearer; Nellie, close behind him, likewise whistling and repeating his cry, "Come on, Rover!"

Rover came on; but, not altogether in the way his young master and mistress wished.

Galloping now in front, now in rear of the two, and then prancing towards them sideways, but always out of reach, he whirled his heavy chain about like a lasso, to the danger of everybody around; many of the passengers being still on the platform looking after their belongings or waiting for cabs, most of the vehicles that had been drawn up on the cab rank having already driven off loaded.

"Do catch hold of him, Bob!" cried poor Nellie in accents of alarm. "He'll trip up somebody."

Rover seemed to hear and understand what she said; and, as if anxious to oblige her, at once twirled his clattering chain round the legs of a fat old lady, who, with her arms full of a number of parcels, was waiting for one of the porters to extract yet more from the carriage in which she had come down.

"Look out, ma'am!" said the Captain, seeing what was coming. "Keep clear of the dog, ma'am, or he'll foul your hawse ."

But, he was too late for the warning to be of any use; for, at the same instant, the old lady was whirled violently round and round like a teetotum and fell to the ground, uttering the while a series of wild shrieks, coupled with the smothered exclamation "My good gracious!"

"I thought so!" ejaculated the old sailor as he hastened up to her rescue, and, with the aid of the porter, succeeded in placing her on her feet again; while Nellie and Bob set to work collecting her parcels which were scattered in every direction. "I hope you are not hurt, madam," Captain Dresser added when the lady was, as he expressed it, 'all a taunto' once more. "I hope you are not hurt!"

However, she did not pay any attention to the polite inquiry, displaying more solicitude for her portable property than her person.

"Who's to pay for my 'eggs, I'd like to know?" was all she said. "I s'pose they be all bruck to pieces!"

She evidently alluded to the largest of her parcels, which still lay close to her on the platform, neither Bob nor Nellie having yet reached this to pick it up; for, a thick yellow fluid was oozing out from the wrappings, plainly betokening the nature of its fragile contents and their fate.

"Oh, never mind your eggs, ma'am," cried the Captain impatiently. "We'll reimburse you for their loss, as the dog has caused the mischief. I was thinking of your bones!"

"Drat my bones and the dog, too!" said the old lady with equal heat. "One doesn't get noo laid 'eggs every day, I'd 'ave yer to know, sir, and I was a taking these a puppose for my darter, which I brought all the way now from Gi'ford only to 'ave 'em bruck at last!"

"Never mind, never mind," replied the Captain soothingly; and on Mrs. Gilmour at the same time telling her that she kept fowls and would send her some more fresh eggs the very next morning, to replace those broken, if she would give her address, the old lady was finally pacified.

She went off presently, with all her remaining parcels, in a cab, which the Captain insisted on paying for; the good dame beaming with satisfaction and looking as if she thought she had made rather a good thing than not by the mishap!

Meanwhile, Bob and Nellie had to interrupt their task of parcel collecting to go after the truant Rover, who, not satisfied with the damage he had already done, was in active pursuit of the traffic manager's favourite cat, right through the station.

The roving delinquent ultimately 'treed' his prey in one of the waiting rooms, where poor pussy sought refuge on the mantelpiece, knocking down a glass water bottle and tumbler in jumping thither out of the reach of the frantic Rover, who scared half to death the occupants of the room as he dashed in, all in full cry!

Then a most delightful concerted duet ensued.

"Mia ow, phoo, phit, phiz!" screamed pussy with all the varied expression of which the cat language is capable, running up the gamut into the treble and dying off in a wailing demi semi quaver. "Mia o w!"

"Bow, wow, wuff!" chanted Rover, singing his portion of the refrain in deep bass notes that produced a hollow echo through the waiting-room, making the noise seem to proceed from twenty dogs instead of one. "Wough!"

Nor was Rover long content merely to take part in a musical performance only.

Bent on more active hostilities, he jumped up at the angry cat in her retreat on the mantelpiece standing up on his hind legs for the purpose; and then, being only able to sniff near enough for puss to slap his face energetically with her paws right and left with a sharp 'smick smack,' Rover uttering an agonized howl that came in at the end of the chorus and must have been heard all over the station.

A catastrophe was avoided, just in time, by Bob and Nellie appearing on the scene of action; when, catching hold of the end of Rover's chain, they bore him away captive again to where their aunt and the Captain were waiting and wondering at their long delay.

Nemesis followed behind the trio in the shape of one of the railway police.

He came in the ostensible interests of the hunted cat and damaged property belonging to the waiting room; but the elders of the party regarded him to be more intent on obtaining 'hush money,' wherewith to blot out Rover's misdeeds and line his own pockets at the same time.

"Here's a pretty to do, children," cried the Captain, taking this view of the matter and slipping a shilling into the man's hand to avoid any unnecessary explanations. "That dog of yours is like a wild elephant in an Indian jungle!"

"He's a fine dorg," observed the railway policeman parenthetically, pacified by the coin he had received and willing on the strength of it to forget alike the onslaught on pussy and the broken glass. "Finest dorg I ever seed for a retriever, sir."

"Ah, handsome is as handsome does!" replied the Captain sententiously. "Dogs, like children, ought to be taught to behave themselves."

Nellie, however, did not like this sort of slur on Rover's character.

"Oh! Captain Dresser," she exclaimed. "It was only his playfulness on getting out of confinement."

"Humph!" ejaculated the old sailor "playfulness, eh? A playful dog like that once bit me playfully in the calf of the leg, stopping all my play for a fortnight!"

"Oh, Rover wouldn't do that," said Bob "No, not he!"

"Wouldn't he? I'd be sorry to give him the chance," answered the other with a laugh, as he assisted Mrs. Gilmour into an open fly, into which the children's luggage had been already put by the attentive Dick. "There'd be precious little of me left, I'm afraid, if he once tackled me!"

Nellie and Bob then got into the fly, the Captain following them on their aunt's pressing invitation to escort them all down to her house on the south parade; while Dick, after having, with the help of the cabman, lifted Rover, who behaved like a lamb during the operation, on to the box-seat, where he was wedged in securely between the trunks and the driver's legs, climbed up himself and away they all started 'packed as tightly as herrings in a barrel,' to use the Captain's expression.

In the evening, after dinner, the whole party went down to the shore, where Bob and Nellie made their first acquaintance with the sea; a distant view of which they had a glimpse of previously from the balcony of their aunt's house on the parade.

Both were in ecstasies of delight as they gazed out on the undulating expanse of blue water, with the tiny little wavelets rippling up to their feet caressingly, as if inviting them to wade in over the glittering pebbles of the beach that glistened like jewels where wetted by the tide.

"Jolly, isn't it?" cried Bob enthusiastically. "Don't it make a noise though!"

"Not a noise," said Nellie, shocked at his unromantic description. "The waves seem to say 'Hush!' and speak, to me, as softly as if they wanted to send me to sleep!"

"Bravo, young lady!" put in the Captain, overhearing her remark. "'Rocked in the cradle of the deep,' as the old song runs, eh? Though I've almost forgotten all my Greek knocking about the world, or rather had it knocked out of me in a midshipmen's mess, if I recollect aright, old Homer describes the noise of the waves nearly in your own words, my dear. His term for it is πολυφλοισβοιο θαλασσης the 'murmuring of the many voiced sea!' Grand, isn't it; grand, eh? But, let us walk round the castle, and then you will see and hear it better."

They accompanied him, accordingly, around the sloping rampart; Mrs. Gilmour walking by the side of the old sailor, while Bob and Nellie lingered behind with Dick.

On their way round the castle, Master Bob occasionally pitched in a piece of stick for Rover to fetch out of the sea, which the energetic dog did with the utmost gusto; barking with glee as he dashed into the water and coming out sedately with his coat all dripping, to deposit the stick at his master's feet, with a shake that sent a shower of drops like rain all over them, making them laugh in glee as great as his.

The stragglers presently came up with the seniors of the party who had seated themselves on a little ledge of the wall on the highest point of the glacis at the back of the old forti fication, from whence away to the west the sun could be seen setting in a glory of crimson and gold behind the dockyard, with the masts of the ships standing out in red relief, as if on fire.

In front were the purple hills of the Isle of Wight, with the white terraced Ryde lying in between, its houses lit up likewise by the rays of the sunset, and their windows all aflame; and, under their feet, stretching away to where it met the hills opposite and to the harbour's mouth and Haslar breakwater on the right, with the now twinkling Nab light on the extreme left, was the dancing, murmuring, restless sea, its hue varying every instant, from the rich crimson and gold it reflected from the western horizon to the darker shades of evening that came creeping up steadily from the eastward, blotting out by degrees its previous bright tones.

Two or three merchant ships were anchored at Spithead; but there was not a single sail moving in sight.

All was still; and, as if in harmony with the scene, the Captain and Mrs. Gilmour sat in silent contemplation of the sight before them, neither uttering a word.

The children, however, were not quiet long.

"Hi, Rover, fetch it, good dog." cried out Bob presently, pitching the stick into the water that laved the base of the sloping rampart. "Fetch it out, sir; fetch it."

Rover raced, slipping and sliding, down the slope, plunging in with an impetus that sent him souse in head and ears under the surface; but, he soon re appeared to view and, swimming out to where the stick floated, gripped it valiantly and made his way back to the shore, holding it in his mouth crosswise.

Now, however, poor Rover experienced more trouble in

climbing out than he had probably anticipated; for, it being deep water at the foot of the ramparts and the stones being slippery, as the animal got his fore paws on the stonework and tried to raise his hind legs, back he would slip again into the sea.

"Poor fellow!" said Bob. "Why, he can't get up. I will go and help him."

So saying, he began to clamber down the slope.

"Stop, boy, stop!" cried the Captain excitedly. "You will fall in!"

"Come back, Bob, come back!" screamed Nellie and her aunt together. "Come back!"

But, hardly able to keep his footing, it was out of Bob's power either to arrest his rapid descent of the downward slope or to retrace his steps.

The very cries of warning, indeed, of those above brought about the result they sought to prevent; for, looking up and waving his hand to reassure them, Bob all at once lost his footing, rolling over and plunging into the water right on top of Rover, his yell of dismay being echoed by a howl of pain from the dog.

CHAPTER IV

DICK TO THE RESCUE.

"Gracious heavens! The boy will be drowned!" exclaimed Mrs. Gilmour, wringing her hands frantically and rushing forward at once; while Nellie, equally excited, burst into tears, clinging to her aunt's side. "Oh, what shall I say to his mother? He's lost; he's lost!"

"No, he isn't not a bit of it; no more drowned than I am," cried the Captain, laying his hand on Mrs. Gilmour's arm, and putting both her and Nellie back, to prevent any rash impulse on their part. "You just keep as cool as the young rascal must be now! I'll fish him out in another minute, if you'll leave me alone; and, he'll be none the worse, barring a wetting."

With these words, the spry old gentleman, who was more active than many a younger man, began making his way cautiously down the treacherous slope of the rampart, aided by his trusty malacca cane, poking his stick between the niches of the stonework to act as a stay, and so prevent his slipping on too fast.

But, quick as he was in his movements, hardly had he made a dozen sliding steps down the decline, the action of the whole scene being almost instantaneous, when he felt, rather than saw, some one else glide swiftly past him still more expeditiously; and then, there was another heavy plunge in the water below, where Bob and Rover were struggling for dear life.

"Bless my soul!" ejaculated the Captain, halting abruptly with the assistance of his sheet anchor, the malacca cane, as he half turned round. "The woman's never such a fool!"

He thought it was Mrs. Gilmour.

But, he was mistaken.

Dick had anticipated them both.

Bob's unlucky slip and cry of alarm as he fell into the sea, his aunt's exclamation of terror, the Captain's movement to the rescue, and the grateful Dick's perilous jump, for it was almost a leap from the top of the castle wall, were all, as has been already pointed out, the work of a moment; the chain of incidents taking much longer to describe than to happen.

So, there, before you could cry 'Jack Robinson,' as the Captain afterwards said, two boys, instead of one, were struggling with the dog in the water; and of all these three, to heighten the excitement of the scene, Rover alone was able to swim!

Bob, of course, had plunged in unwittingly, while Dick's only thought was to help one from whom he had received such unexpected kindness; the lad not having reflected for an instant on the danger of the task he was undertaking.

Now, therefore, although on reaching the water the grateful boy succeeded in carrying out his object of catching hold of Bob, both immediately sank under the surface.

They came up the next moment locked together, spluttering and splattering for breath and holding up their hands for aid, an action which naturally sent them down again; the tide meanwhile sweeping them away from the shore.

Rover was master of the situation that is, he and the Captain, who by this time had scrambled down to the last ledge of the rampart, and took in the position of affairs at a glance.

"Hi, Rover, good dog, fetch them out!" cried the old

sailor, at the same moment throwing off his coat and preparing to go into the sea, too, if need be. "Fetch 'em out!"

But, there was no necessity for this appeal to Rover, who did not require any orders or directions as to his duty

The dog, like the Captain, was quite aware of the perilous position of his young master, and had already determined in his own mind what was best to be done under such circumstances.

Master Bob having come down flop on top of him as he was trying to clamber out, had in the first instance somewhat obscured his faculties; and the subsequent appearance of Dick on the scene, as he was just recovering from this douche, did not tend to make matters clearer to the retriever, whose eyes and ears were full of water, besides being moreover tired out by his previous exertions.

Any hesitation poor Rover might have felt, though, barely lasted an instant; for, the sight of two figures battling for life in the sea there under his very nose, and the knowledge that one of these was his young master, brought in an instant all his sagacious instincts into play.

He did not need the Captain or anybody else to tell him what to do. Not he!

Giving his head a quick shake to clear his eyes and uttering a short, sharp bark, as if to say, 'Hold on, my boys, I'm coming to help you!' the dog appeared to scramble through the water by a series of leaps, rather than to swim, towards the spot where the two unfortunates were struggling.

Reaching the pair, he at once gripped Bob's collar in his powerful teeth and proceeded to tow him to land, Dick hanging on behind; and Rover's muzzle was already turned shorewards, dragging his double burthen astern ere the Captain's cry of encouragement came to his ears, although on hearing it the noble animal redoubled his efforts.

It was, however, a terrible ordeal; nay, almost a hopeless one!

Had the boys been conscious, Rover would have had comparatively easy work of it, as then one of them might have held on to his collar and the other to his tail, and he could have pulled them both out without much trouble; as it was, now, they clung so frantically to each other and to him that they retarded in lieu of assisting his gallant attempt to save them.

But, help was at hand.

Just as the Captain called out, a couple of coastguardsmen were coming round the corner of the castle on their beat towards the east pier; and, hearing his shout to Rover, they stopped.

"Hullo!" cried one of the men, observing that Mrs. Gilmour was in a state of great agitation, with Nellie sobbing beside her and the Captain at the bottom of the sloping rampart in the act of taking off his coat—"Anything wrong, mum?"

Mrs. Gilmour's heart was so full that she could not speak at once, and the man who addressed her jumped to a wrong conclusion from the absence of any explanation at the moment.

"Oh, I see, mum, he's a going to commit sooacide? We'll soon spoil his little game, mum. Bear a hand, Bill, will ye?"

So saying, the speaker and his comrade, with a catlike ease that came naturally to them from their practice at sea, where they had a rolling deck beneath their feet much more difficult to traverse than the slippery slope they were now on, had reached the spot where the coatless old sailor stood almost as these words were uttered, leaping down the steep descent in a sort of 'hop skip and jump' fashion.

"None o' that!" exclaimed the elder of the two men who had previously spoken, grasping hold of one of the Captain's arms while his mate, or 'Bill,' caught hold of the other. "A going to make away with yourself, eh? Not if we knows it, sir!"

At the same instant, however, Captain Dresser turned round with a face on which the animated expression produced by his determination to try and rescue the boys was mingled with a puzzled look of astonishment at being tackled in this unceremonious manner when on the very point of action.

His black eyes twinkled and his bushy eyebrows moved up and down at a fine rate as he looked up indignantly to see who had dared to lay hand on him.

"My stars!" ejaculated the coastguardsman Bill, dropping hold of the Captain's arm as if it had been a hot poker, "I'm blest if it ain't the old cap'en!"

The other man also recognized him at the same time, releasing the old man equally hurriedly.

"Beg pardon, sir," he said. "Didn't know it wer' you, sir!"

But the Captain made no reply to this apology.

He only pointed to the water just below where they were standing, and where the head of Rover could be dimly seen in the gathering dusk of the evening, now rapidly closing in, splashing his way to the shore.

"Boys save quick drown!" he stammered out brokenly. "Quick, quick!"

The men did not require any further explanation or incentive.

Without stopping to doff a garment, in they both plunged, boots and all; and, before the Captain knew that they were gone from his side, they had reached poor Rover, now quite exhausted, gallant dog though he was!

Then, one of the men grasping hold of Bob and the other catching hold of Dick, they swam with the two boys between them, still locked together, to the end of the rampart wall that jutted out over the water.

Here the Captain was ready and waiting to lean over and lend them a hand, keeping the while a steady purchase to his feet by the aid of his malacca stick, which possibly had never been of such service before; and, presently, the coastguardsmen, the boys, and Rover, who would not let go his young master's collar and was lifted out along with him, were all once more again on firm ground.

By this time, a small crowd of spectators had collected on the spot, composed principally of persons who had come out for a walk round the castle and had their attention arrested by the scene passing in the water below.

The majority of these now, in company with Mrs. Gilmour and Nellie, hurried to the lower part of the rampart, which, on the side nearer the harbour, did not shelve down there so abruptly, broadening out by degrees to a wide flat surface where it joined the esplanade bordering the beach.

At this spot, the coastguardsmen laid down the rescued boys, who were quite insensible from their long immersion; when Rover, at length satisfied that his young master was ashore and in safe hands, was persuaded to loose his grip of Bob's collar, contenting himself by venting his joy in a series of bounds and barks around his inanimate form and licking his apparently lifeless face.

Both Mrs. Gilmour and the weeping Nellie thought they were dead.

"Poor boys!" sobbed the former, her tears falling in sympathy with those of the little girl, who was too stunned to speak. "But, what shall I say to Bob's mother? How can I tell her he is drowned?"

"Drowned? Not a bit of it no more drowned than you are!" repeated the Captain, somewhat snappishly, his anxiety and excitement preventing him from speaking calmly, as he turned and bent over the inanimate bodies. "Help me, men, to rouse them back to life.'

The coastguardsmen bent down, too, and lifting the boys up were proceeding to lay them down again on their faces, when the Captain stopped them.

"You idiots!" he exclaimed "What are you going to do, eh?"

"Why, to let the water run out of 'em, sir," replied the elder of the two, looking up in his face and touching his forelock with his finger in proper nautical salute. "Ain't that right, sir?"

"Hullo! that you, Hellyer?" cried the old gentleman, recollecting him as a former coxswain. "Glad to see you again. By Jove, you came just now in the very nick of time to save these youngsters! Excuse me though; but, you've got hold of the same foolish idea a lot of other people have, that turning a poor half-drowned body upside down to empty him, as if he were a rum cask, is the best way to recover him!"

"What should we do, sir?" asked the man with a grin. "I allers thought it were the right thing, sir?"

"Why, turn the poor fellows slightly a oneside and then rub them smartly to restore the circulation," said the Captain promptly, suiting the action to the word; and, the next instant, he and the men were busily shampooing the boys till their arms ached. "Rub away, Hellyer; rub away!"

Rover growled at first on their touching Bob, apparently thinking the operation to mean an attack on his young master he didn't mind what they did to Dick. But, presently he altered his opinion on the subject, helping so far as he could by means of barking and licking Bob's face and feet alternately to bring him back to consciousness.

In a short space, although to the anxious onlookers it seemed hours, the efforts of the Captain and coastguardsmen were rewarded by Bob drawing a deep breath, which, it must be confessed, was sadly impregnated with the odour of tobacco from the air which Hellyer had puffed into his lungs to induce respiration!

This tobacco made poor Bob cough, but it likewise caused him to get rid of the greater portion of the sea-water he had swallowed; and after that, he opened first one eye and then the other and, finally, his mouth, exclaiming, much to the delight of Rover, who was just then in the act of licking his face, "Good dog!"

"Bravo!" cried the Captain, stopping his shampooing process on Bob's body and rubbing his own hands instead, in great glee. "Now we'll do!"

As for Mrs. Gilmour and Nellie, they expressed their delight by almost hugging the little newly recovered life out of Bob and giving way to fresh tears, only this time they cried for joy and not from grief; while Rover could not contain himself, whining in a sort of hysterical fashion between his loud yelps, and jumping up on every one around as if to say, "Oh, I am so glad, my young master's all right again!"

Aye, Bob was soon all right, getting on his feet and being able to stand without assistance, the only effect of his ducking being that he looked pale, as far as could be seen in the twilight.

He was, besides, most unmistakably, as wet as a drowned rat!

Dick took a little longer time to recover; but, shortly after wards, he, too, was himself once more.

When things had arrived at this happy stage, the Captain, who had been put in a fidget by the crowd clustering round— 'a pack of star-gazing fools' as he whispered pretty audibly to Mrs. Gilmour—thought it was time to make a move.

"Hellyer, you and your shipmate had better call round at my house in the morning," he said to his old coxswain, the elder of the two coastguardsmen. "You know my house, eh, the same old place?"

"Aye, aye, sir," replied the man, saluting as before. "We knows it well enough!"

"Then, good night to you, and thank you both for your timely assistance," said the Captain, turning away with a touch to the brim of his hat in acknowledgment of their salute. "Come on, boys, you'll have to hurry home fast to prevent catching cold after your swim."

So saying and offering his arm to Mrs. Gilmour, who was feeling faint after all the anxiety she had gone through, the brisk old gentleman led the way round the castle.

He insisted that Bob and Dick should run races across the common on their way towards the south parade, in which gymnastic display Miss Nellie and Rover both joined, for company sake as well as to set a good example, the big black retriever going over more ground than either of the competitors ere they reached 'The Moorings,' as Mrs. Gilmour's house was christened.

"Won't you come in?" said Mrs. Gilmour on their getting to the door, when the Captain raised his hat in token of adieu. "Do come in and have a rest, me dear Captain?"

"No, thanks, not up to cribbage to night," he replied, shaking his head and chuckling. "Feel my old bones too sore from sliding down that confounded rampart. I mustn't keep you chattering here, however, for you've got to see about those youngsters. You are sure you don't mind the trouble of putting up my foundling Dick for the night, eh?"

"I should think not, especially after his jumping into the sea so nobly after Bob; and the poor boy, sure, not able to swim either!" said she warmly. "Dick shall not only stop in my house to night, but as long as you please to let him, I tell you; and sure it's always grateful I'll be to him."

"Well, then," cried the Captain, "there's no use my stopping yarning here like an old woman now that point is settled. You'd better go and see after the boys at once."

"Oh, I'll say after them," she answered, laughing at his impatience, as he almost pushed her within the doorway and rushed down the steps towards the gate "I'll say after them, never fear!"

"Mind you put them between the blankets, and give them each something hot to drink when they turn in," he shouted back over the railings. "I'll come round in the morning and give them a lecture to wake 'em up!"

With these last words, off he went; his malacca cane coming down with a thump on the pavement at every third step he took, until the sound died away in the distance—"Stump, stump, Thump! Stump, stump, Thump! Stump, stump, Thump"

CHAPTER V.

BOTH 'SUITED.'

DICK was now 'in clover!'

Running away from a poor home and the tyranny of a cruel step father, he had, in the first instance, providentially succeeded in getting 'a free passage,' as the Captain expressed it, to Portsmouth, the goal of his fondest ambition.

Then, after thus successfully overcoming the obstacles that lay in the way of his going to sea, so far as this initial stage to that ultimate end was concerned, the lucky fellow, in addition to gaining the Captain's favour and making the acquaintance of Bob and Nellie, put the finishing touch to his good fortune by winning over Mrs. Gilmour to his side a lady who, as a friend, was worth perhaps all the rest, she being true as steel and thoughtful and considerate in every way.

For the Captain's sake alone, she would willingly have given the poor homeless lad house room; but, beyond that, she had taken a strong fancy to Dick from noticing his willing manner and anxiety to oblige those who had been kind to him at the station, an impression that was more than confirmed subsequently when she witnessed his gallant conduct in plunging into the water to try and save the impulsive Bob.

So, Dick was in clover!

Like Master Bob, he had his wet clothes stripped off as soon as he got within doors, and wrapped in warm blankets was put into an equally cosy little bed; a hot treacle posset being afterwards given to each boy when comfortably tucked in by Mrs. Gilmour herself, which drink even Bob, accustomed as he was to good things, said was 'not so bad, you know,' while to poor Lazarus like Dick it tasted as nectar!

Nor was this the end of our runaway's good fortune.

In the morning, after a sound sleep which effectually banished all the ill effects of their impromptu ducking from both Bob and himself, Dick awoke, or rather was awakened by his hostess in person, to be told that the Captain was waiting and wanted to see him particularly.

"I think too, my boy, it really is time for you to get up," added the lady kindly. "Do you know it's past ten o'clock?"

"Law, mum!" exclaimed Dick, ashamed of his laziness, having been accustomed at Guildford to turn out at sunrise, that is if he went to bed at all; for his unkind step father often locked him out of a night when in an especially angry mood. "Law, mum, whatever be I a doing of a lying here in broad daylight! I humbly asks yer parding, mum."

"Oh, never mind that, you're not so very late, my poor boy, considering all you went through yesterday and last night," said Mrs. Gilmour smiling. "But, come now, you mustn't keep the Captain waiting, or we'll have him trotting upstairs after you himself. Dress as quickly as you can; I have had your things dried at the kitchen fire, and here they are in this chair near the door."

So saying, Mrs. Gilmour left the room, and Dick hopped out of bed immediately afterwards, proceeding to put on his clothes; thinking, poor fellow, as he did so, how shabby and ragged they were, and that they and he were altogether sadly out of place in an apartment which, to his rustic eyes, used only to the surroundings of his village home, appeared a palace.

As soon as he was dressed and opened the door of the room, he found, waiting on the landing, a maidservant, who, first taking him downstairs to the kitchen, where she gave him a good breakfast, afterwards showed him the way to the parlour.

Here Mrs. Gilmour and the Captain, with Bob and Nellie, were all assembled, apparently ready to go out, the ladies having their walking things on.

"A pretty time of day for a youngster like you to be getting up," cried the old sailor jocularly as he entered. "I wonder the bright sun hasn't scorched your eyes out long before this, sir!"

Dick was commencing an abject apology, but Mrs. Gilmour stopped him.

"Oh, never mind the Captain," she said laughing at the poor lad's look of contrition. "He's only 'taking a rise' out of you, as he would call it."

"Humph! is he?" growled the Captain, blinking away and pretending to be very serious. "But, come now, we must be off. I want you to go along with me into Portsmouth; so, get your cap and we'll start at once."

"Mayn't we come too?" shouted Bob and Nellie in one breath together. "Do say yes, Captain Dresser!"

"Well, I don't know about you, Miss Nellie, for I may have to go into places where little girls may be in the way; besides which, I don't think you would like to leave your aunt all alone, eh?"

"Of course not, dear Captain, I forgot that," said Nellie, accepting this quiet suggestion of the old sailor as a final settlement of the question, without betraying a particle of ill temper or dissatisfaction. "I will stop with auntie."

"Ah, you shan't lose anything by doing it, me darlint," smilingly said Mrs. Gilmour, giving her an approving little pat on the cheek by way of caress. "You and I, Nell, may have a little expedition of our own, perhaps."

"But I may go with you and Dick," interposed Bob, by no means content to be left behind. "Mayn't I, Captain?"

"Oh yes, you may go or come, just as you please to call it," replied the Captain, making a move towards the door, with an energetic thump of his malacca cane on the floor. "Look sharp, though, or it will be midday before we're out of the house ! "

This contingency, however, did not happen, for within a minute or so he and the two boys were out on the parade; the party being further increased by the presence of Rover, who had been lurking in the passage and followed them out unobserved.

Not a bark or a gambol betrayed that he was after them, until the Captain on turning round suddenly saw him in their rear, close up to Bob's heels.

"Hullo!" he exclaimed; "I can't have that dog with us. Rover is a very fine fellow and a brave animal too; but, he's somewhat skittish as yesterday's proceedings at the railway-station showed me. I don't want to get into any more scrapes with him, such as knocking down harmless old women —she was a tartar, though, by Jove! Besides, I may have to go into the dockyard, and they do not allow dogs in there."

"Don't they?" asked Bob, catching hold of Rover's collar and preparing to take him back to the house. "Not even if they're well behaved?"

"No, my boy, they draw the line at puppies! I mean those jackanapes of midshipmen and sub lieutenants, as they call mates now, with their dandified airs. In my time, the reefers weren't half so conceited and didn't try to turn themselves into land swabs as they do now a days," said the Captain grimly, he being, like most sailors of the old school, a thorough believer in the times gone by. "But, go back now, and take that rascal of a dog in. Dick and I will wait for you at the corner."

Rover did not like this arrangement at all, but he had to submit to the force of circumstances; so, Bob disposing of him within doors and closing the outside gate as well for additional pre caution, all presently made a fresh start for their destination.

While crossing Southsea Common, the boys were delighted with the sight of the soldiers of the garrison mustered for brigade drill, the troops marching and wheeling and countermarching to the music of the bands, which played such inspiriting airs that

even the old Captain could not help keeping step, his trusty
malacca coming down with a thump on the springy turf, in
time with the rub a dub dub of the drums.

Bob had seen a regiment or two before in London, at parades
in front of the Horse Guards, or when reviewed on a small scale
in Hyde Park; but, never previously, had he witnessed so many
battalions marshalled together in all the pomp of war as now
the men formed up in double columns of companies, with the
sunlight glinting on the bayonets of their sloped rifles and
their legs looking like those of gigantic centipedes as they
stepped forward in changing ground to the left, first the red
stripe showing on one trouser-leg and then only the dark cloth
of the other.

"How funny they look!" exclaimed Bob, lost in admiration
as he took note of these little details, not a thing escaping him,
the hoarse commands of the officers, the galloping to and fro
of mounted *aides de camp* and 'orderlies,' the tooting bugle
calls, each in turn attracting his attention. "All move as if
they were one man!"

"Aye, they march well, my boy," replied the Captain, taking
advantage of the opportunity to point a moral lesson. "But,
recollect it's all owing to discipline and obedience to orders!"

Beyond the troops, the blue sea could be seen reflecting the
hue of the cloudless sky overhead, its surface dotted here and
there with the white sail of some yacht or other, passing
between Cowes and Spithead, or beating out into the Channel
in the distance; while, in the more immediate foreground,
anchored abreast of one of the harbour forts, was a modern
ironclad man of war.

"What is that?" inquired Bob, pointing in the direction
where the vessel lay, looking like some marine monster asleep
on the water.

"Humph! you may well ask the question," growled the
Captain, jobbing his stick down with an extra thump. "That
is what they call a 'ship' now a days! She's an 'armour-clad'

of the latest type, with all the improvements, though very different to the craft I and your Uncle Ted were accustomed to see in the good old times when ships were ships!"

"Why, Captain Dresser," said Bob sympathetically, "she's just like the roof of a house!"

"You're not far out, my boy. They all resemble floating barns more than anything else," grumbled the old sailor, bewailing the gallant frigates and three deckers of the past. "But, come on now, let us get to the dockyard, and I will show you one or two vessels of the right sort that we still have got left, thank God, to remind us of what England's navy once was!"

With these words, he dragged the boys, much against their will, away from the busy scene on the common and past the last remaining bastion of the old fortifications that once en circled Portsmouth; and, finally getting into the town he dived through all sorts of queer little streets and alleys, and then along the new road running by the side of the Gunwharf until they reached the Hard.

Here, stopping outside an outfitter's shop not far from the dockyard, the Captain seized hold of Dick and pulled him forwards towards the door.

"Do you know what I'm going to do with you, eh, you young rascal?" he asked him, with a chuckle which took all the sternness out of his threatening tones. "Can you guess?"

"No, sir," replied the lad ; but, evidently did not anticipate anything very dreadful, for he grinned all over his face. "I carn't!"

"I'm going to give you a new rig out," went on the other. "Do you know what that is, eh?"

"No, sir," again answered Dick, thinking though that the Captain perhaps meant something to eat. "I dunno."

"Well, come in here and you shall see."

So saying, the old sailor led the way into the shop, where on his giving a few short, sharp, and curt directions to an attendant, Dick was taken in hand and twisted this way and that and measured; the whilom ragged runaway being in the end apparelled in a bran new suit of navy serge that made him look like a smart young reefer, very different indeed to the ragged runaway who had forced his way into the railway carriage frightening Bob and Nellie during their journey Portsmouth wards from Guildford twenty four hours before.

"There, what do you think of yourself now?" asked the Captain, wheeling him round in front of a cheval glass so that he could see his reflection in the mirror. "Eh, you rascal?"

Dick did not say anything; but, the look, of mingled wonder, self satisfaction and gratitude, that overspread his speaking face more than rewarded the good-hearted sailor for his thoughtful generosity.

"He only wants his 'air cut and a pair o' decent boots, sir, and then he'll be a reg'ler tiptopper," suggested the shopman. "I wouldn't know him now for the same chap ag'in, sir!"

"Thank you, my friend, for the hint," said the Captain politely. "You can fit him with some boots, and we'll see about the ''air' when we get outside!"

Bob, of course, went into convulsions of laughter when the Captain thus mimicked the man's disregard of his aspirates.

The shopman's failing in this respect was all the more amusing from the fact that the poor fellow was quite unaware of his 'little weakness'; and, one boy's merriment affecting the other, while the Captain joined in from sympathy, they all went out of the shop in the highest of spirits, the old sailor before leaving directing the attendant to send home another suit of clothes with a complete sailor's kit, so that Dick might have what he called 'a regular rig out.'

Subsequently, Dick had his hair cut, after which the Captain took him into the dockyard, with the intention of his being entered for service in the Navy, the boy having expressed so strong a desire to go to sea.

However, as he was not broad enough in his chest measurements, although sufficiently tall for his age, his joining a training ship had to be postponed until our runaway had, as the old warrant officer at the depôt said, 'Stowed a lot more beef and bread in his skid.'

But, even beyond this material point, Captain Dresser was reminded by this courteous veteran of something he had entirely forgotten; namely, that Dick would have to produce a certificate of birth to show his proper age, and also a paper containing the written consent to his going to sea of his parents, or guardians in the case of his being an orphan which he was nearly if not quite before Dick would be permitted to join 'Her Majesty's Service.'

These documents, it may be mentioned here, slightly anticipating matters, Captain Dresser subsequently obtained through the clergyman of Dick's parish at Guildford, to whom he wrote, and who gave the young runaway the best of characters.

This gentleman stated that the lad was not only honest and truthful, but the steadiest scholar he had in his Sunday school; and he added that the good news which he had been able to tell Dick's mother after hearing from the Captain, of his having fallen into such friendly hands, had made up in some way for her sorrow at being forced to part with her dear son.

"Well, what shall we do with you now?" said the Captain to Dick on their leaving the dockyard, where, in addition to going on board the training ship attached to the port, the boys had seen most that was to be seen going over the smithery; the building sheds, in which ponderous leviathans of iron, that would anon plough the deep, were being welded together; the mast and rigging houses; the sail loft; they had gone over everything in fact! "You see they won't have you yet in the Navy, my lad; so, what is to be done with you, eh?"

"Dunno, sir," answered Dick, scratching his newly shorn head reflectively and staring in the face of the old sailor, who had stopped abruptly just outside the dockyard gates to ask him the question. "I'll leave it to yer for to settle anythink yer likes."

"Humph! I tell you what, we'll wait a bit and then try

again for the training ship three months hence, or so; when, perhaps, you'll have better luck," decided the Captain, who it need hardly be told had already made up his mind on the subject. "But, in the meantime, my lad, you shall stop with me and see if you can make yourself of use."

"Oh, sir," said Dick with tears in his eyes and his voice broken with emotion. "I can never thank yer, sir, for all as ye've done for me! I'll work day and night, sir, and do anythink as yer tells me!"

"We'll see, my lad," replied the Captain, walking on again, the watermen along the Hard touching their hats to him. "I shall probably take you on board my yacht by and by, when the racing season begins. You will, thus, learn something of your future profession; and be able to pull a rope and box the compass before the time comes for you to join the training ship."

"O o—o—h!" exclaimed Bob, the vista of delight thus presented being almost too great for words; for the sight of the sea, now that he had seen it and been actually on board a ship, had made him long for a sail, his involuntary dip of the previous night not having any deterrent influence. "Won't that be jolly, Dick?"

Dick grinned a sympathetic grin, his own peculiar way of showing how pleased he was.

"I only hopes as how I'll suit the Capting," said he earnestly. "I'll try to that I will!"

"Suit me, eh?" cried that worthy with a chuckle, and his little black eyes twinkling away. "That will be 'changey for changey, black dog for white monkey,' as the niggers say. You will have to suit me in return for my having *suit*ed you, my lad, eh? Ho—ho—ho!"

CHAPTER VI.

"Oh, dear! Oh, dear." cried Bob presently, stopping on their way homewards at a nice looking pastry cook's shop hard by the dockyard gates, whose wide green windows framed an appetizing display of cakes and buns which appealed strangely to his gastronomic feelings; while a fragrant odour, as of hot mutton pies, the speciality of the establishment, a renowned one in its way amongst middies and such like small fry who frequented the neighbourhood, oozed out from its hospitably open door, perfuming lusciously the air around "I am *so* hungry!"

"By Jove, my boy, so am I, too, now I think of it," said the Captain, likewise coming to a halt and proceeding to enter the shop, followed by his eager companions. "Let us pipe down to lunch at once. This is a famous place for pies; and you may rely on having mutton in 'em and not puppies!"

The old Captain 'stood treat,' of course, and the boys had such a glorious 'tuck out' that they were behind time when they got back to Mrs. Gilmour's house on the south parade.

'Aunt Polly' and Nellie were both ready and waiting for them outside, dressed in walking attire; while Rover was frisking round the ladies, though he darted up to his young master the moment he caught sight of him, forgetting, with all a good dog's magnanimity, the ill-treatment he had received in not being allowed to accompany him to the dockyard.

"Sure, you're very late, Captain dear," began Mrs. Gilmour

when the old sailor came near, with Dick following in his wake; but, suddenly not'cing the latter's wonderful transformation of appearance, she stopped her laughing reproaches anent the Captain's dilatoriness, exclaiming in admiring tones— "My good gracious! Dear me! Who is this young gentleman?"

Bob was in ecstasies.

"We were sure you wouldn't know him, auntie!" he cried, as little Miss Nellie joined him in a gleesome dance of triumph round the blushing, new fledged Dick, and Rover gambolled behird the pair, barking loudly, in sympathetic accord. "We were sure you wouldn't know him!"

"Sure, you're right, me dears, I wouldn't really have recognized him for the same boy at all, at all!" cheerfully agreed Mrs. Gilmour, as she turned towards the ex-runaway and scrutinizing his altered guise in detail, critically but kindly. "Are ye, really, Dick, now?"

"Yes, mum, I bees the same b'y, surely," replied Dick, with a broad grin that spread over his face from ear to ear. "It's the Cap'en, God bless him, mum, as made me for to look so foine that my own mother wouldn't know me, leastways nobody else   thanks be to the Cap'en, mum."

"Pooh, pooh, there's nothing to make a fuss about," interposed the old sailor, anxious to let these personalities be dropped, being very shy of any of his good actions being noticed. "The boy's all right. He has only changed his rig, that's all, the same as you put on a new dress on going out walking, ma'am."

"That's a nice thing to say of an economical person like me, sir!" said Mrs. Gilmour, shaking her parasol at him in jocular anger. "One would think I was one of those fine ladies who have a new dress every day in the week, and milliners' bills as long as your old malacca cane."

"Well, well, I apologize, ma'am, for I know better than that, as you are far too sensible a woman to spend all your money on finery," said the Captain, with a low bow. "But where are we going to now, for I see you are dressed for walking?"

"Down to the sea, of course," she replied. "Nell and I went up to Landport this morning, while you and Bob were 'transmogrifying' that boy, as my old father used to say. We paid a visit to the old lady whose eggs were broken yesterday by Master Rover's gambols. You may remember, Captain, I promised her some from my own fowls in place of those she lost. Don't you recollect how anxious the poor creature was about them?"

"Yes, yes, I remember," said the old sailor, his face beaming with good humour. "You're always kind and thoughtful."

"Whish!" cried Mrs. Gilmour playfully. "None of your blarney!"

"Oh, Bob!" exclaimed Nellie, interposing at this juncture, while they still all stood talking together in front of the house, neither Mrs. Gilmour nor the 'old commodore' having yet given the signal for sailing, "she has got such a dear little place of her own."

"Who's 'she' the cat's mother, Nell?"

Nellie laughed.

"I mean the old lady who had the broken eggs."

"Aye," put in the Captain, "and who nearly had broken legs likewise!"

This made Nellie laugh again.

"Oh, you know who I mean very well, Bob," said she, when she had ceased to giggle. "She has got the dearest little cottage, you ever saw. It is fitted up just like the cabin of a ship inside; her husband, who was a ship's carpenter, having done it all. Why, the walls are covered with Chinese pictures and shells and curios which he picked up in all sorts of outlandish places, bringing them home after his various voyages. Oh, Bob, you never saw such funny things."

"Didn't the woman say something of having an invalid daughter?" inquired the Captain "I think I heard her speak of one yesterday at the station."

"Yes, poor thing," said Mrs. Gilmour. "She's got spinal complaint, and we saw her lying on the sofa in the queer little parlour crammed with curiosities that Nell took such a fancy to. She seems a very nice girl, so happy and contented although in such a helpless state! Her old mother, whom I know you thought fussy and selfish, is quite devoted to her."

"Humph!" ejaculated the Captain, taking no notice of Mrs. Gilmour's allusions to his original impression of the stout personage with whom Rover had, so to speak, entangled them into an acquaintance. "Perhaps some of that old port wine of mine would do the girl good, eh, ma'am?"

"Not a doubt of it, she looks so pale and delicate," replied Mrs. Gilmour. "But there will be plenty of time to think about that to morrow. Let us go on now to the beach, or it will be too late for us to do so before dinner."

"Come on then, I'm yours obediently," said the Captain with his usual chirpy chuckle. "By Jove, though, I think I've had pretty nearly walking enough for one day for an old fellow turned sixty."

This time they steered clear of the castle, the exciting memories of the previous evening being too vivid in Mrs. Gilmour's mind to allow the boys to go near the treacherous footing of the rampart again.

Instead of going thither, they turned their footsteps rather to the eastern portion of the shore; where a shelving, shingly beach sloped gradually down to the water, and thus no danger to be feared of Master Bob or any one else plunging in suddenly without warning, as happened unfortunately before.

Here, everything was new to the young people; the wet pebbles glistening like jewels after a last polish from the receding tide; the masses of many hued seaweed; the quaint shells; and the rippling waves, laughing in the sunshine, and sportively throwing up in their joyous play little balls of foam or spendrift, which the buoyant south westerly breeze, equally inclined for fun and frolic, tossed about here and there high in the air, until they were lost to sight in the distance beyond the esplanade.

One or two silver grey gulls, with white waistcoats on, as if going to some nautical dinner party, were hovering above and occasionally making dashes down in their swooping curvilinear flight to pick up stray titbits from the tideway, to assuage their hunger until the grander repast to which they were invited was ready; while a whole colony of their kindred, the black, brown, and dusky-coloured gulls, not so fortunate in being asked out to the festive banquet, were anon floating about in groups on the water close inshore, anon suddenly taking wing and flying off, only to settle down again on the surface further out.

Even more impressive, however, than all these evidences of moving life around, there was the sea, that touched their feet almost, and yet stretched out in its illimitable expanse away and away to where?

It was Nellie to whom these thoughts occurred; as for Bob, he was engaged in chasing little green crabs as they scuttled over the shingle, busily collecting as many as he could get hold of in a little pond he had scooped in the sand.

This pond would now be filled as some venturesome wavelet broke over its brink; and then be drained as the tide fell back, leaving the poor little crabs left high and dry ashore to repeat their scrambling attempts at escape, only to tumble over on top of each other as they tried to climb the precipitous sides of Bob's reservoir.

"Isn't it jolly!" cried that young gentleman, looking up at the Captain, who, leaning on his stick, stood near, watching his futile endeavours to restrain the vivacious, side walking, unwieldy little animals that seemed gifted with such indomitable energy, and equal perseverance to that of Bruce's spider. "Isn't it jolly, sir?"

"Not very jolly for the crabs, though," observed the old sailor smiling. " I don't think they would say so if you asked them the question ! "

"I'm not hurting them," said Bob in excuse. "I only want to see them closely."

"I suppose you think they are all alike and belong to the same species, eh?" asked the Captain. "Don't you?"

"Well, I don't see much difference in them," replied Bob hesitatingly. "Do you, Captain Dresser?"

"Humph! yes. I can see in that little pond of yours, now under my eyes, no less than three distinct varieties of the crab family."

"Never!" exclaimed Bob incredulously. "Why, they all look to me the same queer little green backed things, with legs all over them that they do not know how to use properly."

"While you think, no doubt, that you could teach them better, eh?" said the Captain chuckling; but, the next moment, raising his hat and a graver expression stealing over his face as he looked upward towards the blue vault overhead, he added earnestly—"Ah, my boy, remember they have a wiser teacher than you or I! However, you're wrong about their being all similar. The majority of those you've caught are certainly of the ordinary species of green crab and uneatable, if even they had been of any tolerable size; but, that little fellow there is a young 'velvet fiddler' or 'swimming crab.' If you notice, his hind legs are flattened, so as to serve him for oars, with which he can propel himself at a very good rate through the water if you give him a chance. Look now!"

"I see," cried Bob eagerly. "He's quite different to this other chap here with the long legs."

"Oh that is a 'spider crab.' He is of very similar proclivities to his cousin though he lives ashore. The cunning fellow uses his sprawling long limbs in lieu of a web, and will lie in wait in some hole between the rocks, artfully poking his claws out to catch unwary animals often those of his own or kindred species as they pass by his den.'

"What is this queer little chap?" asked Nellie, pointing to

another, which was partly concealed in an old whelk shell. " He seems to want to get out and can't."

" Why, my dear, that is the 'hermit crab.' He does not want, though, to leave that comfortable lodging he has secured for himself, as you think. He's an 'old soldier,' and knows when he's well off! He belongs to what is called the 'soft-tailed' family, and being defenceless astern he has to seek an artificial protection against his enemies, in place of natural armour."

" How funny !" said Nellie, watching the little animal more closely. " What a queer fellow ! "

" Yes," continued the Captain —" and, that is the reason why he goes prowling about for empty shells. Often, too, really he's such a pugnacious fellow, he will turn the rightful tenant out, taking forcible possession. Just look at his tail and see how it is provided with a pair of pincers at the end. He is enabled by this means to hold on firmly to any shell, no matter how badly it may fit him, which he chooses for his temporary habitation."

As he spoke, the Captain extracted with some little difficulty the buccaneer crab from the whelk shell, showing its peculiar formation, quite unlike that of the others. A young shrimp who had lost his latitude was also found in Bob's pond, and the discovery led the old sailor to speak of these animals that form such a pleasant relish to bread-and-butter; and he told them that one of the best fishing-grounds for them was off the Woolsner Shoal, some four miles further along the beach to the eastwards, while another good place was Selsea Bill, more eastward still.

While the Captain was giving this little lecture about the crabs and their congeners, Rover was prancing around and barking for some one to pitch in a stick or something for him to fetch out of the sea.

Presently, in bringing back a piece of wood which Bob had thrown into the water, Rover dragged ashore a mass of seaweed, a portion of which was shaped somewhat like a lettuce and coloured a greenish purple.

The Captain pounced on this at once.

"Hullo!" he exclaimed "why, it is laver."

"Isn't that good to eat?" asked Mrs. Gilmour. "I fancy I've heard people speak of it in London, or somewhere."

"I should rather think it was!" he replied. "It is, too, one of the best sorts, the purple laver, a variety of some value, I believe, in the London market."

"I can't say I should like to eat it," said Nellie, squeezing up her nose like a rabbit and making a wry face. "It looks too nasty!"

"Wouldn't you?" retorted the Captain. "I can tell you, missy, it is very good when well boiled, with the addition of a little lemon-juice. It tastes then better than spinach."

"Do all these sorts of seaweed grow in the sea, Captain Dresser?" asked Bob. "I mean in the same way as plants do in a garden?"

"No, my boy," replied the other. "They attach themselves to the rocks at the bottom of the sea, not to draw their sustenance from them in the same way as plants ashore derive their nourishment from the earth through their roots; but, simply to anchor themselves in a secure haven out of reach of the waves, getting all their nutriment from the water, which is the atmosphere of the sea in the same way as air is that of the land. Of course, some of these weeds of the ocean drift from their moorings, like that bladder wrack there with the berries."

"Don't they pop jolly!" observed Master Bob, popping away as he delivered himself of this opinion. "Pop! There goes one!"

"You are not the only boy who has found that out, or girl either," said the Captain with a smile to Nellie, who was industriously following her brother's example. "But, look here, children, I can now see something stranger than anything we've noticed yet."

"What?" exclaimed Bob and Nellie together, stooping down to where the Captain was poking about with the end of his malacca cane in the sandy shingle. "What is it, sir?"

"A pholas," he answered. "It is one of the most curious burrowing animals known, and has been a puzzle to naturalists for years, until Gosse discovered its secret, as to how it succeeded with its soft and tender shell in penetrating into the hardest rocks, within whose substance it is frequently found completely buried, so that, like the 'Fly in Amber,' one wonders how it ever got there!"

"What did you say it was?" asked Mrs. Gilmour. "A 'fowl,' sure? Faith it's a quare-looken bird, Cap'en dear!"

The Captain smiled, but he was not to be tempted away from his hobby.

"The pholas, I said, ma'am," he replied. "The 'pholas dactylus,' as scientific people call it, which, until Gosse, as I said, discovered its mode of action, was quite a puzzle to every one; although, now that the mystery is out, all wonder it was not cleared up before! If you look at the head of the shell, you'll see it is provided with a regular series of little pointed spines at the end of the upper portion. These spines are of a much harder material than the main part of the shell, and are fixed into it, as you could notice better with a microscope, just in the same way as the steel points for the notes of any air are attached to the barrel of a common musical-box, projecting like so many teeth."

"Yes, I can see them," observed Bob, who was listening attentively. "Look, Nell!"

"Well, then," the Captain went on, "besides this toothed head of his, the animal is provided with a sucker at his mouth, by which he can hold on to any wooden pile or stonework he may wish to perforate so as to make his nest inside; and, gripping this firmly with his sucker and working the head of his shell slowly backwards and forwards with a sort of circular rocking motion, he gradually bores his way into the object of his affections, getting rid of the refuse he excavates by the aid of a natural siphon that runs through his body, and by means of which he blows all his waste borings away—curious, isn't it?"

"Very," said Mrs. Gilmour, while the children, equally interested, wanted to learn not only all the Captain could tell them of this peculiar little animal, but also everything he knew of the other wonders of the shore. "Sure I wish I knew all you do, Captain!"

But, if the Captain was learned and good natured, the children taxed his patience, Miss Nellie especially.

She had not lost any time in setting about making that collection of shells which she had mentioned to him in confidence when coming down in the train it was her intention to begin as soon as she got to the sea; and, all the time he had been speaking of the little crabs and other things, she had been busily gathering together all sorts of razor shells, pieces of cuttle-fish bone, cast off lobsters' claws, and bits of seaweed, which she now proudly drew his attention to, expecting the old sailor's admiration.

He was, on the contrary, however, extremely ungallant.

"All rubbish!" he exclaimed on her asking him if he did not think her pile of curiosities nice. "But, those corallines, young lady, are good. They were long supposed to belong to the animal world, like the zoophytes; instead of which they are plants the same as any other seaweed. When that little branch you have there is dry, if you put the end of it to a lighted candle, it will burn with an intense white flame, similar to the lime light, or that produced by electricity."

"We'll try it to night!" said Bob emphatically. "We'll try it to night!"

"But, the Captain says it must be quite dry," interposed his sister, somewhat appeased by the praise bestowed on her corallines for the wholesale condemnation her collection had received. "Isn't that so, Captain?"

"Right you are, my deary," said he. "They would not burn unless they're just like tinder."

Dick, who had meanwhile been listening to all that was being said, without intruding on the conversation, busying himself in picking up shells for Miss Nell, and, occasionally, diverting Rover's attention by throwing a stick for him into the sea, happened to come across, just at this juncture, a queer looking dark coloured object that resembled an india rubber tobacco pouch more than anything else.

"What be this, sir?" said he, holding up the article for inspection. "Be he good for aught, sir?"

"Why, it's only a piece of seaweed, of course!" declared Master Bob, settling the question in his own way. "Any one can see that."

"You're wrong," said the Captain. "You're quite wrong, Master Sharp!"

"It's a fairy's pillow case," cried Nellie. "Isn't it?"

"Your guess is the nearer of the two, missy," decided Captain Dresser, thumping his malacca cane down to give greater effect to his words. "Strange to say, you've almost hit upon the very name; for, the fisher folk hereabouts and down the coast call the things 'mermaids' purses.' They once contained the egg of some young skate or shark, who, when he was old enough, hatched himself, leaving his shell behind; and this being elastic, like gutta percha, closed up again, so that it cannot be told how he got out."

"Dear me!" exclaimed Mrs. Gilmour. "I've often wondered what those things were, and never knew before."

"It's never too late, ma'am, to learn," said the Captain. "I myself only took up natural history, gathering the little knowledge I possess, after I was put on half pay. Indeed, it was all owing to poor Ted, your husband and my old ship mate, that I ever thought of reading at all. He said it would be something for me to fall back upon for occupation when the Admiralty shoved me on the shelf; and, by Jove, he was right!"

"Poor Ted !" sighed Mrs. Gilmour somewhat sadly. "Poor old Ted !"

"Not 'poor,' ma'am," said the Captain reverently, taking off his hat and looking upwards as he had done before when calling the children's attention to Him who taught the insects. "He's 'rich' Ted, now ; and better off in his snug moorings aloft than you and I here below ."

"Yes, I know that, but it is hard to be content," replied the other, appearing lost in thought for some moments ; until presently, recovering herself, she looked at her watch, when, seeing what time it was, she said they must start back for home at once. "Come along, children, time's up !"

"O o o o h !" exclaimed Bob and Nellie in great constern ation. "Why, we've only just come !"

"O o o o h !" mimicked their aunt, amused at their woe begone faces. "Do you know that we've been down here nearly four hours ! If we stop much longer, you'll be 'oh ing' for your dinner, when it will be too late to get any, and how would you like that ?"

"Humph ! I thought I was feeling a bit peckish," said the Captain, wheeling about and preparing to head the return procession home, accepting Mrs. Gilmour's remarks as a command. "Come on, children, we've got our sailing direc-tions ; so let us up anchor at once, for you'll have plenty of the beach before you see the last of it. I tell you what, though, I'll do for you if you are good."

" What, Captain ? " cried Bob and Nellie, hanging on to his coat tails as he stumped over the shingle by the side of their aunt, the faces of all now set homeward. "What ?"

"Ah, you must wait till to morrow !" was all that they could get out of him, however, in spite of their wheedlings and coaxings as they crossed the Common, with Dick and Rover following behind ; the latter being too hungry even to bark, and only able to give a faint wag of his tail now and then when especially addressed by name. "Wait till to morrow !"

CHAPTER VII

A SOUTH EASTERLY GALE.

"OH, Nell!" cried Bob to his sister the same evening, some time after dinner, which, through their explorations on the beach, was somewhat later than usual "I do wonder what that mysterious 'something' is the Captain keeps promising us for 'to morrow.' Can he be thinking of taking us for a trip on the sea in his yacht, or what?"

"I wonder," was all Nellie could say in reply to her brother's remark, echoing, so to speak, his own words—"I do wonder what he is going to do, Bob?"

Their anxious curiosity, however, availed them naught; the old sailor keeping provokingly silent and being as mute as the Sphinx on the subject, in spite of their wistful looks and watchfulness.

Throughout the evening the Captain only opened his lips to say to Mrs. Gilmour, with whom he was playing one of those postprandial games of cribbage which it had been his wont to indulge in before the advent of Bob and Nellie on the scene to interrupt their regular routine, "Fifteen four and two for his heels," or "I'll take three for a flush, ma'am," as the case might be. He only made use of such like technical phraseology common to cribbage players, limiting his conversation to the game alone; without leaving a loophole for either of the impatient listeners in the corner, who were turning over picture books and otherwise diverting themselves, equally silently, till bedtime, to get in a word edgeways.

It was positively exasperating to Bob; especially as, the moment the old sailor chanced to notice one or other of the children eyeing him more attentively than usual on his looking up from the cards before him, he would smile knowingly and nod his head in the most waggish fashion.

"I don't think he means anything in particular at all," said the restless Master Bob a little later on to Nellie again. "See how funny he looks! He's only 'taking a rise' out of us, as he calls it."

"No, Bob," said Nellie, catching another quizzical look from the Captain just at that moment, "I don't think that. I'm sure he means something from that way he winked at us. Besides, Bob, he promised, and you know that Captain Dresser never breaks his word!"

Presently the report of the nine o'clock gun rolled through the night air, its echoes reverberating fainter and fainter until lost in the distance to seaward.

"By Jove!" exclaimed the Captain, throwing his cards on the table and rising from his seat,—"It's time for me to say good night, or I shan't get any beauty sleep!"

"It's not so very late," said Mrs. Gilmour, rising and going towards the open window looking over the Common. "What a lovely night it is ."

"Aye," replied the old sailor, following her, "the sky is bright and clear enough, certainly."

"Yes, what myriads of stars are out! I can see the 'milky way' quite plain, can't you, children?"

"Where, auntie?" asked Nellie behind her, while Bob stepped out on to the balcony the better to see. "I don't see it."

Mrs. Gilmour showed them the forked pathway leading up from the south and east to the zenith, looking as if powdered with the dust of stars which 'Charles's wain,' as country people term the constellation, had crushed in its lumbering progress through the heavens.

Away beyond this golden 'wake' of starlets the more majestic planets shone in stately grandeur; while the evening star twinkled in the immensity of space, still further away to the westwards.

"But the more you look at them, the further away they appear to go," put in Nellie. "Though, strangely enough, they don't seem to get any smaller."

"Aye, aye," acquiesced the Captain. "It *is* awful to think of the millions of miles they are separated from our globe, and that yet their light reaches us! Why, it is wonderful for us to reflect on this!"

"Hark! I hear a church bell ringing," cried Bob suddenly at this point. "It sounds as if it came from the sea out yonder."

"So it does, my boy," answered the Captain; "but not from any church. It is the bell on the Spit buoy that you hear ringing away to the southward. It is a bad sign for to morrow, denoting as it does a change of wind to a rainy quarter?"

"Oh dear!" exclaimed Bob, in such lugubrious tones that even Nellie laughed, although sharing his feelings about the prospect of a wet day, with the more than probable contingency of their being confined to the house. "What shall we do?"

"Cheer up, my lad, it may not be so bad after all," cried the Captain heartily. "But, really, I must be going now; for, it is close on ten o'clock and I shall lose all my beauty sleep, as I said before. Where is young Dick?"

"Down in the kitchen with Sarah," replied Mrs. Gilmour to this question, ringing the bell as she spoke. "He'll soon be ready if you insist on taking him away with you."

"Humph!" ejaculated the other, "as he's going to be my valet or factotum by the agreement we made to-day, I don't think we'll be able to tell whether we suit each other, ha ha! if he remains in one house and I in another, eh?"

"Perhaps not," said Mrs. Gilmour, smiling in response with the chuckle he indulged in at the recollection of his old joke on his way home from the dockyard; and Dick entering the room at the same moment, with a broad grin on his face as if he knew what they were talking about, she added "Sure, here he is to spake for himself! Are you ready to go home with the Captain, Dick?"

"Yes, mum," answered the lad promptly. "Sarah told me as how the good gentleman allers went away sharp at nine o'clock, and so I comes up as the bell rung."

"That's right, sharp's the word and quick's the motion; so we'd better be off," said the old sailor, taking his hat and stick which the housemaid, Sarah aforesaid, brought in from the hall. "Good-night, ma'am, good night, chickabiddies!"

"Good night!" replied Mrs. Gilmour, Nellie echoing her aunt's adieu with a parting injunction of her own. "Pray be sure and bring back Dick to-morrow morning, Captain!"

"Perhaps, too, you'll tell us then what you are going to do if we are good?" said Bob entreatingly, "though you would not to night."

"We'll see how the cat jumps!" replied the Captain with his cheery chuckling laugh as he marched out of the hall and down the steps with Dick after him; their retreating footsteps gradually dying away until they rounded the corner of the parade, the last sound heard being that of the ferrule of the Captain's malacca cane as it rang on the pavement, keeping time to the rhythm of his tread, and his voice repeating in the distance his quizzing rejoinder, "we'll see how the cat jumps!"

The 'cat' evidently did not 'jump' properly the next day, or, if it jumped at all, it executed that movement most decidedly in the wrong direction; for, when morning broke, much to Bob and Miss Nell's disgust, they found that a stormy south easterly gale had set in, accompanied by smart showers of rain, which very unpleasant change in the aspect of the weather put all ideas of their going out entirely out of the question

During the night, the wind, which had veered more to the eastwardly, rose considerably, drowning the clanging knell of the Spit buoy bell and rattling the windows and doors, like some desperate burglar on thoughts of plunder bent trying to effect a forcible entry.

Not satisfied with this alone, 'Rude Boreas' sent one of his imps down the chimney to frighten poor Nellie, who lay trembling in bed, by flapping up and down the register of the grate ; while another would every now and then boldly rush up and grip hold of the house, shaking it viciously and causing it to rock from roof to basement the rebuffed rascal then sailing away with a shriek of disappointed spite and rage, moaning and groaning like a creature in pain as it went off to vent its malice elsewhere !

Ere long the sea, unable to keep its temper under the bad treatment it received from the wind, which blew in its face most insultingly and kept continually 'pitting and patting it,' baker man fashion, in a very aggravating way, began to boil up in anger, lashing itself into a passion and roaring with fury ; while the noise Neptune made by and by deadened the roar of his assailant as he flung himself aloft in his struggles to grapple his nimble foe, and, missing his aim, rolled onward his boiling waves until they broke on the beach with the shock of an earthquake, amid a hurricane of foam !

The awesome sound of wave and sea combined kept Bob awake nearly all night, the same as it did poor Nellie ; the noise being so strange to their London ears, although, in some respects, somewhat similar to that of the street traffic of the metropolis.

Not only did it keep him awake, but the battle of the elements made Master Bob get up much earlier than usual ;

for he came down to the drawing room before Sarah had time to finish dusting the furniture.

Here he was soon afterwards joined by Nellie, who was equally 'spry' in her movements; and the pair amused themselves till breakfast was ready in looking out of the windows at the busy scene which the offing presented, so different to that of the previous evening, when all was quiet and calm, with Neptune gone to sleep and Boreas speaking but in a whisper!

The whilom glassy surface of the deep was now, however, a mass of short choppy waves, the sea king's 'white horses' leaping up friskily in every direction and chasing each other as they rolled in landward, throwing aloft clouds of feathery spray in their sport, as if champing it from their bits. Such was the scene far as the eye could span away to the eastward, where the sky was lit up by a stray gleam or two from the long since risen sun, who, though trying to hide himself behind a bank of b'ue black clouds, was not quite able to conceal his whereabouts.

Out at sea opposite, facing south and almost on the horizon line, a lot of vessels could be seen scudding down Channel, under short canvas but outward bound, just coming in sight beyond St. Helen's to make sure of their landfall and then disappearing the next moment behind the Isle of Wight, which shut them out from view; while, to the left, snugly sheltered under the lee of the Ryde hills, several others had run in and anchored off the Motherbank, waiting for a change of wind before proceeding on their voyage up, along the coast, to the river 'the river' of the world, the Thames!

As Bob and Nellie gazed out, taking in all these varied details of the scene by degrees, they could not help being pleased, everything was so novel; but, they saw something else beyond the prospect which cast 'a damper' over their spirits, theoretically as well as practically.

This was the rain, which came in squalls, the smart showers

hurtling down in pattering intensity, momentarily shutting out the sea and its surroundings from sight; while the swollen raindrops dashed against the window panes like hail, trying, like the whirling stormblast, to force a passage into every nook and cranny that lay open to attack.

"Oh dear!" sighed Bob dismally, his nose pressed like a piece of putty against the glass. "It's awful rain, Nell; I don't think it will ever stop!"

"Oh dear!" sighed Nellie, in responsive echo; but, just then their aunt bustled into the room, her face the picture of good humour, in marked contrast to theirs, and she caught the mournful exclamation "Oh dear!"

"Why, what's the matter?" asked Mrs. Gilmour, in a cheer ful tone, on their turning round as she entered. "To look at you both, one would think that something dreadful had happened!"

"It's raining," said Bob, in a melancholy tone. "It's rain ing, auntie!"

"So I can see," retorted Mrs. Gilmour. "Haven't I got eyes of my own, sure, me dear?"

"But we shan't be able to go out, auntie," cried Nellie, in the most broken hearted way. "We shan't be able to go out!"

"You need not be so disconsolate about that, dearie," said the other smiling. "It may not rain all day; and, if so, you'll be able to get out between the breaks when it holds up. But, there's Sarah ringing the bell, so, children, let us go downstairs now to the parlour; perhaps by the time we have finished breakfast it will have cleared up and be quite fine."

These cheery words, combined possibly with a savoury odour of frizzled bacon and hot coffee that came up appetizingly from below, had the effect, for a while at least, of banishing Bob and Nellie's gloom, and without further ado they accompanied their aunt to the breakfast-room downstairs.

Here, stretched on the hearthrug before the grate, in which a bright cosy little fire was blazing and looking uncommonly cheery, although it was now summer, lay Rover.

Without rising, he lazily greeted them by flopping his heavy tail, albeit he lifted his nose in the air and sniffed, as if in anticipation of sharing the coming meal with the welcome guests who so opportunely appeared.

"Well, I declare!" cried Mrs. Gilmour, "I hope you make yourself at home, sir?"

Rover only flopped his tail the more furiously at this, his appealing brown eyes saying, as plainly as dog could speak, that he was hungry, and that if she meant to be kind he would prefer actions to words.

After breakfast, as the rain still continued, Bob got grumpy again and Nellie mopy from not being able to go out on the beach as both longed to do.

In this emergency, their aunt suggested that the unhappy children should occupy themselves in sorting and arrang'ng in an old album, which she gave them, some of the best bits of seaweed they had collected the previous afternoon, the good lady advising them first to soak the specimens in a bowl of fresh water, so as to get rid of the salt and sand and other impurities, besides enabling the specimens to be laid flatter in the book for subsequent pressing.

By this means, the time passed so pleasantly that Master Bob and Miss Nell were much surprised when Mrs. Gilmour, who had meanwhile been busying herself about household matters, came to tell them, anon, that they must clear their things off the parlour table on account of Sarah wanting to lay luncheon.

"Why, auntie," cried Bob, looking up from the basin in which he was busy washing the last lot of seaweed, "we've hardly begun yet!"

"You've been a long time beginning then, sir," replied Mrs. Gilmour. "Do you know that it is past one o'clock; so that you've been more than three hours at your task? See, too, my dears, the rain has cleared off, and it looks as if it were going to be fine for a bit."

"How nice, aunt Polly!" said Nellie, the neat handed, carefully lifting up the album out of Sarah's way so that she might spread the cloth. "I declare I never thought once of looking out of the window to see if it were still wet. Did you, Bob?"

"No," he answered, "I was too busy helping you, Nell."

"Ah, my dearies," interposed Mrs. Gilmour, taking advantage of the opportunity to point a moral, "you see what it is not to be idle and having something to do! If you had not both been so engrossed with your task, you, Master Bob, would have been 'Oh ing' all over the house and going to each window in turn to see if the rain had stopped, looking like a bear with a sore head; while you, Miss Nell, would probably have shed as many tears as would have floated a jolly boat, as Captain Dresser would say in his sailor language!"

"Oh, auntie!" exclaimed Bob impetuously, "I never say 'Oh' like that, do I?"

"Sure you've answered the question yourself." replied Mrs. Gilmour, speaking in her racy brogue. "That's just what I should have had to listen to all the morning but for my thinking of that album, which I'm glad has amused you both, my dears, so well. Ah, children, children, there's nothing like having something to do. I'll tell you something one of the poets, Cowper I think, has written about this in his homely verse :—

> ' An idler is a watch that wants both hands ;
> As useless as it goes as when it stands ! '

What d' you think of that, me dears, for an illustration of a person without occupation for mind or body does the cap fit anybody here, eh?"

Bob was silent; but, Nellie took the lesson to heart.

" Yes, auntie, I know it's true enough," she replied. "I like
those lines; papa taught them to me when I was a tiny little
girl.   I wonder if he learnt them first from you?"

" No, dearie," said Mrs. Gilmour, drawing her towards her
with an affectionate caress.   " Our father, your grandpapa
that was, taught that little verse to us years ago, when your
papa and I were of the same age as Bob and yourself; and I
have never forgotten them, as you see, dearie.   But, sit down
now and have your luncheon.   Bob, come to the table ; Bob !
What on earth are you staring so out of the window now for,
I wonder?   Bob, I say !"

This repetition of his name in a louder key made the
delinquent jump; and he turned round in a hurry.

CHAPTER VIII.

"I REALLY beg your pardon, aunt Polly, for my inattention!" cried Bob, in a state of great excitement. "It's the Captain!"

"Sure, you don't mean that, my dear," said Mrs. Gilmour, equally flurried, rising at once from the seat she had just taken at the head of the table. "Is it him, really?"

"Oh, yes, auntie," replied Bob, returning to his post of observation in the corner of the window. "There he is coming along the terrace, with Dick at his heels."

"Indeed, now?" said Mrs. Gilmour, who had come up to Bob's side. "Let me look for meself. Sure and you're right. It's him and none other, and he's coming along at a grand pace, too!"

"Hurrah!" shouted Bob. "Isn't it jolly, auntie?"

"Very jolly," agreed Mrs. Gilmour, more sedately, laughing at Bob's ecstasies, the boy, like most youngsters, being all extremes. "I call it very nice of him, Nell, don't you?"

"Delightful!" chimed in Nellie, catching hold of Rover's forepaws and making him dance round the room with her in high glee, Rover barking to express his sympathy with her excitement. "How good he is I mean Captain Dresser; not you, Master Doggy!"

"It is well we know what you do mean," said her aunt smiling, as Nell and Bob, with Rover dashing madly after their

F

heels rushed into the hall to open the door. "Ah, the young flibbertygibbets!"

In company with the Captain and Dick, as it still continued fine, all presently sallied down to the sea, where the young holiday makers were much surprised at the size of the waves, which seemed much bigger on nearer view than they had appeared from the drawing room windows in the morning.

Now they were so close to the waves that the spray splashed over the little party; and, it being high-water, the incoming tide, aided by the stiff south easterly wind, which was still blowing half a gale, rolled the billows in upon the shore, dashing them against the sea-wall and rampart at the back of the castle with a mighty din, and breaking them into sheets of foam that flew over the moats and fortifications, reaching to the Common beyond the spent water, driven back by the rocky embankment, sullenly ret ring, a seething sea of soap-suds, as if Davy Jones were having a grand 'washing-day.'

Much as this sight pleased them, strange and wonderful to their unaccustomed eyes, they were not allowed long to enjoy it; for, the Captain declaring that another squall was coming, presently made them hurry back to the house, laden, however, with seawrack and spindrift.

It was the same on the following day and the day after, the gale lasting until the close of the third; when it completed its course and died away as suddenly as it began, winding up with a grand thunderstorm, in which the lightning flashed and the thunder pealed through the heavens in a manner whose like, the Captain affirmed, he had never seen on that coast before.

"No, never, ma'am," cried he, emphasizing the assertion with a thump of his malacca cane that almost made a hole in Mrs. Gilmour's best drawing room carpet. "Not since I first joined the service at Portsmouth here, forty years ago, or more!"

Satisfied apparently with the 'blow' it thus had, the weather subsequently was all that could be desired; setting in bright and fine, while it was warm enough to be almost tropical.

Thenceforth, therefore, there was no more confinement to the house for the young people.

Bob started off early every morning across the common to the beach, where, under the superintendence of the Captain, he and Dick were taught how to swim, the boys, it may be mentioned, learning the art all the more quickly from the fact of the old sailor's telling them that "until they were able to keep afloat," to use his own words, "he'd think twice before he would take 'em afloat!"

So, as both were anxious to go out rowing and sailing, this threat acted as a spur to their efforts.

Nellie, too, had a bathe each day; and, much she liked bobbing up and down in the usual girl-fashion from the end of the rope of the machine. By and by, also, when she had gained a little courage, she learnt to swim like Bob, whose boastings on the point had put her on her mettle; and the bathing woman informed Mrs. Gilmour one fine morning, when she accompanied Nellie to the beach and entered into conversation with her teacher, that she was "the smartest young leddy to learn as ever was."

This fact Miss Nell at once proved by swimming there and then some forty yards, more than double the distance Master Bob could accomplish, in spite of all his 'tall talk,' after a similar period of tuition.

"You ladies can always beat us if you only try," said the Captain gallantly, when he heard this. "I believe a woman can do anything she likes."

"You're too complimentary, I'm afraid," remarked Mrs. Gilmour. "You don't mean all you say."

"Don't I, by Jove!" replied he. "Lucky for us men you do not set your mind to it; for, if you did, no poor fellow would ever have a chance of commanding his own ship!"

"That's a base slander," cried Mrs. Gilmour, laughing. "I thought you were paying us rather a doubtful compliment."

The old sailor chuckled.

"I had you there, ma'am, I think, eh?" said he, blinking away with much delight. "By Jove, I had!"

"But, when are you going to take us on the water?" asked Bob at this point, before his aunt could give the Captain 'a Roland for his Oliver' in reply to his aspersion on her sex. "You said you would, you know, when I and Dick knew how to swim."

"And I know how to, as well," put in Nellie. "Don't I, auntie?"

"Don't bother me, children," growled the Captain, pretending to get in a rage. "I must be off now. I have an appointment in the Dockyard this afternoon."

"You shan't go! you shan't go." cried the two together, hanging on to him on either side. "You promised to take us somewhere or do something if we were good, and that was to be to morrow."

"To morrow comes never!" ejaculated the old sailor, chuckling and blinking away. "'Hodi mihi, cras tibi.' What is that, Master Bob?"

"Eh, sir?" said Bob, making a wry face. "Why, it's Latin."

"Thank you for nothing, you young shaver!" retorted the Captain drily. "What I want to know is, what does it mean?"

Bob hesitated a bit, as if puzzled to translate the phrase; but in a moment memory came to his aid.

"Ah yes, I recollect now," he said in an assured voice. "It means, I think, 'to-day it is my turn; to morrow it will be yours.'"

"Very good, my boy," said the Captain with a chuckle. "That's my answer to your question just now."

"But you promised us, Captain," cried Nellie, taking up the cudgels now that poor Bob was routed so ignominiously. "You know you did, sir—didn't he, auntie? And the 'to-

morrow' you meant was a long time back, before the storm
and everything!"

"Then I'm afraid, Miss Nellie," he replied, making for the
door, so as to secure his retreat, "it must be a very stale one;
a sort of 'to morrow' I wouldn't have, if I were you, at any
price!"

Nellie was not to be beaten so easily, so she followed him
out into the hall as he was leaving the house.

"Do tell me, dear Captain," she pleaded earnestly. "Do
tell me what this wonderful something is that you have in
store for us."

"I will, my dear," replied the old sailor, succeeding by a
dexterous twist in releasing the lappel of his coat from her
restraining hand. "I will, my dear. I'll whisper it to you
I will tell you to morrow!"

With this he skipped down the steps as nimbly as a two-
year old, slamming the gate behind him to secure his retreat;
and Nellie could hear his hearty "Ho ho!" as he went along
the parade towards Portsmouth.

"What a tiresome man the Captain is!" she exclaimed
petulantly, on returning to the drawing room, where Mrs.
Gilmour had remained with Bob. "It is always 'to morrow,'
and 'to morrow,' and 'to morrow'; and when the 'to morrow'
comes, he never tells us anything."

"Fie, Nellie, you must not be impatient, my dear," said
her aunt, on hearing this outburst. "Recollect how kind and
good natured Captain Dresser has always shown himself, who
ever since you two came down here for your holiday, putting
himself out in every way to suit your convenience, and never
regarding anything as a trouble which could conduce to your
pleasure. I confess I am surprised at my little niece Nell
speaking in such a way of so good a man. If the Captain
keeps you in suspense, depend upon it his purpose is to make
you enjoy the treat he has in his mind ten times more than
if you knew all about it beforehand."

"But I hate being kept in suspense, auntie!" cried Miss Nellie rather naughtily, tossing her head indignantly, and throwing back her golden curls as if she were metaphorically pitching them at the offending old sailor. "I like to know the best or worst at once. I say, Dick, has the Captain told you anything about the treat he has for us?"

Poor Dick, who had been thoughtfully left behind by the old sailor, on account of Mrs. Gilmour having expressed her intention of going down to the beach with the young people in the afternoon, hardly knew how to answer the question.

He did not like to tell an untruth by saying that he had no knowledge of the Captain's plans, nor did he wish to disoblige Miss Nell, so his answer was of the non committal order a sort of 'I don't recollect' in its way.

"I can't tell, miss," was all he said, but, fortunately enough for him, it sufficed to throw Nellie off the scent and prevent her trying any further to worm the secret out of him; although, there is no doubt, she would have succeeded had she persevered, and Dick was on thorns until she went upstairs to get ready for going out, the little lady having an insinuating manner of her own that was well nigh irresistible.

By the time she came below again, equipped for walking, Nellie's passing fit of ill temper had disappeared, and she was not only her bright cheerful little self once more, but full of a project for adding to her collection a specimen of the 'sea cucumber,' which the Captain had told her she might find if she only hunted diligently enough.

These strange marine animals belong to a species of 'Triple Alliance' of their own, being connected in a greater or less degree with the anemones, the ringworms, and the 'sea urchins'; albeit, the sea cucumbers possess one very great advantage over these cousins of theirs, in being able, when they so please, to turn themselves inside out and dispense with their stomachs, as well as what would be considered other equally necessary portions of their corporate frames.

When in this transformed, or 'turn coat' stage of his existence, the animal consists only of an empty bag, or pocket, that has at the broadest end an apparently useless mouth, but which he still continues to make use of for feeding purposes; and, by and by, when my gentleman feels disposed to return to his original state, seemingly by the mere effort of will, his tentacles sprout out one by one, the mouth-end of his bag becomes surmounted by a sort of mushroom head, his interior person gets filled up, and the sea cucumber is himself again, 'all a-taunto!'

The Captain had advised Nellie to search amongst the old wooden piles of the pier, as a likely situation to find these animals, and others he named quite as curious, such as the 'beroe' and the 'balanus,' which while looking as if inanimate yet are 'all alive,' and, if not 'kicking,' certainly may be seen fishing, either with natural lines of their own or with a sort of trawl-net, very similar to which we human bipeds use.

But, although Miss Nellie, with Dick acting under her direc tions and Bob, too, assisting in a desultory way when the superior attractions of crab hunting on his own account did not beguile him from the pursuit, all hunted everywhere, finding every variety of young whelks, cockles, and other shell fish ova on the pier-piles, which they were able to examine at their pleasure, it being low tide, no sea cucumbers to be seen anywhere.

Nellie was in despair at her failure and felt almost inclined to cry; but, Dick at the last moment, when the search was just about to be given up, raked out a perfect specimen from a hole in the rockwork beneath one of the buttresses that was nearly awash with the water a darksome dungeon, isolated from the vulgar herd of barnacles, and common but kindred anemones with which the stuck up sea cucumber was too proud to associate.

Naturally enough, Miss Nellie was delighted with her capture, and, she tenderly bore him home in triumph to be added to her extensive marine collection, which had now increased so considerably, that her aunt declared laughingly that she would have to build a room especially to contain it presently, her house not being big enough for the purpose.

"Rubbish!" the Captain had called her first attempt at collecting, but, since then, she had learnt something under the instruction of the old sailor and displayed greater discrimination in the objects of her zeal; although still, perhaps, inclined to err in the matter of quantity over quality, leaning fondly, as most enthusiasts do, to common things.

Not only was the album which her aunt had given her pasted as full as it could hold of different sorts of seaweed, known and unknown alike to Bob and herself; but she had a pile of shells big enough to build a rockery.

In addition to these, her accumulation of pet specialities included a seven fingered starfish, which is supposed by the ignorant to be peculiarly inimical to the adventurous cat that swalloweth it; and a ring horned pandalus or 'Æsop prawn,' which queer creature Master Bob appropriately christened 'The Prawnee Chief,' much to the annoyance of Miss Nell, who had become quite grand now in her language, becoming 'puffed up,' as Bob said, with her newly acquired 'knowledge' a 'little' of which, as the proverb tells us, is 'a dangerous thing.'

The Æsop prawn, by the way, gained the prefix to his name from having a hump on his back like the Phrygian slave, the fabulist. He is, also, distinguished by the most exquisite little rings or bands of scarlet, which seem to en circle his body; but the picturesque effect is really produced by his antennæ, which the pandalus has the happy knack of arranging round his little person in the most graceful fashion.

Beyond these rarities, precious above price, Nellie had gathered a quantity of cuttle fish 'bone,' as it is erroneously called, sufficient to have supplied Bob and herself for a lifetime with ink erasers a purpose for which it is generally employed.

The substance, however, is not really 'bone,' but is composed of thin layers of the purest white chalk, which, when the cuttle fish is living, is embedded in the body of the animal, running through its entire length.

The cuttle-fish in which this so called bone is generally met with, is the same species from whence the well known colour sepia used in painting is usually obtained.

To make a long story short, the rest of Miss Nellie's collection consisted of most of the various members of the crustacean family found along the south coast, which she, with the help of Bob and Dick, had picked up promiscuously.

"A good deal of rubbish stil , my dear," was the Captain's comment when he came round in the evening and Nellie showed him the latest additions to her store; "but, you've got one or two good things. I'll tell you what you want, though."

"What?" she asked excitedly. "What do we want, Captain? Hush, Bob!"

"An aquarium," said he. "You see, my dear——"

"Why, we've got one. We've got one already, Captain ." she cried out triumphantly, clapping her hands as she interrupted him. "Aunt Polly bought one this very morning for us."

"That was very good of her, more than you young torments deserve," said the Captain, with his customary chuckle. "However, now you've got an aquarium, you must have something to put in it. Something living, I mean. These dead and gone dried up old chaps here are of no use; although I wouldn't be surprised if that starfish there could still tell the number of his mess if placed in water. I'm sure he's yet alive, my dear."

"Why!" exclaimed Nellie, astonished at this, "we've had him hanging up like that for a week ! "

"Never mind that," replied the Captain. "Those funny, fat, seven fingered gentlemen have a nasty habit of 'shamming Abraham,' or pretending to have 'kicked the bucket' when they are all alive and hearty ! "

"How funny!" said Nellie, laughing. "But, what shall we get to put into the aquarium besides, Captain dear, crabs and little fish, like those we see swimming about in the sea below the castle?"

"Crabs and little grandmothers!" ejaculated the Captain in great disgust. "A nice aquarium you would make of it, missy, if you hadn't some one to look after you! Why, the crabs would eat your little fish before a week was out and then turn round and eat you!"

"Dear me, that would be dreadful!" cried Nellie laughing still more, the Captain did look so comical. "But, what may we have for our aquarium, if we must not have these?"

"Get? Well, let me see," said he, blinking away furiously and moving his bushy eyebrows up and down for a moment, as if deliberating. "We'll have some sea anemones, to commence with. No proper aquarium is complete without them; and, when you once see them expand, showing their red and purple hues, and watch their wonderful way of moving about, you will soon be convinced that they are really animals and not vegetables, which, as I believe I told you before, many wise people for a long time supposed them to be! You just wait, missy, and you will find this out for yourself and learn more about them, too, than I can tell you."

"Oh, yes," interposed Bob. "I saw one this morning when I was swimming, and it looked just like a big dahlia."

"Lucky for you it wasn't a jelly-fish, or you'd have felt it as well as seen it!" rejoined the Captain grimly—"Avast there, though, we were talking about sea anemones and other similar fry; and I was thinking that the best place for us to go to get them would be   why, by Jove, it's the very thing!"

"What's the matter now?" said Mrs. Gilmour, who had been reading a letter she had just received by the post, looking up at his sudden exclamation. "Dear me, Captain, is anything wrong?"

"Nothing, ma'am, nothing," he replied, turning round to

her "only I've this moment thought of a way of 'killing two birds with one stone.' I promised these youngsters, you know, if they were good——"

"I know, I know what's coming now," cried Miss Nell, again interrupting him. Really she was a very rude little lady sometimes. "You're going to tell us at last!"

"What, missy?" said the Captain chuckling, as she and Bob executed a triumphal dance round him, while Dick stood grinning in the background, his face, which had filled out considerably in the last week or two, making him look very different to the lantern jawed lad they had encountered in the train, all one smile. "What, missy?"

"You're going to take us out somewhere," Bob and Nellie cried in concert. "You promised, you know you did."

"But, that was if you were good," he answered, enjoying their antics. "That was the proviso, young people."

"We *are* good," they shouted together. "Auntie says so."

The Captain put his hands to his ears to shut out their voices.

"Are they good?" he asked Mrs. Gilmour. "Eh, ma'am?"

"Well, yes, I think so," said she, smiling. "Good enough as far as such children can be, I suppose! I suppose I must not tell tales out of school, sure, about what a little girl said the other day when somebody, whom I won't name, went away?"

"What, what?" inquired the old sailor, looking from one to the other. "Tell me what she said!"

Nellie put her hand over Mrs. Gilmour's mouth.

"Hush auntie," she cried appealingly. "You mustn't say anything; I didn't mean it!"

"I dare say you called me a sour old curmudgeon?" hinted the Captain, pretending to be very much grieved. "Didn't you?"

"No, I didn't," said Nellie, jumping up and throwing her arms round his neck to kiss him. "I think you are the dearest and kindest old Captain that ever was!"

" Humph ! " he ejaculated in a smothered voice, addressing her aunt. "There's no doubt, ma'am, where she gets the 'blarney' from. It runs in the family . "

" Sure an' small blame to her either," retorted the other defiantly. " It's fortunate for us women that we have some thing wherewith to get the better of you hard men sometimes."

" Sometimes, eh? always, I think," growled the Captain, looking very knowing and laughing the while. " But, I won't argue the point with you, ma'am sure to get the worst of it if I do. Tell you what I'll do, that is if it is agreeable to you. What say you to all of us crossing over to morrow to the Island, eh ? "

" Oh, auntie, how nice . " cried Nellie, hugging her and the Captain alternately.

Bob contented himself with uttering only the single word ' jolly ! '

But, the ejaculation spoke volumes, Bob's highest appreci ation being ever expressed by that expressive but slangy term ' jolly ! '

" Will it do, d'ye think ? " said the Captain to Mrs. Gilmour ; there was no need of his asking either of the children, their faces giving an unhesitating assent at once, as did Dick's. " Eh, ma'am ? "

" Certainly," she replied, " if it suits you."

" Then, that's settled," he decided. "There's a new steamer, called the *Bembridge Belle*, I've seen advertised to run on an excursion to Seaview pier ; and I think she will do very well for us ; especially as she will go partly round the Island afterwards."

" I can't say I like excursion steamers," observed Mrs. Gilmour hesitatingly ; " but if you think, as an experienced sailor, that she will be safe, of course I can have no objection. You know I'm speaking more for the children's sake than my own, being responsible to their parents for them."

" Safe, ma'am, eh? Safe as houses ! " replied the Captain,

with much energy, stamping his foot on the floor as he spoke
to give point to his assertion, his malacca cane not being
within reach at the moment. "Otherwise, ma'am, I wouldn't
let you or the chickabiddies go in her for worlds!"

"You're quite sure, Captain?"

"Faith, I'll take my 'davy,' ma'am, she's as staunch and
sound as the old *Bucephalus*."

"Say no more, Captain," said Mrs. Gilmour. "If she's as
safe as my poor Ted's ship, she must be safe indeed, I know."

"She is that, I believe, ma'am, on my honour."

"All right then, Captain," replied Mrs. Gilmour to this.
"We'll consider the trip arranged, then, for to morrow, eh?"

"Very good, ma'am, there's my hand on it," cried the
Captain, rising to take his leave. "I must say 'good night'
now; for, it's getting late, and I ought to turn in early if you
expect me to turn out to-morrow. Good night, Miss Nell;
good-night, Bob; come along, Dick!"

With which parting words, away he sailed homeward, not
thinking that he had forgotten his game of cribbage with his
fair hostess.

Strange to say, the old sailor never once recollected his
customary diversion throughout the evening!

CHAPTER IX.

A RIVAL COLLECTOR.

NOTHING could have been better than the appearances of wind and weather next morning that long wished for 'to morrow,' which had at last come, in spite of the Captain's perpetual procrastination.

The bright sun was glowing in a clear blue sky overhead, that was unflecked by a single cloud, while a fresh breeze blowing from the westwards to prevent the air from becoming stagnant; and the barometer, at 'Set Fair,' made all prophets of evil, if such there were about, keep their lips tightly closed and say nothing to damp the spirits of the expectant voyagers.

"Hullo, Nell!" shouted Bob, drumming on the balustrade of the staircase outside his bedroom to attract her attention and rouse her up. "Are you awake yet?"

Nellie's answer to this question was a 'staggerer' to Master Bob, as he termed it in his choice phraseology.

She appeared in the passage that passed her door fully dressed.

"I got up when Sarah rose, and have been ready to go downstairs for the last hour," she said calmly, with a conscious pride. "You'd better look sharp with your dressing, Bob, for it is past six o'clock. Unless you start off soon to the beach, too, for your bathe, you'll never be back in time for breakfast, which is going to be earlier this morning so that we may catch the steamer comfortably."

"My good gracious!" exclaimed Bob, jamming his right foot into his left boot in his hurry and wasting a minute or more in wriggling it out again. "I thought I was ever so early, and up before any one!"

"Ah, me dear," cried out Mrs. Gilmour from below; "you'll have to catch a weasel asleep, sure, before you can hope, sir, to get ahead of us in this house. I called Sarah long ere either of you were stirring!"

This was a climax; and so, without making any reply to aunt Polly's pertinent statement of fact, save a stifled laugh at the expense of Miss Nell, who had prided herself on having, as she thought, got the start of them all, Bob expediting his dressing in the most summary fashion, hurried off as speedily as possible across the common for his matutinal dip.

He was accompanied, as a matter of course, by Rover, who was ready and waiting for him on the terrace outside, barking and bounding about like a demented dog who had parted company with his usual stock of common sense.

"Down, Rover!" cried Bob, when the faithful fellow, in the exuberance of his joy on seeing his young master come out of the house, leaped up and licked his face, preventing him from closing the door properly as he was about to do. "Behave yourself, sir!"

Rover, however, thought there were different ways of 'behaving himself,' the chief in his estimation being to show his affection to those who were kind to him, whom he loved with all the intensity of his great canine heart; and so, ranking obedience to orders as only second to this potent law of his life, he frisked and jumped and playfully tousled Bob until he finally made him start at a swinging trot for the beach, the frolicsome retriever galloping in advance one moment, the next stopping in his mad career onward to give out a loud bark and wag his tail in encouragement to his master to try and catch him up, if he could!

Bob bent his steps towards the coastguard station on the

eastern side of the sea wall, near the new pier, which was the regular meeting place for him and Dick every morning for their bathe; and here, punctually at 'Six Bells,' or seven o'clock, he found on the present occasion his fellow swimmer along with the Captain.

The latter, he could hear as he approached, was having an animated discussion with Hellyer, the chief boatman, on the subject of torpedoes, which Hellyer believed in, but which the Captain utterly poohpoohed, saying that in his opinion they were of little, if any, use in naval warfare.

He was laying down the law with great unction when Bob came up to them.

"Don't tell me," he cried, "of your 'Whitehead' going twenty knots an hour and exploding its charge of gun cotton under a ship's bottom; for, where and what would those on board the ship be doing all the time standing still, I suppose, to be shot at and doing nothing in their own defence?"

"Aye, that's true, sir," said Hellyer; "but "

"Remember, too," continued the Captain, "the torpedo, even of the most improved type, can only keep up this speed of twenty knots for a distance of five hundred yards, within which range the boat discharging it would have to approach before sending it off at the vessel attacked, which of course would be fool enough to let it come to such close quarters without riddling it? Oh, yes, you tell that to the marines!"

Hellyer laughed.

"You carry too many guns for me, sir," said he good-humouredly. "I can't stand up against you, Captain, once you tackle me fairly!"

"Too strong, eh?" rejoined the Captain, triumphant at getting the better of his opponent. "Of course I am! Your argument, Hellyer, won't hold water. Besides, should one of those spiteful little inventions succeed in getting near an ironclad without being seen and sunk, the torpedo nets of the ship would prevent the infernal machine, as these new-fashioned fallals were called in the old days, from exploding against her hull. I, for my part, would be quite content to stand the brunt of a torpedo attack on board a ship fitted with protecting nets and quick-firing guns. By Jove, I'd guarantee that Jack Dresser wouldn't be the one that was licked!"

"I'd bet that same, sir," agreed Hellyer heartily, but seeing Bob he added, "Ah, here's the young ge'man I fished out of the sea t'other night. He doesn't look any the worse for being nigh drown ded. He warn' hurt, sir, much, were he?"

"Not he," said the Captain. "He's learnt to swim, though, since then, and the other boy too; so, if they choose to tumble in again off the ramparts and get into deep water, there won't be so much bother in hauling them out; eh, Bob?"

"No, Captain," replied Bob, who was busy undressing; and, within a few moments he had plunged into the sea, and was swimming out with a brave firm stroke in a way that fully justified the Captain's praise of his natatory powers, shouting out at intervals his customary war cry—"Jolly!"

Nor was Dick far behind, although perhaps not quite so plucky in venturing beyond his depth, now that he had no especial motive as on that memorable evening already alluded to by Hellyer the coastguardsman, for running the risk; while, as for Rover, he fairly revelled in the water, paddling round and round Bob and Dick, thereby executing a series of concentric circles never dreamt of by the Egyptian mathematician whose problems have been the torment of the boys of all ages.

The sea was so warm and pleasant that they stopped in such an unconscionable time as to necessitate the Captain's hailing them three times to come out before they obeyed the order, and even then did so lothfully, making the old sailor sing out to them the more imperatively

"Come out, come out of that. you young rascals." he cried, shaking his stick menacingly. "If you are not out and dressed

G

in five minutes, by Jove I'll start without you; for, I can't keep the ladies waiting. By Jove, I will!"

This threat had the desired result of quickening the boys' movements; Dick, if the slowest in the water, being the sharper of the two in getting into his clothes. Rover was even speedier still, having only to give himself one good shake, administering in the action a shower bath of drops to the Captain, when, there he was all ready, with a smart new curly black coat, glistening from his dip, as if he had just been to the hairdresser's and had a brush up for the occasion!

On the way back to Mrs. Gilmour's house to breakfast, the Captain and Dick being specially invited this morning, so that they might leave together immediately afterwards for the steamer without losing any time, the boys had great fun with Rover and the towels.

These the retriever was always in the habit of carrying home, though Bob would not let him have them at once, right out, to take in his mouth as he left the beach.

He would first show them to Rover, with a "Look here, good dog!"

Then Bob would put the bundle of towels in a hole in the shingle, or under some big boulder, which did not improve them, by the way; Rover observing everything his young master did with the keenest attention, barking the while, and with every hair of his mane bristling with excitement.

After thus hiding the towels, if it could be called hiding where every detail of the operation was watched by the dog, Bob would, as he did on the present occasion, set out on his return across the common; Master Rover prancing in front of him, and anxiously keeping his speaking brown eyes fixed on his face, awaiting the order which he knew to be impending for him to go back and fetch the bundle left behind.

It was always a struggle for Bob to keep his countenance steady, the slightest suspicion of a smile being interpreted by

Rover as an intimation that he was at liberty to 'go and fetch,' without a word being uttered; and, this morning, the struggle was intensified by the presence of the Captain, who was in a joking mood, and tried all he could to draw off Rover's attention from Bob.

However, in spite of these difficulties, the latter succeeded in repressing any signs of emotion in his face until they got to the landmark in the middle of the common, when, opening his mouth at last, Bob said, almost in a whisper, the magic words, "Go and fetch!"

Low as was the tone in which the command was given, Rover heard it; and then, in an instant, off he flew, like an arrow from the bow, with his bushy tail stretched out straight behind, bottle brush fashion, making him resemble a dark-coloured fox in the distance, with the hounds in full cry after him.

The last they saw of him was the end of his tufted tail disappearing over the sea-wall at the place where Bob had secreted the towels, so on they went in the expectation of Rover presently overtaking the party with the towels, which he seldom failed to do before the roadway skirting the other side of the common was reached, the retriever being generally very rapid in his movements.

On this occasion, however, the Captain with the boys not only got as far as the terrace, but arrived at the gate of Mrs. Gilmour's house, without there being any appearance of Rover's return.

He and the towels were alike 'conspicuous by their absence.'

What could have happened?

Listening attentively, they could hear presently the sound of a dog barking in the direction of the sea, and to Bob's mind, at least, there was no doubt that the bark was the bark of Rover.

"He cannot get the towels from under the stone," cried Bob, turning back. "It is either that, or somebody has stolen them, or something. I must go and see what's the matter."

"We'll all come," said the Captain.   " I should like to see
the affair out."

So saying, he wheeled round too, and with Dick started off
in pursuit of Bob, who, going at the run, was already some
distance ahead, on his return journey to the beach.

The Captain stepped out well, however, and he and Dick
got up just in time to settle a little dispute, in which Bob,
Rover, and an ugly looking man, very like a gipsy and
evidently a tramp, were the parties interested.

The man had one end of the bundle of towels grasped in
both his hands, while Rover was holding on like grim death to
the other; the dog growling, and tugging away so violently
between each growl, that the tramp had hard work to keep
hold of his prize.

Bob, on his part, had caught up a piece of broken timber,
and was advancing to the faithful dog's aid.

But a boy like Bob, even with the help of such a valiant
protector as the retriever, could do little or nothing against a
burly, ruffianly giant, six feet high, and broad in proportion.

The arrival of the Captain on the scene with Dick, however,
altered the aspect of affairs considerably.

The gipsy tramp, who had sworn to Bob, and at him too,
that the bundle was his own, and that he was walking quietly
along the shore in search of work, when he was assailed by
"that savage dog o' yourn there," now said, on the Captain's
telling him curtly to drop the towels, or he would have him
locked up, that he had "only picked 'em up on the beach,
and didn't mean no harm by it to nobody, that he didn't."

" Then the sooner you are off out of this, the better for you,
my friend," said the Captain, on the man's letting go the
bundle of towels, which Rover at once carried off in triumph
and laid at Bob's feet. " Be off with you, you rascal, at once ! "

The man took his advice, and slouched away round the
castle, soon disappearing from their sight; when, much
excited by the unexpected little incident that they now would

have to detail to Mrs. Gilmour and Nellie, besides being full of Rover's bravery and sagacity, they took their way home again, for the second time, across the common, the clock of old St. Thomas's church in the distance striking as they turned their faces homeward—"One two three four five six—seven eight NINE!"

"Look sharp, lads, or we'll be late for the steamer!" cried the old sailor, as they hurried along, setting the example by hastening onwards as fast as his little legs, aided by his ever-present malacca cane, could carry him. "I'm told that the *Bembridge Belle* will leave the pier at ten o'clock without fail, wind and weather permitting, and it has just struck nine all through your loitering and skylarking in the water, Master Bob and you Dick, and that long palaver we had afterwards with your friend the towel thief."

On reaching the house, where breakfast was all ready awaiting their arrival, the old Captain, while hurrying through the meal, found time to chaff Nellie about this 'rival collector,' as he called the prowling tramp when narrating all about the adventure that had detained them; telling her she would have to look to her laurels, and gather up all the odds and ends she could find, on the beach, or else this gentleman, who had displayed such zeal that morning in trying to add to his collection, would certainly outvie hers.

"Now, children," said Mrs. Gilmour, when breakfast and chaff had both come to an end, repeating the Captain's favourite word of command, "Look sharp!"

Her preparations had all been made beforehand; and without losing another moment, she and the Captain, with Bob and Nellie behind them, started off, Dick, who had been taken care of meanwhile by Sarah in the kitchen, bringing up the rear with a substantial looking hamper on his shoulder.

Almost breathless, alike from excitement and their rapid pace, they made their way seawards, to where the *Bembridge Belle* was blowing off her steam alongside the pier, sounding her whistle to tell belated passengers like themselves that they had better put their best foot foremost if they wished to reach her in time.

"All aboard?" inquired the captain of the steamer from his post on the port paddle-box, hailing the porter of the pier ashore, when they, the very last of the late comers, had scrambled across the gangway; and the porter having signified that no one now was in sight, the blue capped gentleman standing on the paddle box touched the engine-room telegraph, and gave the signal to "Go ahead!"

In another minute, the fore and aft hawsers that had previously made her fast to the pier were cast off, and her paddles began to revolve with a heavy splashing sound, like that of flails in a farmyard threshing out the grain.

"Starboard!" sang out her skipper, now mounting from the paddle box to the bridge above. "Hard over, my man!"

"Starboard it is, sir," replied the helmsman, rapidly twirling the spokes of the wheel as he spoke. "It's right over, sir."

"Steady!" now sang out the skipper, meaning that the vessel's head had been sufficiently turned in the direction he desired. "Steady; keep her so."

"Steady it is, sir," repeated the man at the wheel like a parrot, to show that the order had been understood and acted upon. "Steady it is"

"Port a trifle now."

"Aye, aye, sir," returned the helmsman, reversing the wheel. "Port it is, sir; two points over."

"Steady."

"Steady it is."

Whereupon, a straight course being now laid for the little port to which they were bound on the Isle of Wight opposite, the *Bembridge Belle* steamed ahead, splashing and dashing through the water, that rippled over with laughter in the bright sunshine, lightening up its translucent depths, and leaving a broad silvery wake of dancing eddies behind her.

CHAPTER X.

AFLOAT AND ASHORE.

"Sure, I'm almost dead entirely, with all that hurrying and scurrying!" exclaimed Mrs. Gilmour, when she was at length got safely on board the little steamer and comfortably placed on a cosy seat aft, near the wheel, to which Captain Dresser had gallantly escorted her. "Really, now, I couldn't have run another yard, if it had been to save me life!"

She panted out the words with such a racy admixture of her Irish 'brogue,' which always became more 'pronounced' with her when she was at all excited in any way, that the Captain, even while showing every sympathy for her distressed condition, could not help chuckling as he imitated her tone of voice and accent much to the amusement of Master Bob and Miss Nellie, you may be sure!

"Sure, an' there's no knowin' what ye can do, now, till ye thry, ma'am!" said he. "Is there, me darlint?"

"None of your nonsense," she replied laughing; "I won't have you making fun of my country like that. I'm sure you're just as much an Irishman as I am!"

This slip delighted the Captain.

"There, ma'am," he exclaimed exultingly, "you've been and gone and put your foot in it now in all conscience."

"Oh, auntie!" cried Nellie, "an Irish*man!*"

This made Mrs. Gilmour see her blunder, and she cheerfully joined in the laugh against herself.

Bob, meanwhile, had stationed himself by the engine room hatchway, and was contemplating with rapt attention the almost human like movements of the machinery below.

How wonderful it all was, he thought the up and down stroke of the piston in and out of the cylinder, which oscillated from side to side guided by the eccentric; with the steady systematic revolution of the shaft, borne round by the crank attached to the piston head, all working so smoothly, and yet with such resistless force !

The whole was a marvel to him, as indeed it is to many of us to whom a marine engine is no novelty.

"Well, my young philosopher," said the Captain, tapping him on the shoulder and making him take off his gaze for a moment from the sight, "do you think you understand the engines by this time, eh ? "

Bob only needed the hint to speak ; and out he came with a whole volley of questions.

"What is that thing there?" he asked, "the thing that goes round, I mean."

"The paddle-shaft," replied the Captain; "it turns the wheels."

"And that other thing that goes up and down ? "

"The piston rod," said the old sailor. "It is this which turns the shaft."

"Then, I want to know how the piston makes the shaft turn round, when it only goes up and down itself? "

"The 'eccentric' manages to do that, although it was a puzzle for a long time to engineers to solve the problem not until, I believe, Fulton thought of this plan," said the Captain ; and, he then went on to explain how, in the old beam engine of Watt, as well as in the earlier contrivances for utilizing steam-power, a fly-wheel was the means adopted for changing the perpendicular action of the piston into a circular motion. "Of course, though," he added, "this fly wheel was only available in stationary engines for pumping and so on ; but, when the principle of the eccentric was discovered later in the day, the previously uneducated young giant, 'Steam,' was then broken to harness, so to speak, being thenceforth made serviceable for dragging railway carriages on our iron roads, and propelling ships without the aid of sails, and against the wind even, if need be!"

"But what is steam?" was Bob's next query. "That's what I want to know."

This fairly bothered the Captain.

"Steam?" he repeated, "steam, eh? humph! steam is, well let me see, steam is   steam."

Bob exploded at this, his merriment being shared by Nellie and Mrs. Gilmour, the latter not sorry for the old sailor's 'putting his foot in it' by a very similar blunder to that for which he had laughed at her shortly before; while, as for Dick, the struggles he made to hide the broad grin which would show on his face were quite comical and even painful to witness.

The Captain pretended to get into a great rage; although his twinkling eyes and suppressed chuckle testified that it was only pretence all the time, though his passion was well simulated.

"I don't see anything to laugh at, you young rascal," he said to Bob. "I'm sure I've given you quite as good a definition as you would find in any of those 'catechisms of common things'—catechisms of conundrums, I call them   which boys and girls are made to learn by rote, like parrots, without really acquiring any sensible knowledge of the subjects they are supposed to teach! I might tell you, as these works do, that 'steam was an elastic fluid generated by water when in a boiling state'; but, would you be any the wiser for that piece of information, eh?"

"No, Captain," answered Bob, still giggling, "I don't understand."

"Or, I might tell you 'steam is only a synonym for heat, the cause of all motion'   do you understand that?"

Bob still shook his head, trying vainly to keep from laughing.

"Of course not," cried the Captain triumphantly, "nor would I, either, unless I knew something more about it; and to tell you that would take me all the day nearly."

"Oh spare us," said Mrs. Gilmour plaintively. "Pray spare us that!"

"I will, ma'am," he replied. ' I assure you I wasn't going to do it. Some time or other, though, this young shaver shall come along with me when one of the new ships goes out from the dockyard for her steam trials; and then, perhaps, he will be able to have everything explained to him properly, without boring you or bothering me."

"How jolly!" ejaculated Bob "I should like that."

"You mustn't count your chickens before they're hatched," growled the other, turning round on him abruptly; "and, if ever I catch you sniggering again when I'm talking I'll—I'll——"

What the Captain's terrible threat was must ever remain a mystery; for, just at that moment, Nell, who had been looking over the side of the steamer, watching the creamy foam churned up by her paddles and rolling with heavy undulations into the long white wake astern marking her progress through the water, suddenly uttered an exclamation.

"Look, look, aunt Polly!" she cried excitedly. "Oh, look!"

"What, dearie?" inquired Mrs. Gilmour, bending towards her, thinking she had dropped her glove or something into the sea. "What is it?"

"There, there!" said Nellie, pointing out some dark objects that could be seen tumbling about in the tideway some distance off the starboard quarter. "See those big fishes, auntie! Are they whales?"

It was the Captain's turn to laugh now.

"Whales, eh? By Jove, you'll be the death of me, missy, by Jove, you will, ho ho—ho!" he chuckled, leaning on his stick for support. "What does Shakespeare say, eh? 'Very like a whale,' eh? Ho ho ho!"

Miss Nell did not like this at all, though she did not object to laughing at others

"Well, what are they?" she asked indignantly. "What are they?"

"Pigs," replied the Captain with a grave face, but there was a sly twinkle of his left eye approaching to a wink. "Those are pigs, missy."

"I don't believe it," cried the young lady in a pet, putting up her shoulders in high disdain. "You're only making fun of me!"

"Hush, dearie, you mustn't be rude," said Mrs. Gilmour reprovingly; "but sure, Captain, you shouldn't make game of the child."

"I assure you, I'm not doing so, ma'am," he protested, chuckling though still with much enjoyment. "I've only told her the simple truth. They *are* pigs, sea pigs if you like, commonly called porpoises. But, whales, by Jove, that's a good joke, ho ho ho!"

This time Nellie laughed too, the old sailor seemed to enjoy her mistake with such gusto; and, harmony being thus restored, they all turned to watch the graceful motions of the animals that had caused the discussion, which, swimming abreast of the vessel, were ever and anon darting across her bows and playing round her, describing the most beautiful curves as they dived under each other, apparently indulging in a game of leap-frog.

The *Bembridge Belle* was now just about midway between Southsea and Seaview, and close upon the buoy marking the spot where the old *Marie Rose*, the first big ship of our embryo navy, sank in the reign of bluff King Hal, in an action she had with a French squadron that attempted entering the Solent with the idea of capturing the Isle of Wight. The 'moun-seers,' as the Captain explained to Bob, were beaten off in the battle and most of their vessels captured, a result owing largely to the part played by the gallant *Marie Rose;* though, sad be it to relate, while resisting all the efforts made by the enemy to carry her by the board, being somewhat top-heavy, "she 'turned the turtle' at the very moment when her guns were brought to bear a starboard, to give a final broadside to the French admiral and settle the action, the poor thing then incontinently sinking to the bottom, where her bones yet lie."

"Not far off either," continued the Captain, "the *Royal George* also foundered in the last century, with over nine hundred hands, there being a lot of shore folk in the ship beside her crew. Her Admiral, Kempenfeldt, was also on board, and   "

"Yes," said Mrs. Gilmour, interrupting him; "and, sure, there's a pretty little poem my favourite Cowper wrote about it which I recollect I learnt by heart when I was a little girl, much smaller than you, Nell. The lines began thus

'Toll for the brave, the brave that are no more,'

don't you remember them; I'm sure you must, Captain?"

"Can't say I do, ma'am," he replied   "poetry isn't in my line. But, as I was saying, the *Royal George* heeled over pretty nearly in the same way as the other one did that I just now told you about; and, I remember when I was studying at the Naval College in the Dockyard ever so many years ago, when I was a youngster not much older than you, Master Bob, being out at Spithead when the wreck of the vessel was blown up, to clear the fairway for navigation. I've got a ruler and a paper-knife now at home that were carved out of pieces of her timber which I picked up at the time."

"How nice!" observed Mrs. Gilmour. "A charming recollection, I call it!"

"Well, I don't know about that," replied the Captain, who seemed a little bit grumpy, and was fumbling in his pockets without apparently being able to find the object of which he was in search—"my recollection is not so good as I would like it!"

On Mrs. Gilmour looking at him inquiringly, noticing the tone in which he spoke, the truth came out.

"The fact is, ma'am, I've lost my snuff box," he said apologetically to excuse his snappy answers. "I must have left it in my other coat at home."

He did not give up the quest, however, but continued to dive his hands on the right and left alternately into pocket after pocket; until, suddenly, the cross expression vanished from his face, being succeeded by a beaming smile, followed by his customary good humoured chuckle.

"I've found it!" he exclaimed triumphantly, producing the missing box from the usual pocket in which he kept it, where it had lain all the time; and, taking a pinch, the Captain was himself again. "By Jove, I thought my memory was gone!"

The porpoises all this while continued their gambols about the steamer, now ahead, now astern, now swimming abreast, one after the other, rolling, diving, and jumping out of the water sometimes in their sport.

They seemed to be having a regular holiday of it; and, tired of leap frog, had taken to 'follow my leader' or some other game. At any rate, they did not think much of the *Bembridge Belle*, passing and repassing and going round her at intervals, as if to show their contempt of a speed they could so readily eclipse.

"Do you often see them here playing like this?" asked Nellie of the Captain, who was also looking over the side. "Is that the way they always swim?"

"No, missy," said he, with all his old geniality, "not often, though they pay us a visit now and then in summer when so inclined. Their coming now through Spithead is a sign that there's going to be a change of wind."

"Oh!" cried Nell wonderingly. "How strange!"

"Yes, my dear," went on the old sailor, smiling as he looked down in her puzzled face upturned to his, "I'm not joking, missy, as you think. Those fellows are regular barometers in their way; and, if you note the direction towards which they are seen swimming when they pass a ship at sea, from that very point wind, frequently a gale, may be shortly expected."

"I hope we're not going to have another storm," said Nellie, thinking of their late experience. "I don't like those gales."

"No, no, not so bad as that now, I think," he replied, chuckling away. "There probably will be only a slight shift of wind from the western quarter, whence it is now blowing, to the eastward, whither the porpoises are now making off for, as you can see for yourself."

So it subsequently turned out.

The 'sea-pigs,' as the Captain had at first jocularly termed them, bade good bye to the steamer and its passengers when they had got a little way beyond No Man's fort, and were approaching shoal water, with an impudent flick of their fluky tails in the air as they went off, shaping a straight course out towards the Nab lightship, as if bound up Channel.

They had all been so occupied watching the porpoises that they had not noticed the rapid progress the steamer had been making towards her first port of call on the other side of the Solent; and so, almost at the same moment that the Captain called Nellie's attention to the last movements of the queer fish as they vanished in the distance, she shut off her steam and sidled up to Seaview pier.

"Who's for the shore?" cried out the skipper from his post on the paddle box, as soon as the vessel had made fast, and the 'brow,' or gangway, was shoved ashore for the passengers to land, without any unnecessary delay. "Any ladies or gents for Seaview?"

The majority of those on board at once quitted the steamer, amongst them being our quintet.

As they were stepping on to the pier, however, a slight difficulty arose in connection with one of their number.

It was about Rover.

"Is that your dog?" asked the collector of tickets of the

Captain, as the retriever darted ahead in a great hurry. "That your dog, sir?"

"No," replied the old sailor, "not exactly why?"

"Because, if he is, he'll have to have a ticket the same as the rest," said the man. "Dogs is half price, like children."

"Oh, I didn't know," cried the Captain apologetically, as he put his hand in his pocket and paid Rover's fare, adding in a low voice to Mrs. Gilmour, while they were ascending the steps from the landing stage to the pier above, "I do believe that rascal thought I meant to cheat him and smuggle the dog through without paying, the fellow looked at me so suspiciously."

"Perhaps he did," replied she laughing. "You know you are a very suspicious looking gentleman."

"Humph!" he chuckled. "I think Rover intended to do him, though. He squeezed himself past my legs very artfully!"

"He did, the naughty dog," said Nellie, who, with Bob, had been much amused by the little incident. "He's always doing it in London at the railway-stations whenever we go by the underground line; and papa says he wants to cheat the company. He comes after us sometimes, and jumps into the railway-carriage where we are, when we think him miles away and safe at home! Did you ever hear of such a thing, aunt Polly?"

"No, dearie," she answered as they all stepped out briskly along the rather shaky suspension bridge connecting the pier with the shore, which oscillated under their feet in a way that made Mrs. Gilmour anxious to get off it as quickly as she could to firm ground. "Rover is a clever fellow, sure!"

"He's a very artful dog!" observed the Captain, whereat Rover wagged his tail, as if he understood what he said and appreciated the compliment—"a very artful dog!"

Arrived on shore, presently, the children were in ecstasies at all they saw; for, by only crossing the roadway opposite the land end of the shaky bridge, they at once found themselves within the outlying shrubbery and brushwood of Priory Park, which the kindly proprietor freely threw open for years to the public, without post or paling interfering with their enjoyment, until the vandalism and vulgarity of some cockney excursionists, who wrought untold destruction to the property, led to the rescinding of this privilege!

Although touching the sea, the waters of which lapped its turf at high tide, when once within the park, it seemed to Bob and Nellie as if they were miles away already in the heart of the country; so that, accustomed as they had been only to town life, it may be imagined how great the change was to them in every way.

As for runaway Dick from Guildford, who had been familiarized to rustic scenes from his earliest infancy, he could see no beauty in the various objects that each instant delighted the little Londoners' eyes and ears, for, like the hero of Wordsworth's verse, "the primrose by the river's brim" was but a primrose and nothing more to him!

To Bob and Nellie, however, the scene around, with its salient features, disclosed a new world.

There were great, nodding, ox-eyed daisies that popped up pertly on either side, staring at them from amidst wastes of wild hyacinths and forget-me nots that were bluer than Nellie's witching eyes.

Pink and white convolvulus hung in festoons across the bracken bordered little winding pathways that led here and there through mazes of shrubbery and undergrowth, under the arched wilderness of greenery above.

Rippling rivulets trickling down from nowhere and wandering whither their erratic wills directed, their soft, murmuring voices chiming in with the gayer carols of the birds.

Amongst these could be distinguished the harmonious notes of some not altogether unknown to them, the trill of the lark on high, the whistle of the blackbird in the hidden covert, the 'pretty Dick' of the thrush, and the 'chink, chink!' of the robin and coo of the dove, mingled with the sweet but subdued song of the yellow-hammer and sharp staccato accompaniment of the untiring chaffinch; while, all the time, a colony of asthmatic old rooks in the taller trees of the park cawed their part in the concert in a deep bass key at regular intervals "Caw, caw, caw!"

Bob and Nellie were so delighted and unsparing of their admiration of everything they saw and heard, that Dick fell to wondering at the pleasure they took in things which he held of little account.

If unappreciative, however, Dick was of some service in telling Nellie the names of the principal wild-flowers; while he rose high in Bob's estimation by his lore in the matter of birds' nests, of which the ex-runaway from the country, naturally, could speak as an expert.

Touching the feathered tribe generally, he was able to tell them off at a glance, with the habits and characteristics of each, as readily as Bob could repeat the Multiplication Table more so, indeed, if the strict truth be insisted on, without stretching a point!

"That be a throosh," he would say; and, "t'other, over there's, a chaffy. He ain't up to much now; but wait till he be moulted and he'll coom out foine! I've heard tell folks in furrin' parts vallies 'em greatly, though we in Guildford think nowt of they. I'd rayther a lark mysen, Master Bob."

"Ah!" exclaimed Nellie, who had previously been shocked by Dick's lack of sentiment, much pleased now at this expression of a better taste "you do like their singing then!"

"Lawks no, miss," replied the unprincipled boy. "Larks is foine roasted!"

Nellie was horrified.

"You don't mean to say, Dick," she cried, "that—that you actually eat them?"

"Aye, miss," he replied, without an atom of shame, "we doos. They be rare tasty birds!'

H

She gave him up after this, going along by herself in silence.

"This is jolly!" exclaimed Bob presently, when, after getting a little way within the park and ascending the rise leading up from the shore to an open plateau above, he saw a sort of fairy dell below, at the foot of a grassy slope, the green surface of which was speckled over with daisies and buttercups. "Come along, Nell."

Down the tempting incline he at once raced, with Nellie and Rover at his heels; and, diving beneath a jungle of blackberry-bushes at the bottom, matted together with ropes of ivy that had fallen from a withered oak, whose dry and sapless gnarled old trunk still stood proudly erect in the midst of the mass of luxuriant vegetation with which it was surrounded, Nellie heard him after a bit call out from the leafy enclosure in which he had quickly found himself "Oh, I say, I see such a pretty fern!"

There was silence then for a moment or so, as if Bob was trying to secure the object that had taken his fancy, the quietude being broken by his giving vent to a prolonged "O o-h!"

"What's the matter?" cried Nellie, who had stopped without the briary tangle into which her brother had plunged, noticing that his accents of delight suddenly changed to those of pain. "Are you hurt?"

"I've scratched my face," he said ruefully, emerging from the blackberry-brake with streaks of blood across his forehead and his nose looking as if it had been in the wars. "Some beastly thorns did it."

"Oh!" ejaculated Nellie, in sympathy and surprise; "I'm so sorry!"

"It is 'oh,' and it hurts too!" retorted he, dabbing his face tenderly with his pocket handkerchief. "However, I shall get that fern I was after, though, in spite of all the prickles and thorns in the world!"

So saying, in he dashed again, stooping under the thorny network, and came out ere long with a beautiful specimen of the shuttlecock fern, which elicited as expressive an 'Oh' from Nellie as the sight of his scratched face had just previously done an 'Oh' of admiration and delight. But, as with Bob, her joyful exclamation was quickly followed by an expression of woe.

As she stepped forward to inspect the fern more closely, she put her foot on a rotten branch of the oak tree, which had become broken off from its parent stem and lay stretched across the dell, forming a sort of frail bridge over the prickly chasm below up to the higher ground on which she stood.

Alas! the decayed wood gave way under her weight, slight as that was, and Nellie, uttering a wild shriek of terror, disappeared from Bob's astonished gaze.

CHAPTER XI.

IN A SAD PLIGHT!

THE Captain, who had remained on the plateau above, in company with Mrs. Gilmour and Dick—the latter still in charge of the precious hamper pricked up his ears at the sound of poor Nellie's scream and Bob's expressive cry of alarm.

"Hullo!" he sang out in his sailor fashion "I wonder what's the row now? By Jove, I thought it wouldn't be long before those two young persons got into mischief when we left them alone together."

"I hope to goodness they haven't come to any harm," said Mrs. Gilmour dolefully. "Sure and will you go and say what's happened?"

"Sure an' I'm just a going, ma'am," replied the Captain, keeping up his good humoured mimicry of her accent so as to reassure her; adding, as he scrambled down the slope cautiously with the aid of his trusty malacca cane—"You needn't be alarmed, ma'am, 'at all at all,' for I don't believe anything very serious has occurred, as children's calls for assistance generally mean nothing in the end. They are like, as your countryman said when he shaved his pig, 'all cry and little wool!'"

He chuckled to himself as he went on down the declivity, turning round first, however, to see whether Mrs. Gilmour appreciated the allusion to 'poor Pat'; while Dick, leaving the hamper behind, followed, in case his assistance might also be needed in the emergency.

Arrived at the bottom of the dell the old sailor found it impossible at first to tell what had happened; for, Bob was trying to force his way through the brushwood brake, and Rover barking madly. Nellie was nowhere to be seen, although her voice could be heard proceeding from somewhere near at hand, calling for help still, but in a weaker voice.

"Where are you?" shouted the Captain. "Sing out, can't you!"

"Here," came the reply in the girl's faint treble; "I'm here!"

"Where's 'here'?" said he, puzzled. "I can't see anything of you!"

"I've tumbled into a pit," cried Nellie piteously, in muffled tones that sounded as if coming from underground. "Do take me out, please! There's a lot of wild animals here, and they're biting my legs—oh!"

A series of piercing shrieks followed, showing that the poor child was terribly alarmed, if not seriously hurt; and the Captain saw that no time was to be lost.

"Can you reach her, Bob?" he sang out; "or see her, eh?"

"No, I can't get through these prickly bushes, they're just like a wall!" replied Bob, fighting manfully through to get down to his sister's relief. "I can't see her a bit, either!"

"Humph!"

The Captain thought a moment, rather shirking going amongst the thorns.

"Ha, the very thing!" he exclaimed. "Hi, Rover!"

The dog, who had been barking and running here and there aimlessly, at once cocked his ears and came up to the Captain, scanning his face with eager attention.

"Fetch her out, good dog!" he cried, pointing to the spot where the broken branch of the oak tree had given way, adding in a louder voice, "Call him, Nellie call the dog to you, missy."

A cry, " Here, Rover ! " came from underneath the tangled
mass of brushwood, borne down and partly torn away by Nellie
in her fall to the depths below.   " Come here, sir ! "

No sooner did he hear this summons, faint though it was,
from his young mistress, than any uncertainty which may have
obscured his mind as to what the Captain meant by telling him
to ' fetch her out,' at once disappeared ; and Rover, uttering
a short, sharp, expressive bark, to show that he now understood
what was expected of him, boldly plunged into the thicket with
a bound.

" Chuck, chuck, chuck !   Whir r r r," and a blackbird flew
out, dashing in the Captain's face ; while, at the same time,
another piercing screech came from Nellie—"Ah h h ! Help !"

The old sailor was so startled that he jumped back, his hat
tumbling off into a bramble bush.

" Zounds ! " he exclaimed.   " What the dickens is that ? "

In a moment, however, he recovered himself.

" Pooh, what a fool I am ! " he said, ashamed of the slight
weakness he had displayed, and hoping neither of the boys
had noticed it ; and then, to show how cool and collected he
was, he whistled up the retriever. " Whee—ee up, Rover,
fetch her out, good dog ! "

Rover did not need this adjuration, not he.

Even as the Captain spoke, there was a rustling and tramping
in the thicket, accompanied by the snapping of twigs ; and,
almost at the same instant, the dog dashed out from amidst
the brushwood with Nellie holding on to his tail.

" Oh my ! " ejaculated Dick, rushing to her side ; and, with
the assistance of Bob, who also emerged from the prickly cavern
at the same time, she was got on her feet   " Poor Nell ! "

She presented a sorry spectacle.

Never was such a piteous plight seen !

Her face was scratched by the thorns, her clothes torn, and
her hat had fallen off like that of the Captain, who had, by
the way, in the flurry forgotten to replace his on his head, the

venerable article remaining in a sadly battered condition where it had fallen.

On being released, however, from her predicament, Nellie treated the matter much more lightly than might have been expected.

She was a very courageous little girl now that she knew she was in safety.

But she was also, it should be said, blest, too, with great amiability.

"Oh, never mind the scratches," she replied, in answer to the Captain's inquiries. "I'm not at all hurt, thank you."

"How about those wild animals?" asked the old sailor smiling. "eh, missy?"

Nellie coloured up, but could not help laughing at the Captain's quizzical face, as he took up his hat gingerly and put it on.

"I I made a mistake," she stammered. "I was frightened!"

At that moment, however, very opportunely, Master Rover, who had darted back into the thicket after reclaiming his young mistress, saved her all further explanation as to the unknown beasts that had caused her such alarm by appearing now in full pursuit of an unfortunate rabbit which, putting forth its best speed, escaped him in the very nick of time by diving into a hole on the other side of the knoll, contemptuously kicking up its heels as it did so, almost into his open mouth.

The mystery of Nellie's disappearance was thus satisfactorily solved.

She had fallen into an old rabbit burrow.

The harmless little creatures, whom she had imagined to be making desperate assaults on her legs and about to eat her up, too, were probably even more frightened than she was!

"Oh oh, that's one of those ferocious wild animals, little missy, eh?" chuckled the Captain. "I see, young lady."

"Yes, but they frightened me," pleaded poor Nell. "They moved about under my feet, jumping up at me, I thought; and it was so dark down there that I didn't know what they might be. You would have been frightened too, I think, sir!"

She added this little retort to her explanation with some considerable spirit, a bit nettled by the Captain's chaff.

"Well, well, my dear, perhaps you are right," he replied good humouredly. "I also have a confession to make, missy. Just before Rover cantered up, with you holding on to his tail like Mazeppa lashed to the back of the fiery untamed steed of the desert, a blackbird flew out of your blackberry thicket, brushing past my face, and do you know it startled me so that I jumped back, losing my hat. So, you see, I got a fright too!"

"I see'd yer, sir," said Dick, the Captain looking round as if awaiting comment on his action. "I see'd yer done it!"

"And so did I," cried Bob, the appearance of whose face had not been improved by his struggles with the thorny bushes as he tried to force his way through them to Nellie's rescue. "I saw you too!"

"You young rascals!" exclaimed the Captain, shaking his stick at them. "I thought you were looking at me! I suppose you'll be going and telling everybody you saw the old sailor in a terrible funk, and that I was going to faint?"

"Sure and that's what I feel like doing!" cried Mrs. Gilmour in a very woebegone voice, she having only just succeeded in arriving at the scene of action, scrambling down with some difficulty from the top of the slope, the pathway being blocked at intervals by the struggling creepers which twined and inter laced themselves with the undergrowth, trailing down from the branches of the trees above, and making it puzzling to know which way to go. "I couldn't crawl a step further. What with scurrying to catch that dreadful steamboat, and then my fright of hearing the children scream, and now having to clamber down this mountain, I'm ready to drop!"

"Don't, ma'am, please," said the Captain imploringly;

" you'll be sorry for it if you do. The ground is full of rabbit-burrows, and there are a lot of nettles about."

" Good gracious!" she exclaimed, looking round her in the greatest alarm, and drawing in the skirts of her dress. "Whatever made you bring me here then, Captain Dresser?"

" Well, ma'am," began the Captain; but Mrs. Gilmour, who at that moment first caught sight of Nellie's face, interrupted him before he could get in a word further than, "you see   "

" Oh, my dearie!" cried she, in a higher key, forgetting at once all her own troubles; and, rushing up to Nell with the utmost solicitude, she hugged her first and then inspected her carefully, " what have you done to your poor dear face?"

" Oh, it's not much, auntie," said Nellie, just then busy arranging her dress. "I have only got a scratch or two."

" And your clothes too," continued Mrs. Gilmour, her consternation increasing at the sight of the damage done. " Why, your frock is torn to shreds!"

" Not so bad as that, auntie," laughed the girl, but with a look of dismay on her face the while. " It is rather bad though."

" Bad," repeated her aunt, "sure, it's scandalous! And, say your brother, now—whatever have you both been about? His poor face is all bleeding, too!"

" Now, don't you make matters worse than they are," interposed the Captain. " A little water will soon set them both right."

" And where shall we get water here?" she asked. " Tell me that!"

His answer came quick enough, the Captain being seldom 'taken aback.'

" You forget, ma'am, the little rivulet we passed on our way. Dick," he added, " run and fetch some for us, like a good lad."

Nell had brought with her from home a little tin bucket, which she usually took down to the shore for collecting sea-anemones and other specimens for her aquarium; so, catching hold of this, Dick started off in the direction of the tiny brook they had crossed some little time before, returning anon with the bucket brimming full.

Miss Nell and Bob thereupon set to work in high glee at their extempore ablutions; and, when they had subsequently dried their faces in their pocket handkerchiefs, both presented a much improved appearance.

With the exception of a few scratches, they bore little traces of the fray, the blood stains, which looked at first sight so very dreadful, having vanished on the application of the cold water, as the Captain had prophesied.

"There, ma'am," cried he now exultingly; pointing this out to Mrs. Gilmour, "I told you so, didn't I? 'All cry and little wool,' eh, ho, ho, ho!"

"That may be," retorted she; "but, water won't mend Nellie's dress."

"Well then, ma'am, I will," replied the Captain. "You'll always find a sailor something of a tailor, if he's worth his salt!"

He laughed when he said this, and his imperturbable good humour banished the last vestige of Mrs. Gilmour's vexation at the children's plight.

"Sure, and you shan't do anything of the sort," she said smiling. "I'll run up Nell's tatters meesilf!" As she spoke she produced from her pocket a handy little 'housewife,' containing needles and thread, as well as a thimble, which useful articles the good lady seldom stirred out without; and, sitting down on a shawl which the Captain spread over a bit of turf that he assured her was free from nettles, and ten yards at least from the nearest rabbit burrow, she proceeded to sew away at a brisk rate on the torn frock of Miss Nellie, who sat herself demurely beside her aunt.

"Will you be long?" inquired the old sailor, after watching her busy fingers some little time, getting slightly fidgety. "Eh, ma'am?"

"I should think it will be quite an hour before I shall be

able to make the child decent," she replied. "Why do you ask?"

"Humph!" ejaculated the Captain, as he always did when cogitating some knotty point, "I'll tell you, ma'am. If it's agreeable to you, ma'am, the boys and I might go on to Brading and see the remains of that Roman villa I was talking about yesterday. That is, unless you would like us to wait till you've done your patchwork there, and all of us go together, eh?"

"No, I wouldn't hear of such a thing," answered Mrs. Gilmour, looking up but not pausing for an instant in her task. "I wouldn't walk a mile to see Julius Cæsar himself, instead of his old villa, or whatever you call it."

The Captain appeared greatly amused at this.

"I'm not certain that the place ever belonged to that distinguished gentleman," he said. "It is supposed, I believe, to have been the residence of a certain Vespasian, who was governor of the Isle of Wight some period after its conquest by the Romans; but how far this is true, ma'am, I can't vouch for personally, never having as yet, indeed, seen the spot."

"But, I assure you, I've no curiosity to go. I feel much too tired, and would rather sit comfortably here. Would you like, Nell, to go with the Captain and Bob?"

"No, auntie, I'd prefer stopping with you. I want to get some ferns and lots of things after you've mended my dress for me," replied Alice. "I like flowers better than old ruins."

She said this quite cheerfully, as if she didn't mind a bit not going with the boys.

This surprised the Captain somewhat, for he thought she would not like being left behind, and would have looked at all events a trifle cross.

But, seeing how she took the matter, the old sailor's mind was immensely relieved.

"Well then," he cried smiling, with his eyes blinking and winking away, "the sooner we're off, why the sooner we'll be

back. Hullo, though, I've forgotten the hamper! Run up,
Dick, and fetch it down here."

Off scampered the lad, coming back quickly with the hamper,
which he placed carefully by Mrs. Gilmour's side.

"There ma'am," said Captain Dresser, "you can look after
the luncheon while we're away. Come along, boys hi, Rover!"

"Oh, please leave him behind," implored Nellie. "We want
him."

"What, who?" asked the Captain. "Dick or the dog?"

"Rover," replied Nellie promptly. "He'll protect us in
your absence in case anything happens."

"What's that, eh" quizzed the old sailor. "I suppose
you're thinking again of those ferocious wild animals you
encountered awhile ago, eh, missy?"

"It's a shame, auntie, for the Captain to tease me so!"
exclaimed Nellie, as the chaffy old gentleman went off
chuckling, followed by Master Bob and Dick, the three soon
disappearing amidst the greenery. "Never mind, though, I
have got you, my good doggie; and I shan't forget how you
came to my help, nor how glad I was to catch hold of your
poor tail, you dear Rover, when you dragged me out of that
horrid hole!"

"Be aisy, me dearie," remonstrated Mrs. Gilmour, as Nell
reached over to hug Rover in a sudden caress of affection, and
caused by the sudden movement a breakage of the thread, thus
interrupting her aunt's handiwork. "Sure, if you go wriggling
about like an eel with that dog, I shall never get your frock
mended!"

"All right, auntie, I beg your pardon. I'll be very good
now, and promise not to move again till you tell me to."

So saying, Miss Nell resumed her former position, and,
making Rover lie down at her feet, remained 'as quiet as a
mouse,' as her aunt acknowledged, until the latter had completed her task of gathering up the rents in the damaged
garment that the envious blackberry thorns had made.

CHAPTER XII.

'THE DEVIL'S BIT.'

"Now, me dearie," said Mrs. Gilmour, replacing her needle and thimble, with the reel of thread, in her little 'housewife,' and putting that carefully back into her pocket, "sure, we'll have a jollification on our own account as our gentlemen have left us. We'll show them that we can do without them, sure, when we like."

"How nice, auntie!" cried Miss Nellie, agreeing thoroughly in the sentiment her aunt had expressed, the desertion of the Captain and Bob, in addition to the fact of Dick having been also taken away, having affected the young lady more than she had acknowledged. "What shall we do first to be 'jolly,' as Bob says?"

"I'll soon show you, me dearie," replied Mrs. Gilmour. "Sure, you'll say in a minute, Nell. Come now, me darlint, and help me."

Then ensued a pleasant task, one in which Rover especially evinced the keenest interest, the sagacious retriever watching their every movement with an attention that never faltered.

Needless almost to say, the agreeable occupation in question was that of unpacking the hamper containing all the good things which Sarah had packed and Dick had brought from the house for their picnic in the woods.

Aye, it was in the woods; and under the woods, too!

Encircled by a hedge of green shrubbery and thicket undergrowth, amidst which the wild flowers of the forest stood out here and there, their brightest tints gleaming with a wealth of colouring which nature's gems alone display, Mrs. Gilmour selected a nice smooth stretch of velvety turf for their table.

On this, she proceeded to lay a damask cloth, whose snowy whiteness contrasted vividly with its surroundings; for, a clump of silver birches joined in handclasp with a straggling oak overhead, sheltering the grass plot with their welcome shade from the heat of the noonday sun, w ile, over all, a lofty spreading elm extended its sturdy branches, like outstretched arms, above its lesser brethren below, as if saying paternally, "Bless you, my children!"

Having daintily arranged the contents of the hamper to the best advantage on the open air banqueting table, an enormous veal and ham pie, their chief dish, in the centre, Mrs. Gilmour and Nellie surveyed their handiwork with much complacency.

"Sure, and I don't think a single thing has been forgotten," observed the former with pardonable pride, after a critical inspection of the various viands. "At most of the picnics I have participated in, either the salt, or the mustard, or something else has been left behind; but, to day, I believe Sarah has remembered everything!"

"Yes, I'm sure she has, auntie dear!" cried Miss Nellie with equal enthusiasm. "Here's the kettle for us to boil; and the teapot, and teacups, too, all ready for our tea, auntie, after lunch."

"She is a good girl, Sarah, and I will reward her for this," said Mrs. Gilmour, giving a final pat to the table cloth after smoothing it down and pulling the corners straight. "I'm afraid, though, dearie, we'll have to wait a precious long time before Captain Dresser and the boys come back; and, laying the table has made me feel quite hungry, I declare."

"So am I, auntie," laughed Nell. "The sight of all the nice things is too much. Let us go away and pick some wild-flowers till the others come back, eh, auntie?"

"But, how can we leave the things here?" questioned the other. "Suppose some stranger, passing by, should take a fancy to our nice luncheon? What a terrible thing it would be to come back and find it gone! Again, too, just think, your friends the rabbits, dearie, might take it into their comical little heads to play at hide and seek amongst the dishes, besides nibbling what they liked. How would you like that, eh?"

"Oh, auntie, how funny you are!" cried Nell, quite overcome at the idea of the bunnies making a playground of their well arranged table-cloth. "But you can trust Rover to guard everything safely if we go away."

"Are you sure, dearie?" inquired her aunt. "Quite sure?"

"Certain, auntie, dear, nobody would dare to come near the spot while he's here, for he'd pretty soon bark, and bite, too! And, as for the poor rabbits, one sniff of his would send them all scuttling back into their burrows, Hi, Rover!" Nell called out, after giving this testimony on his behalf. "Lie down there, good dog, and watch!"

Rover at once cocked an eye and looked in his young mistress's face. Next, he took note of her pointed finger, which she waved in a sort of comprehensive curve embracing the table cloth with its appetizing display of eatables; and then, as if he had made a mental list of all left in his charge, he laid down in a couchant position at the head of the table, if such it could be called, with his nose between his paws, along which his eyes were ready to take aim at any intruder, saying, in their fixed basilisk stare, "Now, you just touch anything, if you dare, my friend. I should like to see you attempt it!"

"We can safely leave now, auntie," said Nellie; whereupon she and Mrs. Gilmour strayed off through the bracken, hunting here and there for flowers on their way.

Almost the first thing to catch their sight, before indeed they had left the little turfy dell where their paraphernalia was spread out with Rover in charge, was the pretty rose-coloured blossom of the 'ragged Robin,' rising out of the grass. A little further off was a cluster of the lilac field madder, named after Sherard the eminent botanist, whose herbarium is still preserved at Oxford. This plant is one of a large family, numbering over two thousand varieties, from which the well known dye, madder, is obtained, though, of late years, aniline colouring matter has somewhat depreciated its commercial value.

Mrs. Gilmour presently picked up something better than either of these, at least in appearance. This was a little blue flower resembling the violet, with glossy green leaves that were its especial charm.

"I declare I've found a periwinkle!" she cried "such a fire one too."

"Oh, let me look, auntie!" said Nell, peeping into her hand. "Dear me, do you call that a periwinkle?"

"Yes, dearie. Pretty, isn't it? It blooms all the year; and I've seen it down in Devonshire covering a space of nearly half an acre with its leaves and blossoms. One of the poets, not Cowper my favourite, though one equally fond of the world of nature, describes the flower very nicely. 'See,' he says—

'Where the sky blue Periwinkle climbs
E'en to the cottage eaves, and hides the wall
And dairy lattice, with a thousand eyes!'"

"What pretty lines, auntie, so very like the flower!" cried Nell when Mrs. Gilmour finished the quotation. "But, do you know, auntie, I thought when you said you'd found a periwinkle, you meant one to eat, like those periwinkles I've got in the aquarium you gave me."

"Did you really, though, dearie?" said her aunt, smiling at her very natural mistake. "It is because you feel hungry, I suppose. You may eat this one if you like!"

"No, no, auntie," laughed Nellie, "I'm not quite so

hungry as that! But, oh, auntie, here are some of those lovely big daisies we saw when we first came in the park."

"Those are the daisies that are called the 'ox eye' or moon daisy, my dear," explained Mrs. Gilmour "You might call them the first cousins though only, mind you, a sort of poor relation of the choice marguerite daisy that gardeners cultivate and think so highly of. Here, too, dearie, I see another old friend of mine, whose petals fall just like snow-flakes on the grass."

"It is almost like the honeysuckle," cried Nellie. "How sweet it smells!"

"Like its name, dearie," replied the other. "It is called the 'meadow sweet'; and a delicious perfume can be extracted from it by infusion in boiling water. The roots of the plant are long tubers, which, when ground to powder and dried, may be used as a substitute for flour, should you have any scarcity of that article!"

"I'd rather have the real sort of flour, though, auntie."

"So would I, too, dearie," agreed Mrs. Gilmour. "I only told you in case you may be thrown on a desert island some day, when the information might be of use in the event of your being without bread."

"But, supposing there was no meadow sweet there either, auntie?"

"Sure that would be a bad look out," said Mrs. Gilmour, joining in Nell's laugh. "I think we'd better wait till you get to the desert island!"

Wandering along, they plucked at their will masses of the wild convolvulus, or 'great bindweed,' whose white blossoms, while they lasted, added much to the general effect of the bouquet Nellie was making up with her busy fingers from the spoils of coppice and sward.

These, in addition to the flowers they had just picked, now comprised many other natives of the wood and hedgerow, such as the purple bugloss, the yellow iris, the star thistle, the common mallow; and, a convolvulus which was brilliantly pink, in contrast to his white brother before mentioned. Besides these, Nellie had also gathered some sprays of the 'toad flax' and 'blue succory,' a relative of the 'endive' tribe, which produces the chicory root so much consumed in England, as in France, as a 'substitute' for coffee. A splendid sprig of yellow broom and dear little bunch of hare bells, the 'Blue Bells of Scotland,' with two or three scarlet poppies, a wreath of the aromatic ground ivy and some fern leaves for foliage, completed her floral collection.

Stopping beneath a group of trees further on, to listen to the song of a thrush, which was so full of melody that they approached him quite close without his noticing them, Nell and her aunt were amused by seeing two rooks quarrelling over a worm which they had both got hold of at the same time, one at either end gripping the unfortunate creature; and gobbling, and tugging, and cawing, at once!

One of these rooks had a white head, which he seemed to cock on one side in a strangely familiar way to Nell.

"He's just like the Captain" she exclaimed, tittering at the fancied resemblance. "Look, auntie, why he actually seems to wink!"

"I declare I'll tell him!" said Mrs. Gilmour, enjoying the joke none the less at the fancied resemblance. "Sure he'd be hoighly delighted."

Then, as they wound round back to the dell through the dense shrubbery, they re crossed the little rivulet which they had twice passed over before.

On the banks of this, although it was too small almost to have 'banks,' properly speaking, Mrs. Gilmour pointed out to Nell the 'great water plantain,' with its sprigs of little lilac blossoms and beautiful green leaves, like those of the lily of the valley somewhat. The plant is said to be used in Russia as a cure for hydrophobia, the good lady explained; though she added that she could not vouch personally for its virtues.

Not far from this, too, they found another very curious plant, called in some places the 'cuckoo pint,' and in others the 'wake robin,' or, more commonly, 'lords and ladies.' The leaves of this are of a glossy dark green and the flower very like the leaf; only, more curved and tinted inside, with a hue of pale buff that becomes pinkish at the extremities, the centre pistil being of the same colour. It belongs to the arum family.

Following the course of the brook, Nellie, a little way on, spied out a regular bed of the forget me-not; when Mrs. Gilmour told her the old legend connected with the flower.

How a knight and a lady were sitting by the side of a river; and, on the lady expressing a desire to have some of the bright blue blossoms "to braid in her bonny brown hair," the gallant knight at once dashed in the stream to gratify her wishes. He secured a bunch of the flowers; but, on turning to regain the shore, the current overcame him; and, as the old song goes

> "Then the blossoms blue to the bank he threw,
>   Ere he sunk in the eddying tide;
> And 'Lady, I'm gone, thine own love true,
>   Forget me not,' he cried.
>
> The farewell pledge the lady caught;
>   And hence, as legends say,
> The flower's a sign to awaken thoughts
>   Of friends who are far away!"

" How nice!" cried Nellie "How very nice!"

"Not for the poor knight, though," said her aunt. "However, here, dearie, is another plant not quite so romantic, the old brown scabious, or 'turf weed.' It is a great favourite with bees, while its roots are supposed to have valuable medicinal properties, which the country people well know and estimate at their right worth. In some places they call it the 'Devil's bit'!"

"How funny!" interposed Nellie. "Why do they give it such a strange name?"

"Yes, it is rather a strange title; but I read once somewhere that the story about it is, that the Spirit of Evil, envying the good which this herb might do to mankind, bit away part of it and thence came its name, 'Devil's bit.'"

"Really, auntie," said Nell. "Does it look as if it had been bitten?"

"Yes, the root does," she replied. "But, come, dearie, we must get back now as fast as we can, or Captain Dresser and the boys will be there before us and eat up all the luncheon!"

Without stopping to look at any more flowers or curious plants, they retraced their steps towards the dell, Nellie humming the last line of the song of the forget me not, which she was trying to learn by heart—"Of friends who are far away! Of friends who are far away" when, suddenly, they heard Rover's bark ringing through the woods, its echoes loud and resonant, like the sound of a deep toned bell.

"Come on, dearie," called out Mrs. Gilmour, who was in advance, quickening her pace as she spoke, "come on quick, dearie! There's some one making off with our lunch; and, just think how hungry we are!"

"Don't fear, auntie," said Nell reassuringly behind her; "Rover will not let any one touch it, you may be certain!"

Nevertheless, she hurried after Mrs. Gilmour; and both arrived together, well nigh breathless, at the spot where they had left their feast so nicely laid out.

CHAPTER XIII.

THEY need not have been alarmed.

Indeed, had she but given herself time for reflection, Nellie must have known this without any further assurance than the faithful Rover's bark, which would have been of quite a different tone had any stranger or suspicious person invaded the spot he was left to guard.

In such case, the good dog would have growled in the most unmistakable manner, besides giving warning of there being danger ahead by a different intonation of his expressive voice.

He did not growl now, however, although he who had invaded the sacred picnic ground where their provender was so lavishly displayed was, in one sense, a stranger, being not one of the original members of the festive party who had set out from 'The Moorings.'

The reason for this was that the new comer, really, was not a real 'stranger' in the sense of the word. The intruder was, in fact, Hellyer, the coastguardsman, whom Rover had seen only so recently as that very morning, when of course master doggie had accompanied Bob to the beach for his bathe; and so, naturally, there was every reason for his receiving Hellyer in a friendly manner. Hence, his bark, alarming though it might have sounded at the first go off to Nell and her aunt, was found now to have been a bark of recognition and joy and not one of warning.

Mrs. Gilmour felt such a sensation of relief at the sight of Hellyer that her feelings prevented her from speaking. As she told Nell afterwards, she "couldn't have uttered a word to save her life"; and there she remained, "staring at the poor man," to use her own expression, and one that savoured thoroughly of her country, "as if he were a stuck pig!"

Hellyer, however, did not remain dumb.

"Beg pardon, mum," said he respectfully, doffing his sailor hat and touching his forehead with his forefinger in nautical salute; "but, 'ave you seen the Cap'en anywheres about here, mum?"

"You mean Captain Dresser, I suppose?" replied Mrs. Gilmour, recovering her loss of speech at the sound of his voice, at least so it seemed; the good lady answering the coastguardsman's question in her usual way, by asking him another! "Eh, what, my man?"

"Yes, mum. I've a message for him from our commander, mum; and they told me at the house as how he were over at Seaview, so, mum, I comes across by the next boat."

"Well, he isn't very far off, Hellyer," said Mrs. Gilmour smiling; "I didn't recogn'ze you at first, sure, I was in such a terrible fright on hearing the dog bark, least somebody was making off with our luncheon. I'm really glad it's only you."

"And I'm glad, too, mum."

"So glad you're glad I'm glad!" whispered Nellie to her aunt, quoting something she had seen in an old volume of *Punch*, and going into fits of laughter. "Eh, auntie?"

"Hush, my dear," said Mrs. Gilmour reprovingly, but obliged to laugh too in spite of herself, although she tried to hide it for fear Hellyer would think they were making fun of him; and she turned to him to say, "We expect the Captain, Hellyer, every minute. Why, here he is!"

There he was, most decidedly; and he soon made his presence known.

"Hullo, you good people!" he shouted, while yet some

little distance off, as he made his way down the slope followed by Bob and Dick, "I hope you've got something for us to eat, for we're all as hungry as hunters."

"Come on," answered Mrs. Gilmour, "everything is ready, and Nell and I are only waiting for you loiterers to begin."

"Loiterers, indeed!" retorted the Captain good humouredly, as he hobbled along with some difficulty by the aid of his stick down the uneven path, "you would loiter too if you had my poor legs to walk with! Never mind, though, here we are at last; and, I tell you what, ma'am, that table cloth there and the good things you've got on it is the prettiest sight I've seen to day."

"What!" exclaimed Mrs. Gilmour. "Prettier than the Roman villa?"

"Hang the Roman villa! I beg your pardon, ma'am, but the word slipped out unawares."

After this apology for his somewhat strong expression, the old sailor was proceeding to give the reason for his condemnation of the archæological remains he and the boys had been to see, when he noticed Hellyer standing by in an attitude of attention.

"Why, man," he cried, "what brings you here?"

"I've got a letter for you, sir," replied Hellyer, handing an envelope over to him, and saluting him in the same way as he had done Mrs. Gilmour just before. "Here it is, sir!"

"Humph!" ejaculated Captain. Dresser, opening the missive and running his eyes over the contents. "Here's some good news for you, Master Bob."

"Oh?" said the latter expectantly. "Good news, Captain?"

"Yes," went on the old sailor, "my friend, Commander Sponson, of the Coastguard, writes to me to say that one of the new ironclads is going out of harbour next week on her trial trip; and, if you like, you shall have a chance of seeing what sort of vessel a modern ship of war is."

"Oh thank you, Captain Dresser, that will be jolly!" said Bob, his face colouring up with pleasure. "But, will she fire her guns and all?"

"Certainly," answered the other, "big guns, little guns, torpedo tubes, and the whole of her armoury! Besides, my boy, you'll be able to see her machinery at work, as she will try her speed on the measured mile; and then you can ask one of the engineers all those puzzling questions you bothered my old brains with when we were on board the steamer this morning."

"That will be jolly," repeated Bob; "and——"

"There, there," cried the Captain, interrupting him, "I won't say another word now, I'm much too famished to talk. Mrs. Gilmour, what have you got for a poor hungry creature to eat, eh, ma'am?"

"Anything you like," she responded with a smile. "Pray sit down and begin."

"I will," said he, seating himself with alacrity; and turning to the coastguardsman, he added "I suppose, Hellyer, you could pick a bit too, eh?"

"Yes, sir, saving your presence. But, only after you and the ladies, sir," was Hellyer's respectful reply; and then, with all the training of an experienced servant, knowledge he had gained in the exercise of his manifold duties during several years' service as the Captain's coxswain, he proceeded to assist Dick in waiting, with an "If you'll allow me, sir."

"Some bread, please," called out the Captain presently. "Any your side, Hellyer?"

Hellyer and Dick both looked about the table, seeking in vain for the required article.

"I can't see none, sir," said the ex-coxswain deprecatingly, giving up the quest after a bit in despair. He seemed, from the way in which he spoke, as if he thought it was his fault that the bread was missing. "There ain't any this side, sir."

Dick's search too was equally fruitless.

" Dear me !" exclaimed Mrs. Gilmour, all anxiety. " Look in the hamper again. Sure, we must have forgotten to take it out."

But there also, alas ! no bread was to be found.

The Captain could not help laughing at Mrs. Gilmour's face of dismay ; while Nellie clapped her hands in high glee.

" Oh, auntie," she cried, " I thought you said just now when we were spreading the cloth that nothing had been forgotten, and how good Sarah was to think of everything. Oh, auntie !"

" Oh, auntie !" chorussed Bob, joining in the general laugh. " Fancy forgetting the bread !"

" Aye, to leave out the staff of life, of all things !" put in the Captain, having his say. " I hope 'the good Sarah' has not remembered to forgit anything more importint, sure !"

" I won't have you mimicking me," expostulated Mrs. Gilmour, although she took their joking in very good part. " Sure, mistakes will happen sometimes, and there are biscuits if you can't have bread."

" All right, all right," said the Captain soothingly, " I dare say we'll get along very well as we are. Don't worry any more about the matter, ma'am. We've got your excellent piecrust, at any rate, and that's quite good enough for me."

He chuckled still, though, for some time ; and he chuckled more presently, when something else, quite as important as the bread, was discovered also to be missing.

The discovery came about in this wise. Before sitting down with the others, Bob had rigged up in gipsy fashion, on three forked sticks, a little brass kettle, which he had specially asked his aunt to have put with the other picnic things, in order to carry out thoroughly the idea of 'camping out' as he had read about it in books ; and, besides slinging the kettle artistically in the way described, he also filled it with water from a stone jar which they had brought with them, as a precaution in the event of their not being able to get any of drinkable quality where they intended making a halt, Mrs. Gilmour expressing some little repugnance to his taking any out of the brook, although they had been glad enough previously to use it for washing their scratched faces. She said it had too many dead leaves and live creatures in it for her taste.

Under the filled kettle, too, Bob had lit a fire, for which Nell and Dick collected the sticks; and, long before luncheon was done, this was blazing up quite briskly, and the kettle singing away at a fine rate.

By and by, when the Captain declared he couldn't eat another morsel, and Bob and Nellie also had had enough, Mrs. Gilmour heaped up a couple of plates with the remains of the veal and ham pie for Hellyer and Dick, who had all this time been busily employed ministering to their various wants, and now retired some little distance off to enjoy their well-earned meal.

Then came Bob's turn for action.

"The kettle is boiling, auntie," he cried out, poking fresh sticks in the fire, which crackled and spitted out as the sap in pieces of the greener wood caught the heat, the smoke ascending in a column of spiral wreaths, and making Bob's eyes smart on his getting to leeward of the blazing pile. "Shall we have tea now?"

"Yes, my dear boy," said she in a very pathetic voice. "Do, please, make it as quick as you can, I feel quite faint for want of some, as it is long past the time for my usual afternoon cup."

"All right, auntie," replied Bob, bustling about with great zeal, "I will get it ready in a jiffy. But, where's the tea?"

"It's in the teapot, I suppose, my dear; and you'll find that in the hamper with the teacups. Nellie and I thought we wouldn't unpack them until they were wanted."

Nell, who had been sitting between her aunt and the Captain, on hearing her name introduced, at once got up to help Bob; but in spite of every search, neither of them could find the tea.

As in the case of the bread, the 'good Sarah' had forgotten it; for, neither in teapot, teacups or elsewhere could the tea be seen!

"Well, ma'am!" exclaimed the Captain on hearing the painful news. "That bates Banagher, as one of your countrymen would say."

"I'm sure nobody could be more sorry than I am," pleaded poor Mrs. Gilmour, whom this second mishap completely overwhelmed, "I did so long for a cup of tea!"

"Well, well," said the Captain when he was able to speak, after a series of chuckles that made him almost choke, "the next time that a picnic's in the wind I'd take care, if I were you, to overhaul your hamper before starting, to see that nothing is forgotten."

"It's all 'that good Sarah,' auntie," cried Bob slily; and, then, they all had another laugh, the misfortunes of the day being provocative, somehow or other, of the greatest fun. "Oh that 'good Sarah'!"

It appeared as if Mrs. Gilmour would be the only sufferer in having to go without her tea: but, at this critical point, Hellyer came to the rescue.

"Beg pardon, mum," said he, stepping up to her with a deferential touch of his forelock; "but I knows the woman in the keeper's lodge where you comed in, and I thinks as how I could borrow a bit o' tea from her, if you likes."

"Thank you very much, if it's no trouble," replied Mrs. Gilmour, hailing the offer with joy, "I certainly would like it."

Hardly waiting to hear the termination of her reply, the thoughtful fellow darted off along the winding path through the shrubbery by which they had gained the pleasant little dell; returning before they thought he could have reached the keeper's lodge with a little packet of tea. This Miss Nell took from Hellyer and at once emptied into the teapot, while Bob attended to the kettle and poured the boiling water in; so that Mrs. Gilmour was soon provided with the wished for cup of her favourite beverage.

The good lady's equanimity being now restored, she proceeded to question the Captain about the Roman villa at Brading.

"But, what did you see after all?" she asked; "you haven't told us a word yet."

"Oh, don't speak about it, ma'am," he replied grumpily. "It's a regular swindle."

"But, what did you see?" she repeated, knowing his manner, and that he was not put out with her, at all events. "I want to know."

"See?" echoed the Captain, snorting out the word somehow with suppressed indignation. "Well, ma'am, to tell you the truth, we saw nothing but some fragments of old pottery——"

"Just like broken pieces of flower pots, auntie," interrupted Master Bob in his eagerness. "The same as you have at the bottom of the garden."

"Yes," continued the old sailor, "that's exactly what these much exaggerated 'remains' resembled more than anything else, I assure you, ma'am. Of course, all these bits of earthen ware were arranged in order and labelled and all that; but I couldn't make head or tail of them."

"Perhaps you do not understand archæology?" suggested Mrs. Gilmour, smiling at his description. "That's the rayson they didn't interest you, sure!"

"P'r'aps not, ma'am, he replied with the utmost good temper. "I fancy I know something of seamanship and a little about natural history, but of most of the other 'ologies I confess my ignorance; and, for the life of me, I can't see how some people can find anything to enjoy in the old pots and pans of our great-great-grandfathers!"

"You forget the light which these relics throw on the

manners and customs of the ancients," argued the other. "There's a good deal of information to be gleaned from their mute testimony sure, me dear Captain."

"Information?" growled the Captain "Fiddlesticks! And as for the manners and customs of our ancestors; why, if all I have read be true, they were uncommonly similar to the account given by a middy of the natives of the Andaman Isles, as jotted down in his diary, 'manners, none customs, beastly!'"

"That's shocking," exclaimed Mrs. Gilmour, laughing. "But the criticism will not apply to the Romans, who were almost as civilized and refined as ourselves."

"And that's not saying much!" said the Captain with one of his sly chuckles. "Faith we haven't any to boast of!"

"Speak for yourself," she retorted, "sure that's a very poor compliment you're paying me."

"Present company always excepted," he replied, with an old fashioned bow like that of a courtier. "You know I didn't allude to you."

"I accept your apology, sir," said she with equally elaborate politeness. "I would make you a curtsy if I were standing up, but you wouldn't wish me to rise for the purpose. Did you not see, though, anything at all like the ruins of a Roman villa or house at Brading?"

The Captain took a pinch of snuff, as if to digest the matter before answering her question.

"Well, ma'am," he began, after a long pause of cogitation, "we were shown some bits of brickwork, marked out in divisions like the foundations of a house: and a place with a hole in the floor which, they said, was a bath-room. We also saw a piece or two of tesselated pavement, with a lot of other gimcracks; but I certainly had to exercise a good deal of fancy to imagine a villa out of all these scattered details, like the Marchioness in Dickens' *Old Curiosity Shop*, which I was reading the other day, 'made believe' about her orange peel wine!"

"Then we didn't lose much by not accompanying you?" she remarked. "I was rather sorry afterwards I was unable to go."

"Lose anything?" he repeated with emphasis, "I should think not, indeed! If my poor legs could speak, they would tell you that you've gained 'pretty considerably,' as a Yankee would say, by remaining comfortably here. Hullo, missy, what a splendid posy you've got there!"

"Yes, are they not nice?" replied Nellie, on the Captain thus turning the conversation to her collection of wild-flowers, some of which she had arranged tastefully in a big bunch and placed them in her tin bucket filled with water to keep them fresh. "Aunt Polly helped me to gather them."

"I dare say she told you their names and all about them at the same time, my dear."

"Oh yes, Captain Dresser," said Nellie. "She told me lots."

"Ah." ejaculated the Captain, heaving a deep sigh of regret. "If I only knew as much as your auntie does of botany, missy, what a clever old chap I should be!"

"Don't you believe him, Nell!" cried Mrs. Gilmour deprecating the compliment. "Captain Dresser knows quite as much as I do about plants and flowers, and a good deal more, too. I only wish he had been here to tell you the story of the 'Devil's bit,' for he would have narrated it in a much better fashion than I did, I'm sure."

"The divvle a bit of it, ma'am!" exclaimed the old sailor, bursting into a jovial laugh at his joke, wherein even the staid Hellyer joined. "But, a truce to your blarney, ma'am; or, you'll make me blush. Allow me to inform you that time is getting on; and, unless we make a start for the pier soon, we'll never catch the steamer and reach home to night!"

CHAPTER XIV.

WRECKED.

"How's that, sure?" asked Mrs. Gilmour. "It's early yet, for the sun's still overhead."

"You forget, ma'am, our old friend up there is rather a late bird at this time of year," replied the Captain. "He hasn't crossed the line yet, you know."

"Well, then," argued the good lady, who was sitting at her ease on a pile of shawls and wraps, enjoying a second cup of tea which Nell had just poured out for her, "where's the hurry?"

"Oh, pray take your time, ma'am, I wouldn't like to hasten your movements for worlds, you look so comfortable!" said the old sailor satirically. "Perhaps you'd allow me to mention, however, just in a friendly way, that it is now half past five o'clock, and the steamer starts at six!"

This made Mrs. Gilmour jump up so suddenly that she spilt her tea, which made them laugh; and all set to work in a merry mood to collect their traps for the return journey, the good lady saying she would 'never forgive the Captain' for not telling her the time before.

The coastguardsman had to shoulder the hamper when packed, as well as carry the empty water jar; for, both Bob and Dick, whose respective burdens these had previously been, had rushed off soon after luncheon and when all interest in making a fire and boiling the kettle had ceased, down to the shore, where presently the truants were discovered.

They were wading in the sea, without their shoes and stockings, in high glee, and hunting amongst the rocks for anemones and corallines for the aquarium, having already nearly filled with specimens Nellie's useful little tin bucket, from which her poor nosegay had been ruthlessly removed.

"Hullo, you boys!" sang out the Captain on catching sight of them, after consulting his watch; "you'll have to come out of that at once. Time's up, for the steamer will be due in another five minutes. Look sharp!"

"Do stop a moment," answered Bob, just then busy at the base of a rock close by the pier, which was nearly awash with the incoming tide, "I've found such a jolly sea anemone here. Come and see it, please, Captain."

"Are you sure it's not a weed?" called back the old sailor a trifle impatiently. "We can't waste any time on rubbish!"

"Of course not; I should think I ought to know an anemone by now, sir!" cried Bob, rather indignant at being supposed capable of making such a mistake, albeit his knowledge on the subject, it must be confessed, was but slight and only lately acquired. "It is coloured beautifully, and looks like a purple chrysanthemum."

"By Jove!" exclaimed the Captain, forgetting the steamer and his fatigue alike as he hurried towards the spot where Bob was paddling in the water and Dick standing close by, bucket in hand. "Why, it's the very thing I've been hunting for, missy, to set off your aquarium."

"Mind you don't get your feet wet!" called out Mrs. Gilmour, in great solicitude, as he went off in keen ardour to assist the boys in securing the prize, the good lady adding, as Nellie scampered after him, she contenting herself with remaining higher up on the shore: "Take care, my dearie! I don't want to have you laid up, with your father and mother coming down in a few days, when I want you to look your best."

"Never fear, I'll take care of her and myself too!" sang out the Captain, who by this time, hopping from rock to rock, in which operation he was closely followed and imitated by the giggling Nellie behind him, had reached the boulder where Bob was. "Keep close to me, missy."

"Don't touch it for a little while, my boy, I want your sister to see it expanded, and it will close up if you go poking it about. Look, Miss Nell!" he continued, pointing it out to her with the end of his malacca cane. "The sun is just shining on it through the water, and you can see its colours of pink, purple, and orange. This is one of the actinea, or 'anthozoa,' so called from two Greek words meaning 'living flowers.' A pretty name, missy, isn't it?"

"Yes," said Nellie. "It reminds me of a fairy tale aunt Polly told me of the different flowers in the garden having a party and talking together."

"Precisely, my dear; only the anthozoa can't talk!"

"But, oh, how pretty this sea anemone is!" cried she in ecstasies, not noticing his little bit of satire. "It is wonderful!"

"It is, my dear," replied the Captain; "although it's one of the commonest forms of the actinea family. As Bob said just now, it is very like a chrysanthemum; and, if anything, more beautiful, which you can see for yourself before we try to shift its lodging. It is called by a fearfully long scientific name, which to my mind does a positive injury to the poor beast. What do you think of such a jaw breaker as 'mesembryanthe mum,' eh?"

"Oh!" ejaculated Nell, "what an awful word! I'm sure I shall never be able to remember it."

"You must, missy, if you want to describe properly the inmates of your aquarium, where this gentleman is now going to make a move for. Now, Bob," went on the Captain, turning round to the boys, who were anxiously waiting, all eagerness to commence proceedings, "put that knife of yours, that you have been brandishing all this time, carefully under the base of

K

the poor beggar, and try to peel him off, as I see the rock is
too smooth for us to break away   Mind you don't touch the
animal with the sharp point, though; for the slightest scratch
will kill him."

Nellie watched Bob with eager attention from the top of the
boulder; while Dick held the little tin bucket below the sea
anemone, so as to catch it as soon as it had been separated
from the rock.   At the first touch of Bob's knife, the anemone
shrunk in, showing nothing but a row of blue turquoise like
beads around its top or mouth ; the rest of the animal appearing to be but a dull lump of jelly, all its vivid colours and
iridescent hues having vanished on the instant of its being
assailed by Bob with that formidable weapon of his.

"It's wounded !" cried Nellie impulsively.   "Don't hurt it,
Bob, poor thing ! "

"It's all right, missy," said the Captain, consolingly.   "It
always shrinks like that when any one interferes with it.   But,
look sharp, Bob, there's your aunt waving her handkerchief
like mad from the pier head to say that the steamer's coming
in ; and, by Jove, there she is, rounding the point ! "

They did look sharp ; the boys, after the anemone was
secured, scampering ashore in extra high spirits on account of
the old sailor telling them that they had no time to put their
shoes and stockings on, and would have to go on board the
Bembridge Belle without them, like a pair of mudlarks.

The Captain hurried, too, jumping from rock to rock and
boulder to boulder, a precaution now even more necessary than
before, from the tide having risen considerably even during
their short delay and being now nearly at the flood.

Surefooted himself as an old sailor, though holding Nellie's
hand to prevent her slipping, he found time, in spite of his
hurry, to point out to her, growing on the beach under the
low cliff, beyond where the keeper's lodge stood, a solitary
specimen of the 'sea cabbage,' whose bright yellow flowers
and fleshy green leaves, he suggested, would be an addition to

the general effect of her bouquet, which, by the way, Mrs. Gilmour had taken charge of while she went anemone gathering, after this had been discarded from the bucket.

"It isn't bad eating, either, when on a pinch for green stuff," added the old sailor; "and I've seen boys hawking the plant about for sale at Dover. But, let us push ahead, missy run, boys, run, the steamer's alongside!"

With their shoes and stockings slung over their shoulders, Bob and Dick pattered along the shaky suspension bridge to the pier in advance, making good way in their bare feet; but, old as he was, the Captain was not far behind, going at a jog-trot that made Miss Nell step out to keep pace with him.

However, they were not sorry when they reached the pier-head, for, all the while they were running, the steam whistle of the *Bembridge Belle* was screeching away, as if telling them they would be too late, and threatening to start off without them if they did not hurry.

"Just did it!" gasped the Captain, setting foot on the gangway and jumping on board, dragging poor Nellie almost in as breathless a state after him, Bob and Dick having already preceded them. "By Jove, it was a near squeak, though!"

"Sure, it's your own fault you're not cool and comfortable like mesilf," said Mrs. Gilmour, whom Hellyer had escorted to the pier. He had, likewise, secured a good seat for her in the stern sheets of the boat, as the Captain had previously done; and, here she was now snugly ensconced when the late-comers arrived—"How hot you do look, to be sure!"

"Humph!" growled the Captain, not making any further reply to her rather exasperating remark until he had finished mopping his flushed face with a bright bandana handkerchief of the same red hue; when he added grimly, as if somewhat out of temper, "If I'm hot, ma'am, you're *cool*, that's all I can say!"

Mrs. Gilmour, however, was used to his ways and knew how to humour him.

"Now, don't you go pretending you're angry," she said, laughing merrily. "You needn't, sure, for I know better!"

"As you please, ma'am, as you please, ma'am," he replied, adding with his usual chuckle "I know you are bound to have your own way, ma'am, whether I like it or not!"

They both laughed at this, these little tiffs between them being of frequent occurrence, especially of an evening over the cribbage board; and, matters being again on a comfortable footing, they turned to the children, who were looking out, as before, over the side at the various objects that presented themselves as the *Bembridge Belle* ploughed her way back to Southsea.

The steamer passed quite close to one of the harbour forts in the sea, guarding the approaches to Spithead; and, of course, Bob, who with Dick had now again donned his shoes and stockings, wanted to know all about the imposing structure with its frowning guns, by the side of which the boat they were in seemed a veritable cockleshell, although a fairly good sized vessel.

Equally, of course, the Captain had to tell him what he knew how the fort was built of solid masonry, sixteen feet thick, with two feet of armour plating outside that; and how the little fortress, as it undoubtedly was, had a well dug deep down into the sands below the sea, to supply its garrison with fresh water in the event of communication being cut off with the mainland. To provide against which contingency it was also provisioned and furnished with every requisite to stand a siege.

He was explaining all this, when a large screw steamer, high in the bows and low in the stern, crossed the *Bembridge Belle* making for Portsmouth.

"Hullo, ma'am!" cried the Captain, glad to have the opportunity of a sly dig at Mrs. Gilmour in remembrance of her previous amusement at his expense, "there's your pig-boat!"

"What ." said she innocently. "I don't understand you."

"The Irish pig boat, ma'am," he repeated, his beady black eyes twinkling and his bushy eyebrows moving up and down, as they always did when he said anything funny. "It brings your fellow-countrymen over here twice a week."

"You're very complimentary, sir," said she. "Very complimentary, I declare!"

"Not a bit of it, ma'am," he replied, delighted at the idea of her taking his remark seriously. "Don't you, in your 'swate little island' call poor piggy 'the jintleman who pays the rint,' eh?"

"Sure," she retorted with a smile, taking up the cudgels on behalf of her country, "there are more pigs in England than what come over from Ireland!"

"I cry a truce!" exclaimed the old sailor laughing heartily, Bob and Nell, too, as well as Dick, appreciating the joke hugely; "you had me there, ma'am, you had me there!"

The *Bembridge Belle* was now well across the waterway, rapidly nearing the pier from which they had originally started in the morning, and Mrs. Gilmour was just saying what a very enjoyable day they had passed, in spite of all mishaps, while Nellie was priding herself on the grand collection of wild-flowers she had made with her aunt's help, and Bob and Dick busy over the bucket, showing Hellyer the various treasures they had picked up amongst the rocks on the shore; when, all at once, the bows of the steamer struck against something in the channel, with a concussion that threw nearly everybody off their feet the shock being succeeded by a harsh grating sound as if her hull was gradually being ripped open.

"Good gracious me!" cried out Mrs. Gilmour, "what on earth is that?"

Nobody, however, for the moment, attended to her: nobody, indeed, even heard the question; for the scene of quiet enjoyment which the deck had presented the moment before was changed to one of utter confusion, the shrieks of frightened women and hoarse cries of some of the men mingling with the screams of children and the noise of escaping steam, roaring up the funnel.

Captain Dresser had hastened forwards to the forecastle of the ill fated vessel to see with his own eyes what had happened as soon as the steamer struck, being immediately followed by Dick and Bob, who left Nellie clinging to her aunt in great consternation.

As for the skipper of the poor steamer, he seemed to have lost his head completely, for he was shouting out orders one moment from the bridge and contradicting them the next: while the crew were rushing about the decks aim lessly, one going here and another there, without apparent end or purpose, every one looking bewildered from the want of proper leadership.

"Keep calm, ladies!" the skipper sang out at intervals between his orders to the seamen and firemen, whom the incessant sounding of the engine room gong had brought up from below. "Keep cool; there's no danger, I tell you!"

He himself, however, appeared so perturbed, that his assurances increased, instead of lessened, the panic amongst the passengers, who huddled together in groups like startled sheep; and Nell clasped her aunt's hand tightly, the two awaiting in great anxiety Captain Dresser's return from his inspection of the vessel forwards

They were not long kept in suspense.

After a brief interview, which seemed an eternity, the old sailor reappeared aft.

His face looked very grave.

"I'm sorry for the old *Bembridge Belle*," he said in a low tone to Mrs. Gilmour, so as not to be overheard by the other passengers standing near. "The poor thing has a large hole knocked through her fore compartment, and is filling with water fast!"

CHAPTER XV.

"TELL me, is there any danger?" asked Mrs. Gilmour, speaking quite calmly, in spite of her fears; for, although of a somewhat hasty disposition and apt to be put out at trifles, she was possessed of a strong, natural courage, which, as is the case with most of the so-called 'tender sex,' only displayed itself in great emergencies. "You may disclose the worst. I can bear it!"

"Pooh!" grunted the Captain offhand, rather impolitely. "There's no 'worst' to tell, ma'am. All on board are quite safe, and will be put ashore securely as soon as the boats come off. My fears are for the unfortunate vessel, the loss of which will be a sad blow to her skipper, poor fellow, as he has staked his all in her!"

"But, Captain," she rejoined, "why do you look so serious?"

"Serious?" he repeated after her, the hard lines in his face at once relaxing "so would you, too, look serious, ma'am, if you thought of the matter in the same light. You see, I can't help looking upon a ship as a sort of living creature; and to think of a fine boat like this coming to grief in such a lubberly fashion is enough almost to make one cry."

His eyes blinked furiously as he said this, the bushy eyebrows above moving up and down; and, taking out his bright bandana handkerchief, he blew his nose with vigour, as if to give vent to his emotion,

Nellie, whose pale face had gained a little more colour since the Captain's reassuring words to her aunt, now sidled up to him, catching hold of his hand affectionately.

"But will the poor steamer really be lost?" she inquired timidly; "wrecked, as sailors call it?"

"Yes, I'm afraid so with the pack of nincompoops we've got on board," he growled. "They're talking of beaching her; and if so, with the wind chopping round to the eastwards, as those porpoises you saw this morning told us it will do by and by, for they're unfailing weather prophets always, why, the unfortunate craft will lay her bones on the shingle. She will, at all events, if any sort of a sea get up, or call me no sailor!"

Bob, who on his return from the fore part of the vessel in company with Captain Dresser had stationed himself again by the engine room hatchway, here gave a shout.

"They're moving," he cried; "I see the piston going up and down, and the shaft turning round!"

The rapid beat of the paddle-wheels on the water alongside gave testimony to the truth of Bob's statement; but to Nell's surprise, no churned up foam came drifting by astern as before, and she couldn't make it out.

The paradox, however, was made plain to her by Hellyer, who did not seem to trouble himself much about the mishap, remaining seated on the hamper, which he had placed by the after sponsing of the starboard paddle box. The coastguardsman, indeed, appeared as unconcerned throughout all the fuss as if he were safe ashore in his own little cabin on the beach; while Rover kept close beside him, as he had done since Hellyer took charge of the hamper which he had brought on board the dog evidently considering himself still responsible for all the picnic goods and chattels that his young mistress had told him to watch.

"The paddles is backin' astern," replied Hellyer; "and so, miss, their wake drifts for'ard instead of aft. That's the reason, miss, you sees nothing washing by."

But this movement did not long continue, two strokes of the gong in the engine room being heard as the captain of the steamer moved the brass handle of the mechanical telegraph on the bridge; whereupon, the machinery was suddenly stopped.

Then the gong sounded twice again, the signal being followed by the quick 'splash—splash splash!' of the paddles once more in the water; when Nellie was delighted by seeing the creamy foam tossing up alongside where she and her aunt were now standing again, they having vacated their seats on the first alarm, like others of the passengers.

" By Jove ! " muttered the Captain, half aloud. " The fool of a fellow is actually going ahead again ! "

" What ! " cried Mrs. Gilmour " any new danger ? "

" Oh, nothing," he snapped out, evidently very grumpy at things not being done in the way he thought best. " I was only uttering my thoughts aloud, ma'am. If you must know, I think it very risky of our friend the skipper trying to drive the boat ahead when she's down by the bows. Poor chap, I'm afraid he has lost his head, the same as the vessel has hers! Never mind, though, she cannot go very far in this shoal water, or I'm a Dutchman ! "

Nor did she.

In less than a minute there was another heavy bump that shook the deck fore and aft, making all the passengers tumble about like ninepins. Bob nearly took a dive through the hatchway of the engine-room, into which he was still peering, and Nellie fell on poor Rover, causing him to utter a plaintive howl; while, as for Mrs. Gilmour, she lurched against the Captain as if she were going to embrace him with open arms, treading at the same time on his worst foot, whereon flourished a pet corn that gave the old sailor infinite trouble, which he ever guarded as the apple of his eye.

" O-o-o o o h ! " he groaned, hopping about the deck on one leg and holding up the injured foot with both his hands, " I knew some further mischief would come from what that idiot of a skipper was doing !"

Meanwhile, the steamboat people on the pier, off which they had grounded only some three or four hundred yards away, seeing the predicament of the vessel, set to work sending off boats to land the passengers.

The first of these reached the little vessel just as she struck the sandbank she had run foul of for the second time; then coming to a dead stop as if she meant now to remain there for good and all.

"Are we to go ashore in one of those?" asked Bob, pointing out the fleet of small boats making for the steamer, besides the two that had already come up to her; some being launched by the watermen on the beach in addition to those sent off from the pier. "What fun to have a boat all to ourselves, as I suppose we shall ."

"Yes, I suppose so, if we are to get to land at all," replied the Captain, who had become a little more amiable, his natural good humour asserting itself as the pain in his foot somewhat subsided; "I don't see how we can otherwise, unless we swim for it; the vessel is now stuck quite fast with no chance of her moving until she is lightened of her cargo of passengers."

"That will be jolly !" cried Bob. "Why it's just like a regular shipwreck ."

"Ah, my boy," said the old sailor, shaking his head, "if you ever experienced the realities of one, you would not speak so lightly. A shipwreck, let me tell you, is no laughing matter."

"I didn't mean that," explained Bob, "I was only thinking how jolly it would be for us all to have a row, instead of landing at the pier quietly, as we would have done if nothing had happened."

"Sure, and I don't see where your 'jollity' comes in, Master Bob ." observed his aunt, not by any means relishing the prospect. "It may be all very well for you; but, I can't say *I* like the idea of scrambling down the side of the vessel into one of these cockleshells and running the risk of getting drowned."

"Oh, no, you won't, ma'am," rejoined the Captain chuckling again, her comical consternation soothing the last acerbities of his temper. "You shan't drown yourself if I can prevent you, ma'am!"

There was no necessity, however, for the Captain to exert himself especially on her behalf; for, the boats being hauled up in turn alongside and only a proper number being allowed to get into each, no casualty occurred such as Mrs. Gilmour dreaded. Thus, in a very short space of time, all the passengers were safely transferred from the stranded steamer to the shore, where a large crowd of sympathizing bystanders had now assembled.

"There!" exclaimed the Captain, as he jumped out of the wherry in which their little party had taken passage, "catch me going in one of those excursion craft again! Of all the clumsy lubbers I have ever had the misfortune to be shipmate with, that skipper is about the biggest and most lubberly. You can take the word of an old sailor for that!"

"Why, sure, what could the poor man have done, when the steamer was sinking?" said Mrs. Gilmour, as he assisted her also carefully to land. "It's none of his fault that I can see."

"What could he have done, eh?" retorted the Captain warmly. "Why, anything else but what he did do. When he saw his fore compartment was full of water, he should have backed the vessel; and then he could have taken her stern-end foremost up to the pier, and landed us comfortably without any bother half an hour ago. Instead of that, what does he do but go backing and filling, first with his engines full speed ahead, and then ditto astern, ending by sticking hard and fast at the same spot where he first struck. While now, to clench the matter, he's going to run the steamer ashore and beach her, he tells me, as soon as the tide floats her; the upshot of which will be that she'll break her back and probably become a total wreck."

"Why didn't you advise him?" she asked. "Eh, my old friend?"

"The foolish fellow! I pitied him at first, but I can't say I do so any longer. He wouldn't listen to me. He's just like the intelligent Isle of Wight farmer I've heard of, one of whose calves having got its head entangled in a wooden fence, in lieu of cutting the palings, thought the only way to release the calf was by cutting its head off!"

"Sure, nobody could have been so stupid!" cried Mrs. Gilmour laughing. "What, cut off the poor thing's head in order to extricate it?"

"Sure an' they did, ma'am," said he, mimicking her; "and, I'm sorry to say, our friend the skipper is one of the same kidney!"

While the two were thus talking, Bob and Nell remained down on the beach, awaiting the arrival of Dick and Hellyer, who through want of room in their wherry had to come ashore in another boat.

Rover, such was his strict sense of duty, strange to say, instead of accompanying his young master and mistress, was still intent on keeping in sight of the hamper.

Accordingly, he stopped on board the steamer till Hellyer, the hamper's custodian, left her; when after seeing him and Dick embarked along with the hamper, the retriever jumped over the side of the stranded vessel and swam ashore in company with the boat containing his friends, apparently mistrusting the frail craft, and preferring to rely upon his own powers in the water.

Nor was he far behind, getting to land almost at the same moment that the wherry's keel grated on the beach; when, after shaking himself decorously as he had been taught, so as to avoid wetting his friends by his excessive moisture, Rover barked and pranced round Hellyer and the hamper, and then

round Bob and Nellie, as if to say in his dog language—
"There, my dear young master and mistress, I have discharged
my trust faithfully," scurrying off then to the higher part of the
shore, where Mrs. Gilmour and the Captain were standing, to
tell them the same tale, with a loud 'Bow wow!'

"Come now," cried Mrs. Gilmour, on the little party being
reunited again, "we must be off home at once; for, it is getting
late, and Sarah will be wondering where we all are."

"Well, we mustn't keep 'the good Sarah' waiting," said the
Captain slily, with a wink to Nellie that set her off laughing so
that she dropped the bunch of wild flowers which her aunt was
just har.ding her at the moment, and was obliged to stop to
pick them up. "By Jove! though, ma'am, she may have
forgotten *us* as she did the other things."

"You're too bad entirely!" exclaimed Mrs. Gilmour a little
pettishly. "I suppose I shall never hear the last about that,
ror poor Sarah either. Come on now, dearie; we must
hasten home whether or no."

So saying, she made the Captain wheel round from taking
a last lingering look at the *Bembridge Belle*, whose skipper,
now that she was a bit lightened aft by all the people having
cleared out of her, had backed again into deep water; and
then putting on full steam ahead, was trying to run her up
high and dry ashore.

After this parting glance at the poor vessel, our party proceeded on their way across the common back to The Moorings, Miss Nell, as aforesaid, carrying the bouquet of wild-
flowers, and Bob the tin bucket of sea-anemones, their 'spoil'
of the day, in sporting parlance; while Hellyer and Dick
brought up the rear of the procession with the hamper and
empty water jar, representing the relics of their picnic feast.

Rover on this occasion, it may be added, acted anon as
pioneer of the column when he caracoled for awhile in front
of them all; anon as baggage-guard, when he followed at the
heels of Hellyer, sniffing the empty hamper.

Poor Sarah, 'that good Sarah' whom Mrs. Gilmour had so unhappily praised, her penance was yet to come!

Bob was the first to assail her as she opened the door on their arrival home.

"Who forgot the bread?" he shouted out, so loudly that, starting back with fright, she almost tumbled. "Who forgot the bread?"

"Who forgot the tea?" cried Nellie, immediately behind him, following up her brother's attack and making Sarah jump afresh. "Who forgot the tea?"

"And who forgot her head?" said the Captain from the rear, pressing the charge home; whereupon, they all, Mrs. Gilmour included, halted on the doorstep and roared with laughter. "Aye, who forgot her head?"

This was too much for the girl.

"Oh my, me!" she exclaimed, staring at them in hopeless stupefaction. "Oh my, me!"

"Dear me!" observed Mrs. Gilmour, her laugh subsiding into a broad smile. "Why, you are quite a poet, Sarah."

"Me, mum?" ejaculated the other, more astonished than ever. "Whatever have I gone and done now?"

"Yes," continued her mistress, "you've just supplied 'the missing link' in our rhyme; and, people who make poetry, of course, are poets."

"Oh, auntie, I see, I see!" called out Nellie excitedly, in great glee. "I see it don't you, Bob?"

"No, what is it?" asked that young gentleman. "See what?"

"Oh dear! and you began it, too," cried Nell. "You really are a very stupid boy. Why, it's a regular verse of poetry

> 'Who forgot the bread?
> Who forgot the tea?
> And who forgot her head?
> Oh, my—me!'

Don't you see it now?"

"Oh, yes," replied Bob, adding his usual expression when praising anything "it's jolly!"

"I confess I did not see it either at first; so, I suppose, you'll call me a stupid too, Miss Nellie, eh?" chuckled Captain Dresser. "However, now you've made it all clear to us, I will, if you like, christen your short but sweet poem for you. What say you to 'Sarah's forget-me nots'? Do you think that will do, eh?"

"Splendidly!" said Nell; an opinion which they all seemed to share, excepting poor Sarah, into whose ears the verselet was dinned so incessantly, both by Bob and Nellie, and even by the pert Dick, too, that its repetition, or any specific allusion to any one of the articles she had omitted in making up the historic hamper, would invariably make the unfortunate damsel wince; while if the simple name of the innocent flower which the Captain had adopted were but mentioned, even without any malice prepense, the poor girl would leave the room at once.

"Where are the forget me nots?" said Mrs. Gilmour incautiously, for instance, to Nellie, while arranging the wildflowers in vases shortly before going to bed. "I can't see them at all anywhere. Can you Sarah?"

There was no answer from her, however.

Sarah was off like a shot!

CHAPTER XVI

EARLY next morning, after their usual matutinal swim, Bob and Dick accompanied the Captain for a stroll along the beach to the coastguard station on the eastern side of the Castle, near to which the ill fated *Bembridge Belle* had been run ashore.

Of course, Rover formed one of the party; carrying, equally as a matter of course, his young master's towels in his mouth and wagging his fine bushy tail with even more energy than he generally evinced when performing that function, in order to express his proud exultation at the trust reposed in him.

At the coastguard station they found Hellyer standing by the flagstaff, with his telescope under his left arm and evidently on duty.

"Not much damage done to her hull yet, sir," said he, touching his hat, as he thus anticipated the Captain's inquiry. "She were all awash, though, sir, at high water this morning!"

"Indeed!" cried Captain Dresser. "Then, that forward bulkhead must have started when the fore compartment got full."

"No doubt o' that, sir," agreed Hellyer. "Why, the tide covered her after deck at Six Bells; and the cushions of the settees and a lot o' dunnage were floating about in the saloon below and washing through the ports astern."

"Her fo'c's'le, however, keeps high and dry."

" Aye, now it do, sir," replied Hellyer. " But, not for long ! "

" You're right, my man," said the Captain, after having a good squint at the object of their commiseration. " She has been working already on the shingle, and her frame has been a good deal knocked about since last night."

The coastguardsman gave a shrug to his shoulders.

" I expect a tide or two 'll settle her hash, sir," he observed, after thus relieving his pent-up feelings. " With the water making a clean sweep through her fore and aft every time it rises, the poor thing can't last long, sir ! "

" Aye," said the Captain. " She's bound to go to pieces, now, fast enough."

" So I've reported to the commander, sir, this very morning," continued Hellyer ; " and, he's sent down word as I'm to keep men stationed along the shore so as to pick up any wreckage that mebbe washed out on her."

" Quite right," was the Captain's comment on this. " There are a lot of light fingered gentry about here, whom it is just as well to be on guard against. When will it be flood-tide to night, Hellyer, eh ? "

" Nigh upon nine o'clock, sir," answered he. " Just afore the moon rises."

" Humph ! " muttered Captain Dresser, as if cogitating the matter and speaking his thoughts aloud. " I think I'll come down then. The sea seems inclined to get up a bit ? "

He raised his voice when uttering the last words, as if asking a question ; so, the coastguardsman answered it at once.

" That it do, sir," he said with decision ; " and, if the wind freshen more, as is more 'n likely, considerin' it's been backin' all the mornin', I spects it 'll be pretty rough by night time ! "

" Ah, well, so I think, too, Hellyer. Good day to you, my man ; I will come down again this evening when the tide makes. I fancy she'll break up then. Come on, boys ! " sang out the old sailor in a higher key to Bob and Dick, who had been amusing themselves by trying to walk round the hull of

L

the stranded steamer, now nearly high and dry on the beach; although the venturesome fellows had to clamber over all sorts of obstacles in the way of chain cables and hawsers and other gear, besides wading through various pools of water to seaward, before they could congratulate themselves on effecting their object. "Come on now, my boys! There's nothing more to see at present; and I've promised Miss Nell to help her put those actinea we got yesterday at Seaview into her new aquarium."

"But, you will come down again with us to see the wreck, won't you?" eagerly asked Bob, running after the Captain, who on giving this explanation of his desire of not wasting any more time on the beach just then, had started off already on his way back to the south parade, and was hobbling off at a fine rate across the common. "I do so want to see the poor vessel once more before they take her away, Captain!"

"Humph!" grunted out the old sailor as he puffed and panted onward like a steam-engine, turning the services of his trusty old malacca cane to good account. "I don't think, my boy, you need have any fear on that score. The only shape in which she's likely to be taken away from her present berth will be   in pieces!"

"By Jove, ma'am!" he exclaimed later on, when Mrs. Gilmour and Nell met him at the gate of 'The Moorings,' "I might just as well board with you at once. Dined with you on Monday, to lunch Tuesday; at breakfast yesterday, and again this morning. Why, I'll eat you out of house and home!"

"Never fear, Captain," said Mrs. Gilmour smiling. "Sure, I'll take the risk of that."

"But your servants, ma'am," he argued, as Nell took away his hat and cane. "I'm afraid I give them a lot of trouble, and they'll be springing a mutiny on you."

"I don't know what poor Sarah 'll do, sure; you've taised her so!" replied Mrs. Gilmour jokingly. "But, Molly the cook's your friend, I know. She says you're the only one in the house that properly appreciates her curries."

"Faith and she turns them out well, ma'am; and you can tell her so, with my compliments," said the old sailor with much heartiness as he winked to Nellie. "As for 'that good Sarah,' ma'am, I shall have to make my peace with her by and by, with your permission."

After breakfast, the Captain and Nellie, with the assistance of Bob and Dick, even 'the good Sarah,' too, being pressed into the service, set about preparing the sea anemones and other specimens they had collected the previous day for their new home in the aquarium which Mrs. Gilmour had bought for the purpose shortly before.

This aquarium was in appearance somewhat like an inverted dish cover of glass—one of the best shapes to be had. This sort being free from those leaky joints that are the invariable accompaniment of all square cisterns; while globular ones have not got sufficient space at the bottom for rockwork, or those little hiding places that delight the hearts of the denizens of the deep when they are free agents and in their own waters.

Presently, under the active superintendence of the old sailor, the whilom empty glass receptacle began to assume a more picturesque aspect.

To commence with, a groundwork was constructed of fine white sand and shells, each of the latter being washed in repeated baths of clear and fresh sea water, which had been brought up from the beach in the morning, before being introduced into the aquarium; where, if success be desired, cleanliness is as essential to the well being of its little tenants as it is deemed to be amongst human beings.

The Captain said something to this effect while making Nellie wash the different shells, which he then arranged along the sandy bottom, which was made to slope from the back of the structure down to the centre, forming a sort of hollow there; and then rising again in front.

"So far, so good," said the Captain, placing some bits of rock in the background, which, leaning against each other, formed so many small caverns. "These will do for those crabs, which Master Bob insists on having, to retreat to when some of the other fry pay them too much attention."

On the right and left of the aquarium the old sailor dexterously built up larger pieces of rockwork, intermixed with bits of red seaweed that grows in the form of a feathery plume, called by naturalists the 'bryopsis plumosa,' than which no more graceful marine plant can be found.

Close to this and serving as a contrast, the Captain placed the green laver he had made Nell pick up at the last moment when they were leaving Seaview and running to catch the steamer.

"This chap, styled the 'ulva latissima' by the scientific gentlemen who manufacture such titles, is a capital thermometer," said the Captain on putting in the laver. "You'll find he'll always rise to the surface when the weather is bright and sunny; while he sinks back to the bottom, as I've put him now, on its being damp and overcast."

In the more immediate foreground, a number of little starfish squatted about on the miniature strand that shelved down from the rocks, arranged with much care to the general spectacular effect by Nellie, who was most painstaking in the matter.

To be introduced into this very select marine retreat, the anemones had to go through similar ablutions to the sand and the shells, as well as other things, all of them being at the outset cleansed with the greatest care. When, however, this was done and the actinea put into their future home, the aquarium blossomed out into a garden of live flowers, whose tentacles of various colours resembled so many chrysanthemums, dahlias, and daisies, of the most gorgeous hues ever seen on Nature's palette!

Of course, the actinea did not make themselves at home

in their new lodgings and disclose their beauties all at once;
but, in a few days, none of them having been hurt by Bob's
knife, they seemed to have become acclimatized, putting out
the petals of their flower like bodies as freely as when in their
native pools at Seaview. So, too, did a beautiful rose and
white dianthus, which Dick had picked up adhering to an
ugly old oyster shell; and, the even rarer anthea, whose long
hanging filaments were never altogether withdrawn into its
body when disturbed, as was the case with the other sea
anemones, and which were thus a constant source of alarm to
Bob's little crabs; for, it was ever listlessly waving perilously
near these nervous creatures, making them hurry out of
their way in such frantic haste as their lateral conformation
permitted.

It was a long job arranging the aquarium, engrossing the
attention of all engaged and taking up the entire morning;
aye, and all midday, too!

"Good gracious me!" exclaimed Mrs. Gilmour, coming
into the room when they had just completed the task. "What
a long time you've been at it, to be sure! I believe I could
have made an aquarium by now, let alone fit it up."

"Ah, ma'am, 'more haste, worse speed,'" retorted the old
sailor. "'Rome wasn't built in a day,' you know."

"I thought you had enough of the Romans yesterday," said
Mrs. Gilmour, giving him this little cut in return for his brace
of proverbs. "But, come, Sarah, you must see about getting
luncheon now. I want it ready as soon as possible. You'll
stop, Captain Dresser, I suppose?"

"Oh yes, ma'am, if you'll allow me," he replied with a
chuckle. "I know when I'm well off. You recollect, ma'am,
you said just now the cook was my friend."

"Do you know why I wanted to have lunch especially early
to day?" she asked him anon, when they were seated at the
table. "Can you guess?"

"No, by Jove, I can't!" he snorted out indignantly. "I'm

not a clairvoyant, or whatever else you call those people who pretend to read other people's thoughts."

"Sure, then, I'll tell you," she said, laughing at his quaint manner, "I'm going to see Mrs. Craddock."

"I'm just as much in the dark as ever," he retorted. "Who the dickens is the woman, eh?"

Nell saved her aunt the trouble of answering.

"Why, don't you remember the old lady at the station whom Rover tumbled down and broke her eggs?" she cried out eagerly. "You must recollect, for you sent her some port wine for her poor daughter, which auntie and I took the second time we went to see her; You must remember her!"

"Ah, yes, I remember now," said the Captain, scratching his head reflectively. "So that's her name, eh Craddock, Craddock. Where have I heard it before? By Jove, I've got it now! Why, ma'am, there was a Craddock who was boatswain of the old *Bucephalus* on the West Coast."

"What!" cried Mrs. Gilmour. "My poor dear Ted's ship?"

"The same, ma'am," he answered. "I recollect the man very well now. He was a tall, spare, intellectual looking chap, more like a longshore man than a sailor. He was delicate, too, suffering from a weak chest; and, Ted told me, now I come to think of it, that he volunteered for a second term of service on the African station in order to be in a warm climate. It didn't do him much good, though, for he died on the commission."

"How strange!" said Mrs. Gilmour pensively. "I don't remember poor Ted writing me anything about it, but I've no doubt the man was our Mrs. Craddock's husband, and, if so, that will make me take an additional interest in her. Run upstairs, Nel, and get ready at once, my dear. As soon as you come down we'll start, for I have only got to put on my bonnet."

"Do you want me to come, too?" faltered the Captain,

who, unless visiting a sick bed on an errand of mercy, dreaded going to see any one whom he had been kind to, the old sailor doing all his good deeds, and they were many, by stealth. Indeed, the very idea of being thanked made him always inclined to run away, a thing he had never done from an enemy.

"Well, if you'd rather not, or if you've somewhere else to go, I won't insist."

"Why, I did promise to go down to the Club," he replied, still speaking in a half hesitating way. "I I I ''

"I know," said Mrs. Gilmour, interrupting him, and looking very knowing "you don't want to go to Mrs. Craddock's, because you sent her poor daughter some port wine, and are afraid of being thanked for it that's the reason, I know."

The Captain blushed.

"I assure you, ma'am," he began timidly to remonstrate against her conclusion, when suddenly some little recollection gave him renewed courage. "By Jove, I declare I nearly forgot all about it! I've got to meet Sponson at the Club to see when that ship is going out for her trials; I mean the one, which I'm going to take Bob on board of."

"Well, be off with you to your Club," she rejoined laughing, giving him a little push in joke. "Away with you at once!"

"You see, she turns me out," he said humorously to Bob, in a sort of stage aside. "That's what you might call Irish hospitality."

He hurried out after his insulting remark, but popped in his head again at the door to make a parting request.

"May I come back to dinner, please?" he asked, with his hands clasped in mute entreaty also. "I have breakfasted and lunched with you, so I may just as well make a day of it, and come to dinner."

"Yes, if you're good," she replied. "But why so particularly this evening? I'm afraid it's a Banian day, and Molly will not have anything nice for you."

"Never mind that, ma'am. I want to take you all down to see the wreck at high-water," said he. "It will probably be the last of the old ship."

"Hurrah!" exclaimed Bob, pitching his hat in the air, and catching it dexterously again. "Won't that be jolly?"

On Nell now coming downstairs, they proceeded on their respective ways; the Captain into Portsmouth, and Mrs. Gilmour, with Bob and Nellie, accompanied by Dick carrying a basket, to Mrs. Craddock's old-fashioned cottage, at Fratton —almost in the opposite direction.

Here Mrs. Gilmour, after one or two inquiries, discovered, much to her satisfaction, that the widow and her daughter were the wife and child of her husband's boatswain, whence ensued much talk between herself and the old lady, who declared the invalid to be 'the very image of poor dear Craddock!'

While their elders were conversing, Nellie was also having a chat with the bedridden girl, who, she was glad to see, looked decidedly better than at the time of her last visit; an improvement doubtless due to the Captain's old port, and other nourishing things Mrs. Gilmour had taken her.

Bob meanwhile had been overhauling the various curios in the little parlour, where the invalid was lying, this being the first time he had been there.

"Oh, auntie," he called out presently, "do look at this Chinese idol here! It's just like one I saw at the South Kensington Museum, only it has such funny wooden shoes on."

Mrs. Gilmour came across the room to look at the monster figure squatting down in the corner; but, on Bob's showing her the shoes, she laughed.

"Those are not Chinese, my boy," she exclaimed, "they are a pair of wooden sabots from France, such as are worn by the peasants of Brittany and Normandy."

"You're quite right, my lady," said the widow Craddock, approaching them. "My son, who was a sailor like his father,

found them on board a French vessel he helped that was in
distress in the Channel; so, he brought them home and stuck
them on that there h'image in fun.   Lawk, mum, if them
wooden shoes could talk, it's a queer tale they'd tell ye, fur
they was the means, or leastways it wer' through his boarding
the vessel where he found 'em', that my son Jim, which was
his name, my lady, come to give up the sea; although, mind
you, he's summat to do with it still, being a fisherman fur that
matter.   However, the end of it was that he marries the
French gal as took his fancy when he comed across them
shoes, and went to live at Saint Maller, as they calls it."

"St. Malo, I suppose," corrected Mrs. Gilmour.   "Eh?"

"Yes, my lady, I sed Saint Maller, didn't I?" replied the
old dame, not perceiving where the delicate distinction lay;
and, then, she went on to relate in a very roundabout fashion
all the incidents connected with her son's marriage as well
as talking of everything else under the sun, so it seemed to
Bob, who thought it an interminably long story, and was
heartily glad when old Mrs. Craddock got to the end
of it.

But, little did he think in how short a space of time he
would be brought in contact with that son of hers, Jim
Craddock, in the very strangest manner, and under circum
stances that would never have entered his wildest dreams!

However, he did not know this; and, while the old dame
was spinning her yarn, Bob employed the time by looking at
the model of a ship over the mantelpiece, which brought back
to his mind all about the *Bembridge Belle*, making him feel
on tenter hooks lest they should be late for dinner, and so be
unable to go down afterwards and see the wreck, as the
Captain had arranged.

He need not have been so fidgety, though.

Everything comes to an end in time, as did the old lady's
talk; and then, they were able to start home again, Rover
coming in for much praise from his waiting so patiently for

such a lengthy period outside Mrs. Craddock's cottage, without bark or whine betraying his presence there.

The dinner was not late, much to Bob's joy; and, the Captain being also punctuality itself, they set out for the beach, just when the dim shadows of the fading twilight were mingling with those of night.

There was a stiff breeze blowing from the southward and eastward, almost half a gale, as a sailor would express it, the wind causing the incoming tide to break on the shore with a low, dull roar, as if the spirit of the deep felt half inclined to be angry, and yet had not quite made up his mind!

It was almost dark by the time the little party from 'The Moorings' reached the wreck, and things were beginning to get indistinct a little distance off; but, soon after their arrival on the spot, the silvery moon rising at the full, passing through occasional strata of dark cloud that veiled her light at intervals, illumined the sky with her weird beams, making it bright as day, but with a ghostly radiance that lent a mystic spectral effect to all the surroundings.

What a difference the vessel presented to her appearance of the morning!

Then she was high and dry on the shingle, with the retreating tide going out to sea to flood coasts elsewhere, only indicating that it had not quite gone yet by a faint splash and ripple on the shore; and, deserted by the element that should have supported her and did when she moved and had her being, gliding through the waters 'like a thing of life,' the wretched steamer stood up so gaunt and grim that she seemed more than twice her natural size.

That was in the morning, barely twelve hours ago! But, now, where was she? The tell tale light of the moon explained all, without a word being wanted.

At first no doubt, the breakers! how aptly named! had begun their attack against the poor crippled thing's hull by degrees, little billows leading the assault that could only leap half way up the side of the stranded steamer, falling back with impotent mutterings in a passion of spray; then, as the tide rose, these were succeeded by bigger waves rolling in from the eastwards, which, swollen with pride and brimming with destruction, beat and blustered all about the vessel from cutwater to sternpost, seeking ingress through the timbers that they might fall upon her and devour her.

Through it all the poor *Bembridge Belle* battled bravely, holding her own as long as she could keep her head above the boisterous billows; but, when the tide rose yet higher, and the waters flowed through her fore and aft, her upper deck became submerged, the sea made a clean breach over her, the waves took her in their rough hands and shook her so that she trembled, her hull working to and fro in the shingle, the blustering billows dashed against her, and she began to break up. The loose upper or hurricane deck parted. Then the contents of the main saloon below, of which this deck formed the roof, commenced washing adrift, the broken water round the deck pitching and tossing about cushions and chairs, flaps of tables, and all sorts of pieces of furniture, some of which were cast up ashore near by, and others carried out by the tide to goodness knows where!

The Captain and Mrs. Gilmour, with Bob and Nell, and Dick and Rover, too, watched this sad ending of the steamer's career with almost as heavy hearts as if they were her owners. Rover, indeed, took such a very deep interest in her that he assisted Hellyer and the other coastguardsmen on duty at the spot by helping them bravely in dragging out of the clutches of the waves everything that floated near enough inshore for him to jump at and seize.

"We'd better go home now," said the Captain, when the vessel separated amidships, her funnel and masts falling over into the water. "There's nothing more to see now, poor old ship!"

He spoke quite sadly, as if he had lost a friend; and the

others, too, seemed equally affected by the scene, even Bob turning his back on the beach w thout a murmur at their going indoors so early, as he would otherwise have done; this being the young gentleman's usual plaint. But, if depressed for the moment, on reaching 'The Moorings' the thermometer of their spirits jumped suddenly to fever-heat.

Sarah, 'the good Sarah,' opened the door, as she usually did; but she appeared to perform the task on the present occasion with even more than her usual alacrity, while her face wore a pleased expression that had not visited it since the composition of that celebrated poem in honour of her memory! She actually beamed with delight and looked 'bursting, aye, bursting with good news!' as the Captain said afterwards.

"Why, whatever is the matter, Sarah?" asked Mrs. Gilmour. "Speak, my good girl!"

She paid no attention, however, to her mistress.

"Oh, Master Bob oh, Miss Nell!" she exclaimed. "Who do you think have come, and is now in the house?"

Bob and Nellie both stared at Sarah in surprise.

They thought, for the moment, the poor girl had lost her wits !

An inkling of the truth, however, flashed across their minds the next instant ; and, pushing past the almost incoherent Sarah, who said something which neither of them caught the sense of, the two rushed into the lighted hall in a flurry of excitement.

Here the sight of several corded trunks and other luggage, which had not been there when they went out of the house earlier in the evening, at once confirmed their joyous anticipations.

"Hurrah !" cried Bob, giving vent to his feelings first. "Dad and mother are here at last ! "

Nell, though, got ahead of him in greeting the new comers.

"Oh, mamma !" she said, dashing towards the door of the dining room which opened into the hall and meeting half way a stately lady who was advancing with open arms. "My own dear mamma !"

The Captain and Mrs. Gilmour had now come into the hall, following more sedately the harum-scarum youngsters ; and while the former hung back, waiting to be introduced as soon as the first greetings were over, the good lady of the house advanced eagerly to welcome a tall and bearded gentleman, with a right good pair of broad shoulders of his own, who came forward to meet her, with Bob clinging to one of his arms while the other was round his neck.

"Why, me dear Dugald, it's never you!" exclaimed Mrs. Gilmour as her brother let go Bob and caught both her out stretched hands in his, giving them a fraternal grip. "Sure, is it yourself, or somebody ilse?"

"Mesilf, Polly, sure enough," replied he in a deep baritone voice, that resembled Bob's, but had a very slight suspicion of the Irish brogue in it like her own. "Right glad am I to say ye again, too, mavourneen! Ye're a sight good for sore eyes, sure!"

He laughed as he said this, a racy, genial laugh in keeping with his looks; and the Captain instantly took a liking to him for his own sake, apart from his likeness to his sister, Mrs. Gilmour, who now introduced him, having already prepossessed the old sailor in his favour.

"Me brother Captain Dresser," she said smiling. "I'm sure you ought to know each other by this time, if you don't already."

"Glad to meet you, sir, glad to meet you," cried the Captain in his bluff hearty way. "I've often heard of you, especially since Master Bob here has been down at Southsea."

"Ah! I have to thank you for the kind way in which you've made their stay here pleasant for him and my little girl," rejoined the other warmly as the two shook hands. "But, there was little need, Captain Dresser, for my sister to introduce you. She's told me so much about you, that I seem to have known you already for years!"

"Oh, yes," said the Captain; "your sister is one of my oldest friends."

"What's that you're saying about my being an old friend?" exclaimed Mrs. Gilmour, pretending to be indignant. "You speak as if I were an aged person; but, I'd have you to know, that, although I'm not quite a chicken, sure, I'm not as old as old Methuselah yet!"

"No, no, I didn't mean that," chuckled the Captain; and turning to her brother he remarked on the likeness between him and Mrs. Gilmour. "It is absolutely striking, by Jove!"

"We're almost twins," replied he innocently; "only, I'm ten years older!"

The Captain burst into a regular roar of laughter at this; his sides shaking and his face getting so red that it seemed as if he were going to have a fit of apoplexy.

"By Jove!" he exclaimed, "you ought to be twins!"

It was only then that the other perceived the slip he had made, as did his sister, and the two joined in the Captain's mirth; while Master Bob also lent his help, although witless of what the general merriment was about, the deep ho ho ho! of his father being even more contagious than the catching laugh of his old friend the Captain.

"Sure, Dugald, you're the same careless fellow still," cried Mrs. Gilmour, as soon as she was able to get out a word. "As me poo. dear Ted used to say, you're an Irishman to the backbone. Sure you never open your mouth but you put your foot in it!"

"That is what I'm always telling him, too," said her sister-in-law, whom the laughter in the hall, renewed with such force when Mrs. Gilmour, in trying to set matters straight, made another Irish bull as big as her brother's, had brought out of the parlour, accompanied by Nellie. "Dugald is really incorrigible!"

"That's just what Mrs. Gilmour says I am," observed the Captain, bowing between his chuckles. "You must let me introduce myself. I don't need anybody to introduce you, ma'am; for I'm sure from your sweet soft voice alone that you are little missy's mother. She and I, you know, are sworn friends!"

Mrs. Strong smiled; and, if the Captain had called her voice a sweet one, he could find no words in which to describe the light that stole into her eyes, irradiating the face now.

"I see you can pay compliments, Captain Dresser, although you are not an Irishman," she said pleasantly, caressing Nell, who in the joy of seeing her mother again had never left her side. "I suppose that's the reason this young lady has lost her heart to you?"

"You'd better be wary of him, Edith," interposed Mrs. Gilmour jokingly. "He's a terrible old flirt with all the ladies, young and old alike! But, wouldn't you like to go upstairs and take your things off?"

"No, thanks, not till it's time for bed; and, it must be very near that now."

"Oh, the day's yet young." cried her hospitable hostess, leading the way back into the parlour. "We didn't expect you before to morrow, or next day at the earliest; and Nell, indeed, stopped in all the morning to finish her letter in time, so that you could get it to night in London, as she thought. Still, my dear, I dare say we'll be able to find you something to eat, and your rooms shall be got ready for you as soon as possible."

"Please, mum," said Sarah, who was still waiting in the hall, at hand for whatever the guests might need, "they are quite ready, mum!"

"Ready!" repeated Mrs. Gilmour surprised. "The spare rooms?"

"Yes, mum," replied Sarah, dropping a curtsey, with the proud consciousness of having done well in her mistress's sight. "Me and Molly went up to the rooms and did what you told me I'd have to do to morrow, as soon as ever Mr. and Mrs. Strong came, mum; so, now, they're quite ready. Molly, too, went back afterwards to her kitchen, and is warming up the curry, in case you should like it hot for supper."

"You've done quite right, Sarah, and just as I would have

directed if I'd been at home. Tell Molly from me, that there is nothing my brother is fonder of than curry; and that she may send up supper as soon as she's got it ready."

Sarah hurried off to quicken the preparations of her fellow servant below, her movements somewhat accelerated by Bob shouting out the cruel refrain of the 'forget me not poem!'

"Ah, but," put in the Captain, "the 'good Sarah' did not forget her head this time, at any rate! You'll have to alter your poem, Master Bob!"

Then, of course, ensued a lot of explanations, which led up to an account of the picnic, the elaborate description of which Nellie had taken such pains to write in her letter home to her mother.

All of which pains, alas! were thrown away; for here was her mother by her side, while her graphic letter was lying uselessly in the box at the post office!

A series of questions and answers then followed rapidly in reference to Bob and Miss Nell's doings since they had been down by the sea; interspersed with sundry inquiries after Blinkie, the old dissipated jackdaw left behind at home, and Snuffles, the black cat, who was a martyr to chronic influenza, whence his very appropriate name!

Rover, who was wild with delight on seeing his old master and mistress when he came in damp and dripping from his experiences of the wreck, was not altogether forgotten, you may be sure, just because London friends were thought of! On the contrary, he received many pats and caresses besides getting an unexpected supper; a thing not generally in Rover's line, but which, none the less, did not seem to come amiss to him on the present occasion.

· By this time, it was very late, the 'tattoo' having sounded long since, summoning all truant soldiers into barracks; so, the Captain, declaring that his landlady would 'haul him over the coals' for stopping out so late, stumped away chuckling down the parade with his malacca cane.

M

The exhausted household at 'The Moorings' then went to bed in peace, tired out with their day's doings tired even of talk Bob and Nell composing in their dreams a fresh version, as the old sailor had humorously suggested, of Sarah's celebrated picnic poem; in which, instead of their original quatrain, 'bed' now rhymed with 'head,' in lieu of the unfortunately forgotten 'bread,' and 'curry' with 'hurry!'

The next day, both Mr. and Mrs. Dugald Strong said that they were too fatigued to do anything else save lie in the sun and bask on the beach; but the following morning, the Captain, insisting on their seeing the sights of the place, took them all down to the harbour, when they went on board the *Victory*, Nelson's old flagship, which Mrs. Gilmour said she had been over 'at laste a hundred times before,' although she accompanied them now 'for company's sake, sure!'

If a hackneyed theme to her, this visit to the historic vessel was, however, replete with interest to the others; being full of floating memories of the past, in which the grand figure of the hero of Trafalgar stood out in relief with that wonderfully bloodstirring last signal of his, like a laurel wreath encircling his brows—'England expects every man this day to do his duty!'

To Bob and Nellie it was especially delightful to see the real ship in which Nelson had fought so gallantly that battle of which they had read, knowing, by heart almost, the principal incidents of the glorious day, when the British fleet 'crumpled up the combined squadrons of France and Spain'; and, with the able assistance of the Captain, who made an admirable cicerone, they could, standing there on board the *Victory*, imagine themselves in the thick of the celebrated sea fight. Aye, boarding the *Santissima Trinidada*, with the guns banging about them and the sulphurous gunpowder-smoke filling the air around, hiding everything beyond the ponderous hulls of the enemy's three deckers between which, yard-arm to yard arm, the old *Victory* lay!

"Here it was," said the Captain, pointing out the spot on the quarter deck below the poop, close to a hatchway, and marked by a copper plate let into the planking, bearing a short inscription commemorating the fact, "that Nelson was standing when that villainous marksman in the *Redoutable's* mizzen-top hit him, catching sight of the medals on his breast; for, he would stick 'em on, in spite of the advice of Hardy, who was his flag-captain, you know."

"That was very foolish of him," interposed Mrs. Gilmour. "I suppose he did it to show off, like most of you men; for you're a consayted lot! The same as you punish your malacca cane, Captain!"

"Not a bit of it!" retorted the old sailor indignantly, up in arms at once at the slightest aspersion on his hero's fame. "He wore his medals because, ma'am, in the first place, he wasn't a bit ashamed of them; and, secondly, to encourage his men there, ma'am!"

"That's a settler for you, Polly!" said her brother quizzingly; but, he didn't laugh, the Captain appeared so very much in earnest in speaking of Nelson, whom he regarded with the deepest veneration. "I don't think, my dear, though, it's a subject for joking!"

"I'm very sorry I spoke, sure," pleaded she in extenuation of her offence, "I didn't mean any harm!"

"Well, well, let it pass," replied the Captain, dismissing the painful point in dispute with a wave of his arm and continuing his description of the tragic end of the conqueror of Trafalgar, which Mrs. Gilmour's interruption had somewhat confused in his mind. "We were just where he was shot, eh?"

"Yes," replied Bob, who had been hanging on his words and was all attention and had not lost a word of the narrative. "The French marksman saw his medals."

"Humph!" ejaculated the old sailor, 'making sail again with a fair wind,' as he expressed it in his nautical way. "Well, then, the fellow who shot him was potted immediately

afterwards, you'll be glad to hear, by one of our 'jollies'—
marines, you know   on the poop, who saw the chap aiming at
Nelson, but fired too late to prevent the fatal leaden messenger
doing its deadly work !   The poor Admiral sank down here,
just by that hatchway, and there used to be the stain of his
blood, as they said, on the old timbers of the deck ; but those
have been removed, and, indeed, they've restored the ship so
often that there's hardly one of her old planks left in her save
this with the memorial plate here."

"But, what was done after Nelson was wounded ? " inquired
Nellie, who had been listening as intently as Bob.   "Didn't
they do anything to help him ? "

"Why, they took him down to the cock pit, as they called
the midshipmen's berth on the lower deck, where we're going
now," replied the Captain, leading the way down the companion
and an interminable series of other ladders afterwards, as if
they were descending to the kelson, the space getting all the
narrower and darker as they went down.   "They took him
below—to die !"

Here, in a small, confined apartment, which Bob's father
said looked 'like the condemned cell at Newgate,' and whose
sole apparent advantage, as the Captain explained, was in
its being below the water-line, and therefore the only safe
place in a ship before the days of torpedoes and submarine
warfare, he went on to tell the children, the hero breathed his
last ; his dying moments eased by the knowledge that he had
done his duty to his country and cheered by the news that the
foe was vanquished, Hardy making him smile by saying how
many ships of the line had struck their colours already or been
destroyed.

Nell shivered.

"Let us go upstairs," she said, in a very depressed tone, in
keeping with the melancholy associations of the place.   "Let
us go upstairs ! "

The Captain laughed out at this.

"You'd make a sailor faint, if he heard you ever use that expression !" he cried. "The idea of speaking about 'upstairs' on board a ship, and your uncle a sailor, too, missy !"

"What should I say ?" she asked, looking into his face as well as the dim light would permit. "What should I say instead ?"

"Why, 'on deck,' of course," he replied. "We've got no stairs on board ship. They're either 'companion ways' or 'ladders,' up one of which we'll go now, if you like !"

So saying, he led the way on deck as he had down below, taking them all into the ward room under the poop, where they now saw various relics of the hero, besides letters and orders in his writing, which were framed and hung round the cabin like pictures.

Bob, whose caligraphy was none of the clearest or most legible, had the benefit of a little moral lesson here from his father, who seemed to take a mean advantage of the fact of Nelson writing so well with his left hand after he lost his right; but Master Bob evaded the issue very well by saying that 'when he was similarly circumstanced,' he would try and write as well, too !

"Bravo !" cried the Captain, as they left the ship, going down the 'accommodation ladder,' which, as he was careful to tell Nellie, was not a staircase either, although outside the ship. Then, turning to her father he added, chuckling— "That boy of yours, Strong, is a regular chip of the old block, and a credit to your country !"

They had a laugh at this, of course; and, then, on Mrs. Gilmour suggesting their taking advantage of the high tide to visit Porchester Castle, as the harbour looked its best, the watermen in charge of their wherry were directed to row up stream towards the creek on the northern side, where the old fortress, embowered in trees, nestled under the shelter of the Portsdown hills, a monolith of past grandeur and present decay!

CHAPTER XVIII.

A STEAM TRIAL, AND A GUN BURST.

On their way up the harbour, the Captain pointed out the long line of old hulks moored on either side of the stream that had once, when in their prime, been esteemed the pride of the Navy.

With towering masts and gallant rig they had flown the flag that has borne the battle and the breeze for many a long year.

But, within the last decade, their glory has departed, alas, like the glories of 'Rotten Row,' as this anchorage of broken down ships is called; many of the old historic vessels having been sold out of the service and their places know them no more !

"Ah, these are something like 'Roman remains'!" ex claimed Captain Dresser, when their wherry ultimately glided up to the ruins of Porchester Castle, the base of whose swelling walls was laved by the rippling tide. "That 'villa' at Brading was a regular take in, and I shall always regret that half crown in hard cash, out of which I was swindled !"

"Sure, I don't think you'll ever forget that day," cried Mrs. Gilmour, laughing as she explained the matter more lucidly to her brother and sister in law. "Just as Queen Mary said that Calais would be found engraved on her heart after she was dead, the Roman villa at Brading will be found graven on yours, Captain, sure !"

"I don't mind," said he resignedly, "I like something for

my money; and, here, there is something to see and nothing to pay for it either!"

The boatmen rowed the boat close inshore in order to allow them to inspect the place nearer, as they did not have sufficient time to land and examine it properly. Mrs. Gilmour, while they laid off making thus a cursory inspection of the ruins, became the castle's historian   telling how the Romans originally built the fortress on their invasion of England over eighteen hundred years ago, styling it 'Portus Magnus,' or 'the great port,' it being situated on a tongue of land commanding the approaches to their encampments in the interior of the country—the harbour being then more open to the sea than it now is.

"Aye," corroborated the Captain. "It has silted up considerably, even in my time, in spite of continual dredging."

" The Saxons afterwards called the place Portceaster, whence its present name 'Porchester,'" continued the narrator; "and, subsequently, the stronghold has played an important part in history, from the days of Canute up to the reign of Queen Elizabeth."

"That's something at any rate!" interposed the Captain. "More than you can say for the Brading villa!"

"You mustn't interrupt, sure," said Mrs. Gilmour, tapping him with her parasol as her brother laughed, exchanging winks with the old sailor. "After the time of good Queen Bess, however, the castle is not memorable for much in its history till we come to the early part of the present century; when it was used as a depôt for the prisoners taken in the French . war, some eight or ten thousand being incarcerated within its walls at one time!"

"What a lot!" cried Bob. "It must have cost a heap of money to keep them in food, auntie?"

"It did, 'a lot,' my dear," replied his aunt, adopting his favourite word. "Several men with names distinguished in the Revolution were confined here, among them being the

Irish general Tate, who led that ridiculous invasion of this country planned by Buonaparte, which was routed by a body of Welsh women at Fishguard."

"Hurrah for the sex!" interrupted the Captain again, Mr. Strong joining in his cheer, while the boatmen grinned. "More power to their petticoats!"

Mrs. Gilmour only smiled at this, not venturing to explain that the invaders mistook the red cloaked, tall hatted women of the Principality, who were ranged along the crests of their native mountains, for British regiments on the march to annihilate them; and so, capitulated to avoid capture!

"One of the most comical characters imprisoned in the castle," she went on, "was a seaman named François Dufrésne, who was a regular Jack Sheppard in the way of breaking out of confinement."

"Oh!" exclaimed Bob, pricking up his ears at the mention of the noted celebrity of the Newgate Calendar. "That's jolly! What did he do, auntie?"

"Why, he would, for a mere frolic or for a trifling wager, scale the walls of the castle under the very eyes of the sentries, making his way into the woodlands on the north of Portsdown Hill, where he would ramble at large, stealing all the eggs and fowls he could lay his hands on. He had, as he explained, a great weakness for poultry."

"By Jove, I can quite excuse him," said the Captain in his funny way. "I'm partial to a chicken, myself!"

"So am I, too," remarked Mrs. Strong. "It was only what might be called 'an amiable weakness' on his part, considering that probably the poor prisoners were not too well fed."

"They were not, my dear Edith," replied her sister in law, "if all accounts be true; for the French Government complained of their being half starved! However, be that as it may, Dufrésne used to plunder away amongst the cottagers, until their anger at losing their stock led to his recapture and remission to durance vile. Once he actually made his way

to London; when, calling at the house of the 'French Com
missioner' there, who was the agent for all the prisoners of the
war, he procured a decent dress and a passport, with which he
presented himself again at Porchester and made a triumphant
return to his prison!"

"The governor must have been surprised," said Bob.
"Wasn't he, auntie?"

"He was," assented his aunt. "Very much surprised, my
dear."

"Did they punish him for escaping?" asked Nell. "I
don't think they ought to have, as he came back."

"No, I don't think they did," replied Mrs. Gilmour. "But,
my dear, I think I've told you enough now of the castle and
all belonging to it, and must really stop, for it's time for us
to be going back."

"Indeed we must, ma'am," said the Captain, "that is, if
we're going over the Victualling Yard."

"What, more sight seeing!" exclaimed Mrs. Strong in a
voice of despair. "Can't you let us off doing any more to
day?"

"Well, ma'am," pleaded the Captain apologetically, "only
just one place more and you will then have 'killed all the
lions'; that is, all save the Dockyard, which Master Bob will
have to tell you about."

"Do let us go, mamma! I do so want to see them making
the biscuits. They do it all by machinery, just fancy!" said
Nellie coaxingly. "Do, let us go, please, won't you?"

"Do, please," also pleaded Bob, "it will be so very jolly!"

"I suppose I must give in," sighed his mother. "Oh,
Captain Dresser, Captain Dresser, you have a good deal to
answer for!"

The old sailor only chuckled in response; and, giving the
necessary orders to the boatmen, the wherry, which had
come down rapidly from Porchester, the tide having turned
and being now on the ebb, was pulled in to the Gosport

shore, its passengers landing at Clarence Yard, the great food depôt of the Navy.

Here they saw all that was to be seen, gazing with wonder at the vast stores of things eatable accumulated for the service of the fleet Bob and Miss Nell being particularly interested in the bread factory and bakery, where the attendant who showed them over the place completed their satisfaction by filling their respective pockets with the curious hexagonal-shaped biscuits there made, "thus provisioning them," as the Captain said, "for the remainder of their stay."

They crossed back from Gosport to Portsmouth by the floating bridge, which, of course, Bob wanted to know all about, the Captain explaining to him how it was fixed on two chains passing through the vessel and moored on either shore, so as to prevent the 'bridge' from being swayed by the action of the tide, which runs very strongly in and out of the harbour at the point of its passage.

"But how does the bridge move?" asked the inquiring Bob, full of questions as usual. "I can't see how it can, if it be chained up like Rover!"

"There is a steam engine in the centre of the vessel, as you can see for yourself, there," replied the Captain, pointing to the funnels that bore out his statement. "This engine works a pair of vertical wheels inside that casing between the two divisions of the boat; and these wheels, which are each some eight feet in diameter and cogged, wind in the chains at one end, paying them out at the other."

"I see," said Bob; and the floating bridge having by this time reached its terminus at the Portsmouth side of the water, they all stepped ashore and made their way home, Mrs. Strong declaring that she had had "enough of going about, for one day at least!"

In spite of her exertions, however, she was none the worse for them after dinner; being able, indeed, to accompany the others down to the beach, Rover now forming one of the party, and magnanimously forgiving his young master for leaving him behind all day in the house while he went gallivanting about sight seeing, albeit Dick's company and Sarah's kindness in the way of tit bits somewhat made amends to the poor dog for the neglect of the truant Bob.

"By the way," said the Captain to the latter, on taking his leave in the evening after escorting them back to 'The Moorings,' "you mustn't forget the trial of the *Archimedes* to-morrow, my boy. Captain Sponson told me the other day at the Club that she'd go out of harbour at nine o'clock sharp in the morning!"

"Oh, I'll remember," replied Bob. "Where will she start from, Captain?"

"Why, from Coaling Point, at the further end of the Dock yard; so we'll have to be under weigh half an-hour earlier," cried the old sailor from the doorstep. "You had better call at my place, as it is on the way. Mind you're not later than 8.30 sharp, or she'll be off without you!"

"I'll be there in time, never fear," was Bob's response as the Captain bade him 'Good-night!' and stumped off homeward. "I'll be in time!"

Poor Rover!

He was doomed to another day of desertion; for, much to his surprise, his young master, instead of taking him down to the sea as usual in the morning, started off alone, and without his towels, too, which puzzled Rover more than anything else.

Dogs have their feelings, similarly to other people; and so, his brown eyes filled with tears as he watched Bob rushing out of the house, in a terrible hurry lest he might keep the Captain waiting, or even, indeed, be too late altogether with never a word for him save a peremptory "Lie down, Rover; I can't take you with me; lie down, sir!"

It was really too bad of Bob!

In consequence of this unhandsome treatment, it may be like-wise added, Rover's tail, which he generally carried in a jaunty

fashion, with the trifle of a twist to one side, as became a dog
of his degree and one moving in the best canine society, now
drooped down between his legs of a verity it almost touched
the ground !

This made the deserted animal look such a picture of misery
that, on Nell's drawing her aunt's attention to him, the good
lady of the house not only spoke sympathizing words unto him,
to which the sad dog replied by ever so feeble a wag of his
drooping tail ; but Mrs. Gilmour also, sanctioned, nay, even
directed, his being entertained with a basin of hot bread and
milk served up on the best dining room carpet, an event
unparalleled in the annals of 'The Moorings !'

Bob meanwhile, with never a thought of Rover, was proceeding across the Dockyard with the Captain, who hobbled
painfully over the knobbly paving stones with which that national
institution is ornamented, anathematizing at every step he took
the rulers of the "Queen's Navee," who put him thus to
unnecessary pain.

" I can't think how, in a christian land, people's poor feet
should be so mercilessly disregarded !" he exclaimed, on giving
his favourite corn an extra pinch between two projecting
boulders "I'd like to make ' my Lords' of the Admiralty do
the goose step regularly here for four hours a day ; and then,
perhaps, there'd be a chance of a poor creature being enabled
to walk about the place in comfort ."

Notwithstanding the instruments of torture in the shape of
paving stones of which the Captain complained, and justly, he
and Bob just managed to reach the *Archimedes* before she cast
off from the jetty alongside of which she had been coaling, the
two only having time to jump on board as the gangway connecting her with the shore was withdrawn.   Another moment
and they would have been too late ; for, 'time and tide,' and
ships going out on trial, wait for no man, or boy either.

However, there they were, 'better late than never,' Bob
thought, and he thought further, too, as he gazed round

the deck of the ironclad, which was somewhat begrimed with coal dust, and about the ugliest and most mis shapen monster imaginable, 'Can I really be on board a ship?'

He was, though; and, presently, the sound of the escape steam, that had previously been roaring up through the rattling funnels, ceased; while the fan blades of the screw propeller began to revolve, surging up the water of the open dock in which the vessel lay into a mass of foam, and creating, so to speak, a sort of 'tempest in a teapot.'

Then, a couple of attendant tugs sent their tow ropes aboard, so as to check and guide the unwieldy leviathan in her progress through the deeper channels of the harbour which ships of heavy draught have to take to get out to sea; and, 'going easy,' little by little, with an occasional stop, as some imper tinent craft or other got into the fairway, they finally reached Spithead.

"What is that funny red vessel coming down to us for?" inquired Bob, pointing out a dandy rigged yawl that just then rounded up under the stern of the *Archimedes*, laying to a little way off. "She's coming alongside, I think."

"That's the powder hoy," replied the Captain. "She's brought the ammunition for our big guns here."

"And why is she painted red?" asked Bob again "eh?"

"Just for the same reason that danger signals on railways and warning flags are always red," said the other. "I suppose because the colour is more glaring and likely to be taken notice of; and no doubt, too, that's why our soldiers are clothed in scarlet so that they can be all the more readily potted by the enemy?"

"You are pretty right there, Captain Dresser!" said, laugh ingly, a young naval officer standing near, who kindly took all further trouble off the Captain's hands in the way of answering Bob's questions and showing him round the ship, the machinery of which especially charmed him, being so much more imposing and complicated than that of the poor *Bembridge Belle*, which had interested him only yesterday, so to speak, though now washed to pieces by the relentless sea!

The movements of the eccentric aroused Bob's chief wonder, the two piston rods connected with it and guiding the motion appearing in their working like the crooked limbs of a bandy-legged giant 'jumping up and down,' as he expressed it, 'in a hoppety kickety dance.'

Bob was called up from the engine room by an extraordinary sound that proceeded apparently from the deck above.

This, as he ascended, grew louder and louder; until it became to him really awesome.

"What is that?" he asked the young lieutenant, who had accompanied him below and now followed him up, keeping close to his side. "Has anything happened, sir?"

"No, nothing's happened," replied the young officer, who was a bit of a wag. "That is our steam siren."

"What is that, sir?" said Bob again "I don't understand you."

"It's the siren," explained the other, "a thing like the steam whistle, for signalling to passing ships."

"It makes an awful row," cried Bob. "Don't you think so, sir?"

"It does," said the lieutenant laughing. "A great row!"

"Why do they call it a siren, though?" inquired the insatiable Bob. "The 'sirens' I've read of in my lessons at school used to be mermaids that sang so sweetly and made such beautiful music, as they played on their harps or lyres, that they lured poor mariners to destruction!"

"But doesn't our siren make beautiful music?" asked the lieutenant in a joking way. "It is loud, it is true; but don't you think it sweet?"

"No," answered Bob, most emphatically. "It isn't! It is more like a thousand wild bulls all with the toothache and roaring with pain!"

"That's not a bad description," said the other, laughing

heartily again. "Hullo, though, they are going to fire now! Don't you see they've just run up a red flag on that spar we have forward as an apology for a mast?"

"I see," replied Bob, concentrating his attention on the preparations being made around for testing the machine guns and larger weapons with which the vessel was armed, long cylindrical shot, ribbed with brass bands, being piled by the side of the various batteries, and nicely made cases of cartridges placed ready for the hoppers of the Nordenfeldts and Gatlings. "How awfully jolly!"

The *Archimedes,* after taking her ammunition on board, had steamed out seaward so as to get a good offing where she might fire her guns without the risk of hitting any passing craft; and, by the time Bob had come on deck again from inspecting the machinery, she was well beyond the Nab light and far out into the waters of the Channel.

On the order being presently given to fire, the machine guns went popping away, to test how many shots they can fire off in a minute the report of some of them sounding like an asthmatic old gentleman with a very bad cough.

"What a funny noise!" cried Bob—"Rover barks just the same when he's asleep and dreaming!"

"Indeed!" said the young lieutenant, more intent, however, on watching a party of blue-jackets getting ready a big gun for firing in the bows than paying much attention to Bob. "Look out there, youngster!"

"What are they going to do, eh?" asked Bob "all those sailors there!"

"Why, fire one of our forty three ton guns; so you'd better look out for squalls. Have you got any cotton-wool about you?"

"No," answered Bob. "What for?"

"To put in your ears, so as to deaden the noise of the report," said the lieutenant. "I've got some, though, so it doesn't matter. Here's a bit to stick in your ears you'd better take my advice, it'll save your tympanum!"

Bob did not know what he meant; but he put the cotton wool in his ears, as desired, on seeing Captain Dresser and some other officers standing near doing the same, and that the Lieutenant was not 'taking a rise out of him,' as at first he was inclined to think.

The enormous gun, carrying a charge of two hundred and eighty pounds of powder, with a shot weighing nearly a quarter of a ton, was now loaded; when the officer directing the operation ordered all persons to move away from the vicinity of the weapon, which was about to be fired for the first time—at least on board the *Archimedes*.

Everybody retreated behind the armoured screen bulkhead that formed a sort of 'shelter trench' across the deck; for, if an accident should happen in the way of an unexpected explosion, refuge might be had there from any flying fragments.

Everybody, as has been said, at once, on the order being given, sought this retreat—everybody, that is, but Bob, who, instead of stepping back like the others, stepped forwards.

At the same moment the signal was given 'Fire!'

A terrific report followed, as if the ship and all its contents were blown up, there being none of the reverberating sound, like that usually heard when heavy guns are fired, as of an express train rushing at speed through the air; but a dull, hollow, sullen, sharp roar, succeeded by the heavy swish of some body, or something, falling into the water alongside, while a thick smoke hung over the deck like a pall.

" By Jingo! exclaimed the Captain, " the gun has burst!"

CHAPTER XIX.

BOB GETS 'BLOWN UP.'

THE unexpected explosion, though, caused no confusion, nor indeed any apparent excitement such as would have at once occurred had the accident happened on shore; for, thanks to the admirable discipline always observed on board a man of war that flies the glorious old Union Jack, not a man stirred from his station.

It was only through the unusual stillness that prevailed for a moment or two afterwards, that those not on deck became aware that something out of the common had occurred.

"Anybody hurt?" sang out, presently, the officer commanding the ship from the bridge, near the conning tower, where he had been directing her steering "Anybody hurt there, forrud?"

"No, sir," promptly replied the gunnery lieutenant in charge of the firing party, who was standing close by the exploded gun. "Not a soul, sir!"

"Thank God!" said the other in a tone of deep feeling, the anxious expression clearing from his face. "It's a wonderful escape!"

It was and more. It was a merciful interposition of Providence!

There were three flag officers, four post captains, and several others of lesser rank, in addition to a number of blue jackets in the immediate neighbourhood of the exploded gun when it burst; but, strange to say, although the muzzle of

N

the weapon had been blown off completely from the chase at the trunnions, and some hundred weight of the fragments scattered in all directions, many of them piercing the deck and screen bulkhead, every one fortunately escaped injury.

While exchanging congratulations with the other officers, all at once Captain Dresser looked about him for Bob.

But, nowhere was he to be seen in sight.

"By Jove, he must have been blown overboard, and that was the splash in the water I heard!" he exclaimed in alarm; and, turning to his friend the young lieutenant, as they now advanced further forward to have a nearer view of the still smoking gun, he said, "Where, Neville, did you last see the boy?"

"There!" replied the young officer, pointing to the ledge outside the bulkhead, just over the iron ladder way that led down to the fo'c's'le, the scene of the accident. "He cannot well have fallen overboard from there!"

"No," assented the Captain, doubtfully; still at a loss to account for Bob's mysterious disappearance. "Where can the boy be, though?"

They were just about instituting an organized search through the ship, both in great anxiety; when, who should crawl up from below but the missing young gentleman!

Rover's look of dejection on being left behind at home in the morning was nothing to that of his young master now; the latter appearing, from his blackened face and rumpled collar, not to speak of his soiled suit of flannels, so beautifully white and clean the moment before, to have 'been in the wars' with a vengeance!

"Why, what have you been doing with yourself?" exclaimed the Captain, in blank dismay. "Where have you been?"

Albeit dilapidated in his general exterior, Bob had not lost his voice; his powers of speech being happily still unimpaired.

"I'm all right," he answered with an attempt at a grin. "I'm all right!"

"But where have you been?" repeated the Captain, whom this off hand statement did not quite satisfy. "Where have you been?"

"Oh, I got blown up," explained Bob "When the gun fired I felt an awful pain in my ears, as if somebody was running a red hot needle through them going right down to my boots!"

"You must have long ears, youngster," remarked the young lieutenant slily here. "Very long to reach so far!"

"I didn't mean that my ears went down to my boots," replied Bob, rather nettled at the insinuation; and he then continued the account of his experiences of the explosion. "But, as I was saying, I first felt this pain; and then I seemed to be lifted off my feet, tumbling down this ladder here, and after that through a hole in the deck, amongst a lot of coal dust and oil cans, that messed my clothes a bit."

"A bit?" queried the Captain, chuckling now with much satisfaction at seeing him unhurt "I should say a good deal, judging by appearances, Master Bob!"

"Really?" said he, surveying himself ruefully, turning and twisting so as to get a view of his back. "Well, I certainly am dirty, but I didn't look half so bad before I came up."

"Ah, it's the light that does it," observed the lieutenant, chaffing him. "However, if you will go rolling in the coal-bunkers and making love to the engineer's oil cans, you must take the consequences!"

"I didn't," replied Bob indignantly. "You don't think I tumbled down there on purpose, do you?"

"Perhaps not," said the other, smiling. "But, pray remember, you were told to keep away from the gun; and, if you had obeyed orders, you wouldn't have got into any mischief."

"Well, let us be thankful it is no worse," observed the Captain cheerily. "I hope you are not hurt, Bob, by your roll down the hatchway?"

"No, Captain," he answered, brightening up again after the

snub of the lieutenant anent his disobedience, "I fell on the coal sacks quite softly and haven't got a scratch."

"That's all right then," echoed Captain Dresser in his joking way; adding to the young officer on his other side, "I wonder if all the 'cocked hats' have done examining the gun, and whether there's a chance now for an old retired fogey like myself having a look at the damage?"

"I should think so, sir," replied the young officer. "The Admiral, I see, has gone away, and the fellows also from the Ordnance department; so, you'd better come and have a glance round while the coast is clear."

"I will," was the response of the old sailor, as, in company with the lieutenant and Bob, he made his way through one of the watertight doors in the forward bulkhead on to the fo'c's'le; the trio then grouping themselves round the broken breech of the exploded weapon, all that was left now of the whilom big forty three ton gun!

"Ah! I can see how it happened," said the old sailor, after a cursory inspection of the fractured portion. "The gun was strong enough at the breech, but went at the muzzle. It has given way, of course, at its weakest point."

"Yes," agreed the young lieutenant. "It has parted just here, where the last protecting coil of steel has been shrunk on; the tube of the gun has burst at this unprotected portion of it, right in front of the chase."

"What's the reason, sir," asked Bob, "of its bursting there like that?"

"I suppose because the metal was unable to withstand the strain of the powder charge," said the Captain. "So, Bob, it went!"

"Pardon me, but I don't think you've got it quite right, sir," observed the lieutenant apologetically. "The gun was strong enough for the old 'pebble powder' it was originally intended to be fired with, the force of whose explosion would have been expended in the breech, which you can't say is weak?"

"No," asserted the other, "the gun seems strong enough there."

"Well, that being the case," continued the young officer, "the gun might have been fired as many times as you please with the heaviest charges of that powder without its sustaining the slightest injury. Our wise Ordnance people, however, having taken a fancy to a 'slow combustion powder,' whose force, instead of being expended in the breech, is sustained throughout the whole length of the gun, as the particles of powder ignite and expand, bethought themselves they would, for cheapness' sake, use this 'cocoa powder,' as it is called, without going to the expense of building additional coils round their heavy guns to enable them to resist the extra strain!"

"So this is the result," said the old Captain. "It's just like putting new wine into old bottles!"

"Precisely," replied the lieutenant, joining in his laugh. "But, don't you feel hungry, Captain Dresser?"

"I do," he promptly rejoined. "This sea air gives one the very deuce of an appetite; and I confess to feeling slightly peckish."

"So am I," said the other, leading the way to the nearest hatchway. "Let us go down below and see what they've got for luncheon. Mind how you step, it's all dark here, as they haven't fitted her up yet."

"That's plain enough as I can feel!" muttered the Captain in reply as he stumbled against the projecting ledge of one of the watertight bulkheads, knocking his shins. "These new-fashioned ships are all at odds and ends, it seems to me, in their accommodation below. Give me one of the old sort, where everything was really plain sailing and one hadn't to dive down here and climb up there to get for'ard or aft!"

"Ah," rejoined the lieutenant, holding out a hand to guide him, "you'd get used to it in time."

"Just as the eels do to skinning!" growled the Captain,

rubbing his sore shins. "I'd rather be excused the practice, though, on my part."

Bob sniggered at this; and, passing along a narrow dark passage, its obscurity rather increased than diminished by the solitary illuminating power of a single 'dip' in a ship's lantern hung up against the side, the lieutenant stopped the Captain from any further grumbling by introducing him into the ward room, which, being well lit up with little electric lamps, offered a marked contrast to the other parts of the vessel they had traversed.

To the Captain, indeed, it was like passing from purgatory to fairyland, as he said; the more so from the fact of his seeing a well spread table before him, and there being a savoury smell permeating the atmosphere.

So, he took his seat with alacrity, prepared to do ample justice to whatever viands were brought forward.

Bob, who came in a little later, his curiosity being attracted by the sight of the open torpedo room adjacent, with its stores of Whitehead tubes, gave the witty young surgeon, who was facing the door, an opportunity of cracking a joke at the expense of his smutty face, which he had been unable to wash since his tumble amongst the coals.

"Hullo, Pompey!" cried out this worthy, who by the way had been previously chaffed by his brother officers, such is the levity of sailors in imminent peril, about the gun accident not having provided him with any patients. "Hullo, Pompey, you've forgotten your banjo and bones!"

Bob did not see the point of the joke at first, although there was a general titter round the lower part of the table where the young surgeon was seated; when Master Bob did, however, he blushed pretty red, looking uncommonly sheepish.

But the lieutenant came to his rescue.

"He has left his bones behind advisedly, Phillips," said he to the young surgeon, who was smiling still at his own witticism, "because he knew, if he brought them, you would only carve and saw them about as you served those fossils at the hospital."

This turned the laugh against the other, enabling Bob to sit down in peace and enjoy his luncheon, during which he was much amused at the fun going on amongst the junior officers at their end of the festive board about the splendid chances offered for promotion and 'unfortunately missed' by the bursting cannon.

"Just fancy!" observed one of those, speaking in an undertone, so that those of superior rank at the upper end of the table could not hear him. "Three 'flags,' four 'posts,' half a dozen commanders, and two 'first luffs,' all within range of that blessed muzzle that carried away; and not one vacancy on the list!"

"It's positively awful," chimed in another, in cordial agreement with his brother sub, "we may never have such a chance again!"

The Captain subsequently explained to Bob that they meant that had the several admirals and other officers of rank who stood behind the forty three ton gun been killed or materially injured when it burst, these thoughtless juniors believed they would have 'received a step' on the list, or in other words, would have been probably promoted which Bob thought extremely wicked and reprehensible on their part.

After the explosion, of course, there was no more gun-practice, the *Archimedes* slowly making her way back to Spithead, and then into harbour; the broken breech of the unfortunate weapon that had come to grief being carefully covered over with a piece of tarpaulin, so that those on board an Austrian frigate lying in the roadstead, which the iron-clad had to go by, should know nothing of the burst, at least from passing observation. We do not like to show our failures to our friends only our successes!

The Captain and Bob, naturally, got back all the sooner from the trial trip of the *Archimedes* being thus cut short, reaching 'The Moorings,' indeed, just as Mrs. Gilmour and her guests were going out for a stroll before dinner; when, Rover pranced up to his young master, all affection and oblivious of any 'hard feelings' he might have entertained by being left behind in the morning, repeating his magnanimous conduct on a previous occasion!

"By Jove!" cried the Captain jocularly, addressing Bob's father. "That son of yours is bound to turn out something great."

"Really, what's he been doing now?"

"Why," replied the old sailor with his customary chuckle, thumping the pavement with his malacca cane to give greater emphasis to his words, "he was half drowned almost the first evening he came down here; was wrecked in the poor *Bembridge Belle* the other afternoon; and now, to complete the category, has been blown up to-day."

"Boys are like cats," said the barrister smiling. "They all seem endowed with the same proverbial number of lives."

"How funny, Bob," observed Nellie here. "Papa says you're like a cat; so, you must be like Snuffles!"

Bob, however, did not appear to see the joke of this; though it afforded his sister much amusement, which was increased anon by the Captain asking her a question.

"I say, Miss Nell," he cried out in his jocular way, chuckling the while, "what colour is this celebrated cat of yours, Snuffles?"

"He's black all over, Cap'ain," replied Nellie as distinctly as her giggles would permit. "Only, he has four white paws, just as if he had lamb's wool socks on, like those mamma makes Bob wear in winter."

"Humph!" snorted out the old sailor, his beady eyes twinkling with fire and his bushy eyebrows moving rapidly up and down. "If you had seen Master Bob when he first emerged from the fore peak of the *Archimedes* after his tumble through the fo'c's'le and roll amongst the coal sacks, you would have thought him, missy, more like Snuffles than ever. The only drawback to the likeness was that Bob had but two paws instead of four, and that they were as black as his face !"

"Oh, my !" exclaimed Nellie, shrieking with laughter. "Do you hear that, mamma ? "

"Aye, my dear, I'm not joking," went on the Captain, his face now as grave as a judge. " Do you know he was so black, that they mistook him for one of the Christy minstrels when he came into the ward room afterwards ."

This finished poor Nell; even Bob, too, joining in the laugh against himself.

CHAPTER XX.

THE same evening, while they were all on the pier, listening to the band, and chatting pleasantly together in the pauses between the music, Mrs. Gilmour turned the conversation upon a matter of extreme interest to Master Bob, and one concerning which he had been in much doubt of mind for some time past; although his native diffidence had prevented him from personally broaching the subject in his own right.

Sitting there within hail of the sea, the soft arpeggio of whose faint ripple on the shore seemed to harmonize with the louder instrumentation of the orchestra, which was just then playing a selection from Weber's ' Oberon,' the talk naturally drifted into a nautical channel ; the old sailor dilating, to the delight of his listeners, on the charms of a life afloat and the divine beauty of the ocean, whether in storm or at rest.

"Aye, there's no life like it," said he. "A life on the ocean wave !"

"It sounds nice in poetry," observed the Irish barrister, who although full of sentiment, like most of his countrymen, always tried to hide it under a mask of comedy. "But, I think it must be a very up and down sort of existence. Too uncertain for me, at all events !"

"Oh, Dugald !" remonstrated his wife. "Why, this morning you were rhapsodizing over the sea, and wishing you were able to spend your brief life afloat."

"My brief life, indeed!" exclaimed Mr. Strong. "It's precious few briefs I get, or it would be more pleasant. I wish more of 'em would come in, my dear, to pay for those children's shoes. They've worn out half a dozen pairs apiece, I believe, since they've been down here!"

"Better a shoemaker's bill," said Mrs. Gilmour, "than a doctor's, sure, me dear Dugald."

"Aye, by Jove!" put in the Captain with a chuckle. "There's nothing like leather, you know."

"By the way, talking of that, though I don't mean to say it's made like the old Britons' coracles," observed Mrs. Gilmour slily, "when is that yacht of yours going to be ready, Captain?"

This unexpected inquiry made the old sailor blush a rosy red, for his face was turned westwards towards the setting sun, and all could see it plainly; albeit, he tried to conceal his perturbation by drawing out his brilliant bandana handkerchief and blowing his nose vigorously an old trick of his.

"I—I I'm having her done up," he at length stammered out. "She wanted a lot of repair."

"So I should think," rejoined his persecutor, turning round to the others. "You must know, good people, that I've been hearing of nothing but this yacht for the last two years; and, would you believe it, I've never seen her yet!"

"I—assure you——," began the Captain; but, alas! his enemy, in addition to being a host in herself, had allies of whom he little dreamt; and so he was interrupted ere he could get at a second stammering "I assure you!"

"Why, you promised, Captain," said Nell mischievously, "the very first time we saw you in the train, to take us out for a 'sail in your yacht'; and I have been longing so much for it ever since. We thought that was what you meant when you said you were going to take us somewhere or do something that 'to morrow come never' as you called it!"

"You wicked man, to deceive the poor children so!" cried

Mrs. Gilmour, shaking her finger at him. "Oh, you bad man!"

But, before he could answer a word, Bob, who had been waiting anxiously for an opening, likewise assailed him.

"Ah! Don't you remember, Captain, that day when you took Dick down to the Dockyard to get him entered as a sailor boy on board the *St. Vincent*, and they wouldn't take him because he was too thin, you said it didn't matter, for you would employ him on board your yacht when the racing season began? Why, Dick and I have been looking out for a sail ever since. Don't you remember?"

"Now, aren't you ashamed of yourself, sure?" said Mrs. Gilmour, following up Bob's flank attack; his father and mother enjoying the discussion immensely, coupled as it was with the old sailor's comical embarrassment. "Tell me, now, aren't you ashamed of yourself?"

Taking off his hat and shoving his hands through his hair until he raised it up on the top of his head in a high ridge, he looked at his tormentors appealingly; although, the merry twinkle in his bird-like eyes took off somewhat from his contrition.

"Do forgive me!" implored he in accents that had a very suspicious chuckle about them. "I confess my sins!"

"You must clear yourself completely, sir, before you can hope to obtain absolution for your sins of omission," insisted Mrs. Gilmour, pretending to be very stern indeed. "Now, prisoner at the bar, answer truly, have you or have you not got a yacht?"

"I have," he replied solemnly, entering into her humour. "By Jove, I have, ma'am!"

"Well, I'm glad to hear that at all events," retorted his questioner in rather an injudicial way. "Sure, I didn't think you had one at all, not having seen it after all your talking about it. What sort of a yacht is it, now?"

"Only a half decked little cutter of about two or three tons," answered the Captain abjectly, trying to minimize his offence. "A very little one, ma'am, I assure you."

Mrs. Gilmour burst into a fit of laughter, in which they all joined heartily; the barrister's jovial roar being heard above the music of the band.

"Ah, no wonder you didn't like my seeing it!" she cried with pleasant irony, which, however, made the old sailor wince, this 'yacht' of his being a subject on which he was wont to enlarge amongst his friends. "Why, from what you said, I thought she was a big schooner like the one that took the cup at Cowes last year when we all went over with those horrid Tomkinses to see the regatta! Call that a yacht, a boat of such a size? *I* call it a cockleshell!"

This nettled the Captain very considerably, it must be confessed.

"Well, ma'am, you may call it what you please," he replied shortly, with some little heat, putting on his hat again and jamming it down on his head firmly, using a good deal of force as if expending in that way his latent caloric. "But, cockleshell or no cockleshell, she's big enough for me!"

"But, Captain dear, isn't there room enough for me, too?" asked Nell coaxingly, seeing that he was vexed, and sliding her little hand into his, as if to show that she at all events was not joining in the fun against him. "Won't you take Bob and me?"

Her touch somehow or other banished his pettishness, enabling him to see that Mrs. Gilmour was only joking, and that he had but played into her hands, as he said to himself, by losing his temper over it.

"I tell you what," he now exclaimed, without a single trace of ill humour. "You shall see that I'm not ashamed of my little craft, for I'll have the *Zephyr* brought over from Gosport to morrow. What is more, too, the whole lot of you shall go out for a sail in her   by Jove!"

The Captain was as good as his word, the yacht being

towed across the following afternoon from Haslar Creek, where she had been lying, ever since the last yachting season, on the mud flats that there exist.

The little craft, which was a dapper cutter with an oyster-knife sort of bow and a clean run aft, as if she could race well when heeling over and show a good deal of her copper sheathing, did not exceed the tonnage mentioned by the Captain.

But, in spite of her smallness of size, she appeared to have the making of a good sea boat in her, and gained many admirers amongst the Southsea watermen as they surveyed her at her new moorings; the little craft being anchored off the coastguard station and placed now under the charge of Hellyer, when the Captain was not immediately looking after her himself.

Mrs. Gilmour, however, remained obdurate; for, though satisfied now that the 'yacht' really was an actual fact instead of merely a creation of her old friend's fancy, being somewhat averse to adventuring her life on the deep save in large vessels, and even of these she confessed feeling rather shy since the wreck of the *Bembridge Belle*, she, very aggravatingly, declined going out in the cutter   a want of taste on her part shared by her sister in law, whose weak nerves supplied a more reasonable pretext for not accepting the Captain's usual invitation to make the little vessel's better acquaintance.

Bob's father, however, exhibited no such reluctance; and, as for Bob himself, he and Nellie and Dick were all in the seventh heaven of delight when, a morning or two afterwards, there being a nice nor' westerly breeze blowing, which was good both for working out to sea and running home again, the Captain took them for a sail, managing single handed the smart cutter as only a sailor, such as he was, could.

Thenceforward, Bob's holidays were all halcyon days

He had certainly enjoyed himself before; in his rambles on the beach, in his daily dip and new experiences of the delights of swimming; in the various little trips he and Nellie had taken;

aye, and in the pleasurable occupation of collecting all those strange wonders of the shore, with which they had been so recently made familiar.

But, never had he enjoyed himself to the extent he did now !

There was nothing, on his once having tasted the joy of sailing, that could compare with it for a moment in his mind ; and, if his own tastes had been consulted, he would have been content to have spent morning, noon, and night on board the *Zephyr.*

It was the same with Dick ; and, under the Captain's able tuition, both the boys soon acquired sufficient knowledge of tacking and wearing, sailing close hauled and going free with the helm amidships, besides other nice points of seamanship, as to be able almost to handle the cutter as well as their instructor.

Nellie, naturally, could not enter so fully into these details as Bob and Dick ; but, still, she took quite as much pleasure as they did in skimming over the undulating surface of the water and hearing the gurgling ripple made by the boat's keel.

She felt a little alarm sometimes, perhaps, when, with her mainsail sharply braced up, the *Zephyr* would heel over to leeward, burying her gunwale in the foam ploughed up by her keen edged bow, as it raced past, boiling and eddying, astern.

On one occasion the Captain took them out trawling between the Nab and Warner light ships ; where a bank of sand stretches out to sea, forming the favourite fishing ground of the Portsmouth watermen hailing from Point and the Camber at the mouth of the harbour.

"What is trawling ? " asked Master Bob, of course, when the matter was mooted by the owner of the cutter.

"What is trawling, eh ? " repeated the old sailor, humming and cogitating for a minute or so. "Let me see ; ah, yes, you let down a trawl and catch your fish in it, instead of using a line or drag net."

"Sure, Captain," cried Mrs. Gilmour, laughing at this, "that's as good as your definition of steam the other day! You'll have Bob asking you now what is a trawl, the same as I've got to do; please tell us, won't you?"

"Sure and I will," returned he, imitating her accent and making her brother and herself laugh, Mrs. Strong only smiling faintly, as she had a marked dislike to any allusion to the Irish brogue. "The trawl, ma'am, is a very simple contrivance when it is understood; and, by your leave, I'll try and make it plain to you. It consists of an ordinary net, like a seine, which you've seen, of course?"

"Yes," replied his questioner, "I have seen them dragging the seine, as it is called, down on the beach often."

"Oh, auntie, Nell and I saw them, too, the day after that storm we had when we first came," said Bob eagerly. "I know, because I asked the men what they were doing, and they told me."

"There's nothing like asking for information," observed the Captain approvingly. "It's lucky, though, those men told you at once, or you'd have worried their lives out!"

"Sure and you may well say that," put in Mrs. Gilmour. "You have to suffer frequently from some little people's thirst for knowledge."

"I don't mind," chuckled the Captain, beaming with good-humour. "But, to go on with my description of the trawl. You must imagine, as I have said, an ordinary seine net, which must be a small one, and that looped up at the corners, too, somewhat in the shape of a funnel, or rather in the form of a cone sliced in two. The mouth of this apparatus is kept open on its flat side by means of a pole some ten or twelve feet long, termed the 'trawl beam,' which floats uppermost when the net is down; while the lower side is weighted with a thick heavy piece of hawser styled the 'ground rope,' around which the meshes of the net are woven. A bridle or 'martingale' unites the two ends of the trawl beam."

"Yes, I see," said Bob, who was all attention, and taking the greatest interest in the Captain's explanation. "I see."

"Well," continued the old sailor, "to this bridle there is attached a double-sheaved block, through which runs a hundred-and fifty fathom rope, capable of bearing a heavy strain. But, in hauling this in, great nicety must be observed, for, the slightest hitch or deflection will cause the beam to turn the wrong way; when, if the net 'gets on her back,' as the fisher-folk say, all your catch is simply turned out into 'the vasty deep,' and your toil results in a case of 'Love's labour lost!'"

"But, what do you do with the net and beam, when it's all ready?" asked Bob. "You haven't told us that, yet."

"Why, drop it over the side as soon as you get out to the fishing-ground," replied the Captain laconically; "and now, I hope, you understand all about it?",

"Oh yes," responded his listeners with alacrity; all, that is, but Mrs. Gilmour, who assented somewhat dubiously, as if she could not quite grasp the idea, requiring the whole thing to be explained to her over again, when she declared herself still "all in a fog!"

Her brother, however, the barrister, comprehended it at once.

"I should think it was great fun," he observed; "so I would like to come with you."

"Do," said the Captain, with much heartiness. "You'll be amply repaid for the trouble. It is intensely exciting waiting and watching for what the trawl will bring up. It's just like dipping your hands in the 'lucky bag,' Miss Nellie, at Christmas-time."

"Do you ever find any very curious things, Captain?" she inquired on being thus appealed to. "I mean really curious things!"

"Oh yes, my dear," replied the old sailor. "I was once out trawling with a fisherman off St. Helens, when we dragged up a donkey cart!"

"O o h ." exclaimed Nellie, opening her blue eyes wide with wonder. "Did you catch the donkey as well?"

"Well, no," answered the Captain, smiling at her amazement, her eyes being so big and her face such a study. "The poor man's donkey, missy, had been eaten by the crabs, but the cart was there, shafts, wheels, and all ; and, a nice mess the lot made of the trawl net, tearing it all to pieces !"

"That clenches it then. I'll come with you by all means !" cried Mr. Dugald Strong, a pleased smile creeping over his face as he rubbed his hands with expectant glee. "If you find such strange fish as that, it must be worth going out."

"All right, I shall be glad of your company," replied the Captain; "only, mind, you'll have to work your passage, and help hauling in the trawl."

"I agree to that," said the other ; and, the matter being thus settled, it was arranged that they should proceed the following day on their expedition, if the weather were favourable and nothing occurred to alter their plans. Nellie was specially granted permission to accompany the party, much against the wish of her mother, who declared that she would spoil all her things to a certainty ; saying besides, that, from what she had gathered of the conversation, she did not believe trawling was a very ladylike pursuit, 'for little girls, at all events.'

However, all the same, Miss Nellie was up betimes the next morning, and sallied out with Bob and his father, whose pet she was, just as the early milkman was coming his rounds ; the trio getting down to the beach punctually at seven o'clock, the hour fixed by the Captain for their start.

Here they found the old sailor and Dick, ready and waiting for them ; when, going off in the little dinghy belonging to the *Zephyr*, although the boat had to make a couple of passages to and fro, being only capable of accommodating two passengers besides proud Dick the sculler, they were soon all on board.

The cutter, then, having her jib and mainsail already set, had only to slip her moorings, and was off and away, bowling out seaward before the breeze, which was blowing from the land.

The morning was bright and balmy; and the sun having risen some hours earlier even than the very early risers of the party, its beams by this time warmed the heavens and lit up the landscape, the rose tints of dawn being succeeded by a golden glow all over the sky, the sea dancing in sympathy and sparkling in the sunlight being altogether too merry to look blue.

It did not take the little craft long, running before the wind with a slack sheet, to reach the Horse Shingle shoal, beyond the outlying fort, and near the Warner light ship, where lay the fishing ground, or 'bank,' which the Captain had described as being especially favourable for their sport.

"Now," said the old sailor, "the time for action has at last arrived. We must get ready to 'shoot' the trawl."

"You are not going to fire?' cried Nell in alarm, hearing him use the technical term he had employed. "I'm so afraid of guns."

"No, my dear," he answered chuckling, "I meant pitching the trawl over the side, just in the same way as you say 'shooting' coals or rubbish. Are you ready at your end, Strong?"

"Yes, I'm all right," replied the barrister, who had been ably helping the Captain in arranging the meshes of the net along the starboard gunwale, out of the way of the swing of the boom, and getting the trawl beam across the stern sheets of the cutter; while Bob and Dick attended to the sheets and tiller. "Fire away, Captain Dresser!"

"Well, then, let us heave over," sang out the Captain, in his quarter deck voice, as he called it. "One two three off she goes!"

So, with a dull plunge, the trawl was 'shot,' the old sailor and Mr. Strong quickly pitching over the side, after it, the bunchy folds of the net; when the guy rope fastened to the bridle of the beam was secured to the bowsprit bitts and then again to a thole pin aft, so as to prevent its getting under the keel.

The boat was then allowed to fill her jib and drift out with the ebbing tide, keeping a straight course for the Nab, and steering herself by means of the dragging net astern; neither the services of Bob nor of Dick being required any further at the helm under the circumstances.

"You can light your pipe now, if you like," said Captain Dresser to Mr. Strong, when this was satisfactorily accomplished. "We shall have nothing to do for the next hour or two; for we must have the net down long enough to let something have a chance of getting into the pocket of it."

"I suppose the smell of tobacco won't frighten the fish?" observed the barrister, gladly taking advantage of the permission and striking a vesuvian, his pipe being already loaded and ready. "Fresh water anglers are rather particular on the point."

"Bless you, no!" replied the old sailor laughing, "our fish at sea know what's good for them and like it!"

Miss Nell, who seemed anxious about something, presently hazarded a question when her father had lit his pipe and was smoking comfortably on the forecastle.

"Are we not going to have any breakfast?" said she, in a very grave way, as befitted a matter of such deep importance. "I feel very hungry."

"Dear me, I was almost forgetting breakfast!" cried the Captain, throwing away the end of the cigar the barrister had offered him, which he was smoking rather against the grain, preferring his tobacco in the form of snuff. "Dick, did you bring the things all right as I told you?"

"Yes, sir," replied Dick. "They be in the fo'c's'le, sir."

"Is the coffee on the stove?"

"Yes, sir, and biling."

"That's right," said the Captain, who continued, turning to Nellie, "Now, missy, you can preside over our breakfast table if you like. You'll find all the traps ready in the little cabin for'ard under the half deck."

Thereupon, Miss Nellie, with much dignity, busied herself in pouring out the coffee, which had been kept hot all the while on 'such a dear little stove,' as she called out to Bob the moment she caught sight of it in the fore cabin; the pair constituting themselves steward and stewardess instanter, and serving out, with Dick's help, their rations to the rest of the company.

They were in the midst of breakfast, the trawl having been dragging along the bottom of the sea for not quite an hour, when, all at once, the rope holding it attached to the bowsprit bitts began to jerk violently.

"Hallo!" cried the Captain, starting up from his seat on one of the bunks in the little cabin, which, even with stooping, he and Mr. Strong found it a hard matter to squeeze themselves into. "We've caught something big this time!"

"Do you think it's a whale?" said Nell, jumping up also, abandoning in her hurry her post as mistress of the ceremonies. "It must be awfully big to make that great rope shake so!"

The old sailor chuckled till his sides shook.

"You seem wonderfully fond of whales, missy!" he exclaimed, turning round as soon as he had managed to wriggle himself out of the fo'c's'le and was able to stand erect again. "Don't you remember, you mistook those grampuses we came across the other day when going to Seaview for whales?"

"Yes; and I remember, too, Captain, your making fun of me then, the same as now," replied Nell, smiling as she went on. "I don't mind it though, for I like being here with you and dad!"

"That's right, my dear," replied the old sailor. "There's nothing like keeping your temper. But, we must now see about hauling in the trawl; for the chap who has got into the net is a big fellow, whoever he is, and, if we don't pull him in pretty sharp, he'll knock our net to pieces!"

So saying, the Captain brought the end of the tackle to the little windlass placed amidships; when he and Mr. Dugald Strong, who did not find the task, by the way, as easy as he imagined, began reeling in the trawl rope fathom by fathom, until, anon, the end of the beam was seen peering above the water alongside.

The jerking of the tackle, which had continued all the time they were hauling in, appeared to increase as the trawl was raised to the surface, the net now that it was within view swaying from side to side; and, when Captain Dresser and the barrister leant over the gunwale to lift in the beam with its pocket attached, there was a hoarse barking sound heard proceeding from the folds of the net, like that of a dog in the distance.

"Oh!" cried Nellie, in alarm, climbing up on the thwarts and getting as far away as she could "what is it?"

"What is it?" echoed Bob in the same breath. "What is it?"

The Captain, however, did not immediately satisfy their curiosity.

"I've got my suspicions," he commenced in a leisurely way as he bent a little more over the side to get a better hold of the net; but, what he saw, as the trawl lifted out of the sea, made him quicken his speech, and he exclaimed in a much louder tone "Take care, missy, and look out, you boys! There's a shark in the trawl net, and a pretty venomous beast, too!"

CHAPTER XXI.

THE SPOILS OF THE SEA.

"A SHARK!" yelled out Mister Bob, evincing much greater fright than his sister Nell, although he was very fond of referring to her contemptuously as 'being only a girl,' when manly exploits happened to be the topic of conversation and she chanced to hazard an opinion; and, at the same instant, he jumped madly from the gunwale of the little cutter on to the top of her half deck forwards, climbing from thence into the lee rigging, where he evidently thought he would be safer. "A shark! Won't it bite?"

"Aye, by Jove, it will!" said the Captain ironically. "I'd swarm up to the masthead, if I were you, so as to be out of harm's way. You needn't mind your sister or any of us down here. We can take care of ourselves!"

Th's made Bob a bit ashamed, and he began to climb down again from the rigging, looking gingerly the while over the side, as if expecting every minute that the terrible monster of the deep which his imagination had pictured would spring up and seize him.

"I I was afraid," he faltered. "I I—thought it best to get out of the way."

"So it seems," said the old sailor grimly. "It's lucky, though, that every one was not of the same mind; or where would we all be! Dick, where's that hatchet I gave you this morning to put into the boat?"

" It's in the after locker, sir."

" Look smart, then," cried the Captain excitedly.   " Bear a
hand and get it at once."

At this order, Dick, who, like Bob, had thought 'discretion
the better part of valour,' and got behind the windlass, in
order to have some substantial obstacle between himself and
the trawl-net which the Captain, with Mr. Dugald Strong's aid,
had partly dragged into the well of the cutter, now crawled out
from his retreat ; and keeping over well to leeward on the
other side of the boom, proceeded to the locker in the stern-
sheets, from whence he took out a small axe and handed it to
Captain Dresser.

" Ha !" ejaculated the old sailor, as he gripped the weapon
tightly and belaboured with the back of it, using all the vigour
of his still nervous right arm, the bag, or ' pocket ' of the net,
in which the body of some big fish was seen to be entangled ;
although neither its form nor appearance could be distinctly
distinguished, the folds and meshes being so tightly wrapped
round it.   " I'll soon settle him ! "

" Hold hard !" shouted out Bob's father, at about the second
blow with the head of the axe over the gunwale.   " You
very nearly cut my arm off then !   Lucky for me you were not
using the edge of your hatchet."

" Beg your pardon, I'm sure," apologized the Captain.   " But
these brutes are uncommonly tough."

" More than my arm is," said Mr. Strong ruefully, rubbing
this member tenderly.   " What sort of beast is it   not a real
shark, surely ?   I always imagined those beggars to be very
much bigger."

" No," replied the other, satisfied from the net being now
still that he had ' settled ' his victim.   " It is what is called a
' fox shark,' or dog-fish."

" Ah," exclaimed Bob, climbing down from the rigging now
that he saw all danger was over, " I thought I heard it bark
just like a dog when you and dad hauled up the trawl."

"So did I," chimed in Nellie, likewise coming to the stern again from her place of refuge. "It sounded just like Rover's bark when he's sometimes shut up for being naughty."

"You are both right," said the Captain, who, with the assistance of their father, had now lifted the beam and net over the side into the well of the boat and was busy unfolding the meshes of the net. "The brute not only barks, but bites, too, if he gets a chance."

"Oh!" cried Bob and Nell together; and they, with Dick, waited anxiously to see the monster disclosed a deep drawn "O—o—h!"

"There!" ejaculated the Captain a moment after, when he had extracted the dead body of the dog fish, nearly five feet long, from the net and turned it over with his foot so that they should see its wide shark-mouth and rows of little teeth set on edge, looking like so many small-tooth combs arranged parallel to each other. "What do you say to that for a nibble, eh?"

"Is it any good?" asked the barrister, thinking that the dog fish had a sort of resemblance to a good-sized pike, with the exception of course of its head, which, however, the old sailor had so battered about with his hatchet that the animal would not have been recognized by its nearest relative. "Not up to much, I should think!"

"Well, I have heard of sailors eating shark on a pinch, but I've got no stomach for it myself; and all it's fit for is to be chucked overboard," replied the Captain, carrying out his suggestion without further delay, grumbling as he added "The brute has spoilt our haul, too, confound it, and damaged our net!"

It was as the Captain said, there being nothing found in the pocket of the trawl, beyond the carcase he had just consigned to its native element, save some mud and a few oyster shells.

Fortunately, though, the dog fish had not done quite so much harm as he might; and, after mending a few rents by tying them

together with pieces of sennet, which the old sailor had taken
the precaution of having ready for such purpose beforehand,
the trawl net was as good as ever, allowing them to 'shoot' it
again for another dredge.

This time it remained down till the tide turned, a good three
hours at least; and the hopes of all were high in expectation
when they commenced hauling it in.

"What do you think we'll catch now?" asked Nell. "Eh,
Capta'n?"

"Well, not a whale, missy," said the Captain, with his customary chuckle, which to him formed almost a part of his
speech. "Still, I fancy we ought to pick up something this
time better than a dog fish."

These doubts were solved anon; for after a terrible long
interval of heaving round the windlass, at which Mr. Strong
groaned greatly, declaring that his back felt broken from
having to stoop nearly double so as to keep out of the way of
the swinging boom of the cutter, which swayed to and fro as she
rolled about in the tideway, the end of the trawl-beam once
more hove in sight alongside, bobbing up endwise out of the
water.

"Belay!" sang out the Captain on seeing it, taking a turn
with a coil of the rope round the windlass head to secure it,
lest it might whirl round and let the trawl go to the bottom
again before they could hoist it inboard. "That will do now,
Strong; if you'll bear a hand we'll get our spoil in."

Thereupon he and the barrister leant over the side of the
boat as before; and, catching hold of either end of the trawl-
beam, they lifted it over the gunwale.

The Captain then swished the folds of the net vigorously,
so as to shake what fish might have become entangled in the
meshes into the pocket at the end, Bob and Nellie, and likewise Dick, watching the operations with the keenest interest.

"Now," cried the sailor, "we shall see what we shall see!"

So saying, he and Mr. Strong raised up the net pocket,

which was a goodish big bundle and seemed, from its heavy weight, to contain a large number of fish, for it throbbed and pulsated with their struggles; when, cutting with his clasp knife the stout piece of cord with which the small end of the pocket was tied, the Captain shook out its living contents on the bottom boards in the well Nell giving a shriek and springing up on one of the thwarts as a slimy sole floundered across her foot, thinking perhaps it was a fellow sole!

She was not frightened, however, only alarmed; and, the next moment, she was inspecting with as much curiosity as the others the motley collection that had been brought up from the sea.

" Not a bad lot, eh ? " observed the Captain critically, poking the fish about with the end of his stick, which he took off the seat for the purpose. " I see we've got some good soles, besides that little chap that took a fancy to you, missy."

" I didn't mind it," said Miss Nell courageously, now that she knew that there was nothing much to be frightened of. " It was cold and wet, poor thing; but I knew it would not hurt me."

" Ah, but you screamed though ! " retorted the sailor waggishly, as he turned to her father. " Say, Strong, do you know what to do with a sole, eh ? "

" Why, eat it, I suppose," replied the other laughing. " I don't think you can better that, eh ? "

" Yes, that's all right, no doubt," said the Captain, a little bit grumpy at being caught up in that way. " I mean how to cook it properly ? "

" Boil it," suggested the barrister, at a loss how to answer the question satisfactorily. " I should think that the simplest plan."

" Boil it ? " repeated the Captain in a voice of horror; " boil your grandmother ! "

" Well, you must really excuse me," said the barrister, as well as he could speak from laughing; while Bob and Nell went into fits at the idea of their poor old ' Gran ' being cooked in so summary a fashion. "I'm good at a knife and fork, but really I don't know anything of cooking."

"I see you don't," replied the old sailor triumphantly, his good humour restored at being able to put the other "up to a wrinkle," as he said; "but I'll tell you. The best way, Strong, to do a sole is to grill him as quickly as you can over a clear fire. About five minutes is enough for the transaction; and then, with a squeeze of lemon and a dash of cayenne, you've got a dish fit for a king! No bread crumbs or butter or any of that French fiddlery, mind, or you'll spoil him!"

"I'll remember your recipe should I ever chance to turn cook," said Mr. Strong. "I should think it ought to taste uncommonly good."

"By Jove, you shall try it, this very afternoon!" cried the old sailor energetically. "Dick, see that the gridiron is clean, for we'll want it by and by. Hullo, though, I'm forgetting about the rest of our catch. Let us see what we've got."

While the Captain had been talking to their father, Bob and Nellie had been rummaging in the bottom of the boat, trying to make out the different fish; but, from the fact of all being coated with mud, of which the trawl's pocket was pretty well filled, in addition to its live occupants, these latter seemed all so similar at first glance as to resemble those two negro gentle men, Pompey and Cæsar, described by a sable brother as being 'berry much alike, 'specially Pompey.'

However, the old sailor soon sorted them out.

"Half a dozen pair of good soles, eh? That will be a treat for your aunt Polly," he said to Miss Nell, pitching the fish as he picked them out carelessly on one side. "Some odd flounders, too, I see. They're nearly as good as our soles; and, I see also a lot of plaice and dabs, which are not bad, fried, when you can't get anything better in the same line, and hullo, by jingo, don't touch that!"

"Why, Captain?" inquired Bob, who had just taken up in his hands a soft, jelly like, flabby thing that appeared as if it were a little white owl, some ten or twelve inches high, without any particular head or wings to speak of, although it had a short black beak, resembling a parrot's, projecting from out of its livid hued fleshy body. " What is it ? "

" It's a cuttle fish," cried the old sailor. " Drop it, my boy, at once ! or   "

He spoke too late ; for at the same moment, the cuttle-fish deluged Bob with the inky fluid which nature has provided it with as a means of hiding its whereabouts in the water from its enemies, and from which the Romans obtained their celebrated ' Tyrian dye.'

Nell, also, came in for a share of this over her dress, which did not by any means improve its appearance.

" Never mind, though," said the Captain to them both, by way of consolation. " What's done can't be helped ! "

" Ah ! " remarked their father slily, " if you had been looking after the net, instead of instructing me in cookery, this wouldn't have happened."

" You're quite right, Strong," replied the other, with an air of great contrition ; albeit his eyes twinkled with fun and his manner was not quite that of a repentant sinner. " I've neglected my duties shamefully."

With these words he set to work anew, disinterring a large skate weighing over twelve pounds from amidst the mud and refuse brought up by the trawl.

The gills of this fish, in the centre of its globular body, had the most extraordinary likeness to a human face ; and as the queer looking creature puffed out these gills, it appeared, as Mr. Strong pointed out, just like a fat old gentleman taking a glass of some rare and highly-recommended wine and ' washing his mouth out ' so as to taste it properly.

" Oh, papa, how funny ! " exclaimed Nell. " It is just like that, too ! But look, Captain, there's a ' soldier crab,' isn't it ? "

" Yes, my dear, and we'll keep him for your aquarium ; as well as some new sea anemones and another zoophyte I see here, too. This chap is christened the 'alcyonium' by learned naturalists, but is called 'dead man's fingers' by the fisher-folk along shore."

"What a horrid name!" interposed Nellie, shuddering—"a horrid name!"

"It is so named," continued the Captain, "because the creature has the advantage of having several bodies instead of one, all radiating from a single stem, like fingers or toes. But now, I think, there's nothing much of any good left of our shoot, save a few oysters. Those will come in handy presently, eh, Strong?"

"Yes, I shan't mind," replied the barrister. "I'm beginning to have an appetite, I think."

"We'll have luncheon at once then," said the old sailor with alacrity, as if this would be a labour of love. "I'm not beginning to have an appetite, because I've got one already, and a precious good one, too! Do you think you can pick a bit if you try, eh, young people?"

"Yes, please," replied Nell. Master Bob's response was a shout of "Rather," fully indicative of his feelings; while Dick grinned so much that his face was a study as he said "Y es, sir, sure ly."

Taking all these evidences as proof of the unanimity of the company on the subject, the Captain, all helping, at once set about the preparations for the coming feast. He first, however, tied up the pocket of the trawl again, preparatory to heaving it overboard; so that they could 'kill two birds with one stone,' as he said, and be fishing and eating at the same time.

Each had something to do after this important operation.

Dick began by scraping some soles which the Captain selected from the number he had put aside for Mrs. Gilmour. Next, Master Bob washed these in a bucket of water he had procured from over the side of the cutter in sailor fashion; and then handing them to the Captain, who officiated as 'master of the kitchen,' over the gridiron in the 'fo'c's'le,' the old sailor cooked away quite cheerfully, in spite of having to bend himself almost in two in the little cabin in order to attend to his task properly, his zeal preventing him for the moment from feeling any inconvenience from stooping so much.

Nell, who had been debarred from any share in preparing the fish or looking after its grilling, which, certainly, she would infinitely have preferred, contented herself with arranging the four small plates which were all that the cutter's locker contained in the way of crockery ware, besides a similar number of cups of various hues and shapes.

All of these articles the young lady set out systematically on a board which the Captain fixed across the thwarts to serve as a table; while, as for Mr. Strong, all he did in the way of assistance was to set himself down on the most comfortable seat he could find in the stern sheets, where, lighting his pipe, he beguiled the weary moments until lunch should be ready as best he could, smoking and thinking!

He had not to wait long; for presently, with much dignity the Captain served up his first instalment of soles, which were declared by the barrister to be so good that another cooking was necessary; aye, and another too after that, until there was not a single sole left.

"Poor aunt Polly!" exclaimed Nellie, laughing merrily when they were all consumed, and the bones of the fish chucked overboard to feed their brethren below. "All her soles are gone! What shall we tell her?"

"Why, that we ate them," said the Captain, starting the laugh, and all joining in.

Dick, who was at the moment devouring the last crust of bread left, after finishing his portion of the fish, nearly choked himself by bursting into a guffaw while in the act of swallowing; so, this necessitated the Captain's administering to him a cup of sea water wherewith to wash down the morsel sticking in his throat, which did not taste nice after grilled sole, though the Captain said it was 'as good as grog.'

They did not have much sport after luncheon, the next cast of the net bringing up nothing but boulders and mud, besides an old bottle that must have been dropped into the sea years before and, mayhap, went down with Kempenfelt in the *Royal George ;* for it was encrusted with seaweed and barnacles of almost a century's growth.

After a bit, seeing that nothing further was to be gained by stopping out at sea, drifting with the tide alternately between the Nab and Warner light-ships, like Mahomet's coffin between heaven and earth, the Captain hauled up the trawl and bore away back homeward as well as he could with a foul wind, having to make several tacks before fetching the cutter's moorings off the coastguard station.

In spite of this, however, they reached 'The Moorings' in time for dinner ; when, notwithstanding their hearty luncheon, no deficiency of appetite could be observed in any of the party.

Bob and Nellie were, of course, delighted with their experiences of the day ; for, in addition to the joys of trawling and festive picnic on the water, which they thought even better than their previous one on land, they brought home a splendid 'soldier crab,' who caused much subsequent amusement when admitted to the aquarium, two new specimens of sea anemones, and the 'dead man's fingers,' whose name made their aunt Polly shiver, the good lady declaring it 'quite uncanny, sure.'

Their mother, however, was not quite so well pleased with the result of the expedition.

"There, I told you so !" she exclaimed, on catching sight of them, with the stains of the cuttle fish plainly visible on their clothes. "You will never wish to wear this suit again, Bob ; and, dear, dear, look at your dress, Nellie !"

"It's not so bad, mamma," pleaded she. "I only got a little of it."

"A little of what ? "

"The Tyrian dye, Captain Dresser called it, from the cuttle-fish," explained Bob, who seemed to treat the matter more·

lightly than the spoiling of his shirt front and jacket deserved in Mrs. Strong's opinion. "It's quite classical, mother so the Captain said when I got squelched with it."

"Really, I wish Captain Dresser would not make experiments with his dyes when you two are near him," said she, very plaintively. "He hasn't to look after your clothes, as I have."

Nell smiled at her mother's mistake, while Master Bob fairly screeched with laughter.

"Why, it wasn't the Captain who did it," he shouted out gleefully. "It was the cuttle fish that squirted over us."

Then, on the whole story being told her, Mrs. Strong exonerated the Captain.

But not so Mrs. Gilmour, when she learnt the history of the soles, which had been specially set aside for her and afterwards eaten.

"Oh, you cormorants!" she cried, pretending to be in a great rage. "Fancy eating my soles! Did you ever hear of such a thing? Captain Dresser, I'll never forgive you!"

"Don't be so hard hearted," said he imploringly. "If you only knew how hungry we were, I'm sure you would forgive us with your usual good nature."

"I'm not so certain of that," replied she. "'Deed, and I won't."

"Besides, we enjoyed them so, do you know," continued the old sailor, chuckling away at a fine rate. "Sure they were mighty fine, ma'am. The best soles I ivver ate, sure."

"That makes the matter worse, you robber!" she retorted, smiling good naturedly at his broad mimicry of her Irish pronunciation. "Why, ye're adding insult now to injury, sure."

"Never mind, Polly," interposed her brother, acting as peacemaker between the two. "The Captain will show you how to cook soles properly the next time he catches any."

"Yes," said Mrs. Gilmour drily, "if he doesn't ate them first."

"By Jove, I promise not to do that, ma'am, for I don't like 'em raw," replied the offender, keeping up the fun, and not one whit abashed by these comments on his behaviour. "Really, though, ma'am, I think you ought to forgive me now, and banish your hard feelings, as you've given me a wigging. Besides, if we did eat all the soles, I've brought you home a fine big skate, and lots of plaice, instead."

"Sure, I'll consider about it," said his hostess, showing signs of relenting. "But don't you think, now, skates are rather out of place in this warm weather, eh, Captain?"

CHAPTER XXII.

MISSING !

"HUMPH ! that makes the rubber," cried the Captain late one evening, some little time after the events recorded in the last chapter, when they were winding up the day with a game of whist, which had succeeded the nightly battle of cribbage wherewith Mrs. Gilmour and the old sailor used to amuse their leisure before the advent of the barrister and Mrs. Strong on the scene. "What say all you good people to a trip to Southampton to-morrow? There will be an excursion steamer running there in the morning, starting from the old pier at ten o'clock sharp, I think."

"'All right; now you've beaten us, I suppose you want to appear generous, and divert our attention from our defeat," said Mrs. Dugald Strong, with a fine touch of sarcasm, as the Captain chuckled over the odd trick, and collected the spoils of war, in the shape of sundry little fish counters, which he and his partner, aunt Polly, had won, through the old sailor's successful manipulation of the cards. "I believe we've seen all that is to be seen in the Isle of Wight."

"Indade you have," corroborated Mrs. Gilmour. "We've been everywhere in the sweete little place   no wonder it's called the 'garden of England'! Sure we've seen everything, from the broken grating of the w ndow which poor Charles the First was unable to squaze himself through at Carisbrook Castle, being too fat, poor man, down to the hawthorn bush

at Faringford over against Beacon Down atop of the Needles,
where Tennyson used to hide his long clay pipes after smoking
them, before going out for his walk on the cliff. Sure, and I
don't think, Dugald, there's anything more for ye to see
there at all, at all!"

"Oh, auntie, you have forgotten 'little Jane's' grave in the
pretty old churchyard at Brading, and the cottage in which the
good 'dairyman's daughter' lived at Arreton," chimed in Nellie,
who was more romantic. "Yes, and those dear little Swiss
villas too, at Totland Bay, aunt Polly, peeping out from the
fir trees and bracken, with the fuchsias like big trees in their
front gardens, and the scarlet geraniums growing wild in the
hedgerows!"

"Ah," said Master Bob, "I liked the smugglers' cave at
Ventnor. I wish they hadn't boarded it up, so that a fellow
can't see where they used to hide the cargoes of silk and lace
and kegs of brandy the French luggers brought across from
St. Malo   wasn't that where they ran them from, Captain?"

"Aye," replied the old sailor   "They don't now, though,
my boy. Our coastguardsmen are too sharp for that, and the
mounseers have to find another market for their goods! But
are you all agreed about our paying a visit to Southampton
to morrow, my friends?"

"It's a long voyage," observed Mrs. Gilmour, who, although
she had forsworn her resolve anent excursion steamers in her
desire not to interpose any selfish obstacle, such as her own
wishes, to the enjoyment of the others during their holiday by
the sea in proper seafaring fashion, yet could not forget the
Bembridge Belle catastrophe. "Are you sure the vessel is
safe?"

"Oh yes," answered the Captain. "She's one of the
regular boats, and is as safe as a man of war."

"Then we may consider the expedition arranged," said
Mrs. Strong, who, being anxious to see the city of the great
St. Bevis, had no objection to the trip up Southampton Water;

for, having been already across the Solent, and even voyaged round the Isle of Wight, so to speak, without feeling sea sick or qualmish, she was confident of being a 'born sailor,' as the saying goes, and thus only too pleased to have an opportunity of testing her new experiences further. "If you say it is safe, Captain Dresser, neither Polly nor any of us need be alarmed, I am sure."

The next morning, as the steamer was advertised to start punctually at the hour fixed, Bob was warned of his not having much time to spare when setting out for his bathe before breakfast with the good dog Rover.

"Oh, I'll be back in plenty of time," was his boastful reply. "I'll take some bread and-butter with me for breakfast, and get a cup of milk from the apple woman on the beach; and shall be at the pier waiting for you before you leave the house."

"Take care, my boy; we're rather late this morning, and you are running it pretty close," said his father, looking at his watch, as the young gentleman was scampering through the hall. "You won't have half-an hour altogether to spare."

But, Bob was obstinate, and away he went across the common, with Rover at his heels.

"I know he will be late," sighed Mrs. Strong, looking after him. "I know he will be late."

"Well, if he is, he will be left behind, that's all I can say," said his father, with decision. "I'm afraid Master Bob has too much of his own way; and, it is just as well he should be taught a lesson sometimes."

Thus giving his fiat, Mr. Strong, apparently dismissing Bob for the present from his mind, hurried the preparations of the others, so that they, at least, should be in good time; and, some twenty minutes after the truant had left, he and Mrs. Strong and his sister, with Nellie, started for the pier, arriving there just as the Captain came up in a great hurry, stepping along as briskly as he and his malacca cane could get over the ground.

"Where's Bob?" he at once asked, missing the absentee.
"Where's Bob?"

"He's gone to bathe," replied poor Nell, very disconsolately.
"He said he'd get here as soon as we did, but he hasn't come
yet, and I'm afraid he'll be too late."

"That he will," said the Captain, looking equally distressed.
"I hear the steamer's bell ringing in fact, I heard it before,
and that made me quicken my movements.   The stupid
fellow!   Why did you let him go?"

"Wilful would have his way," answered Mr. Strong, shrugging his shoulders.   "It is his own fault, and he must suffer
the consequences.   Come on, you people; I don't see why
we should sacrifice our trip, at any rate."

Mrs. Gilmour and his wife tried in vain to combat the
barrister's resolution, suggesting that the excursion might
be postponed; but he would not consent to this for a
moment.

"No," he said determinedly, "this is the only day we could
go; for, when the boat next leaves for Southampton, we'll most
probably be back in town."

So saying, he pushed them all through the turnstile before
him, and taking their tickets, including one for Bob, in case he
still contrived to turn up in time, led the way to the steamer,
which was blowing off her steam alongside the pier, as if in the
greatest haste to start.

They were none too soon; for, hardly had they got on board,
ere the engine gong sounded and the steamer's paddles
began to move, the vessel gliding out into the stream as her
hawsers were cast off.

All looked out eagerly, Nellie especially, almost in tears,
hoping to the last that Bob would come scurrying up; but,
much to the general disappointment, no Bob came, nor did
they even have the poor satisfaction of seeing him appear in
the distance after the steamer had left the pier.

"Poor Bob!" bewailed Nell, for whom all the fun of the

expedition had departed with his absence. "I knew he would be too late."

"Never mind, missy," said the Captain to cheer her up, although he, too, felt sorry at the party being thus lessened in numbers; "you'll see him when we return this evening, and will then be able to tell him of all the fine sights he lost by not going with us."

But Nell would not be consoled; for, in addition to Bob's not being with them, Rover was likewise an absentee, while the Captain had left Dick behind to give the cutter a good clean out, as well as perform other duties. He thought that, perhaps, Mrs. Strong might not like the boy being brought with them and treated on an equality with her own children; being taken, apparently, everywhere they went, as he had been before. It need hardly be said, though, that such an idea never occurred to Bob's mother, who knew well how Dick had risked his life to save her son's; the thought, really, was entirely due to the old sailor's ultra conscientiousness!

Under these circumstances, therefore, Nellie did not by any means enjoy the trip; nor did the elders of the party, either, seem happy, all appearing to be equally well pleased after they had seen Southampton, where there was not very much to see after all, and the boat started back for home.

Soon after the steamer passed Calshott Castle and got into the waters of the Solent, late in the afternoon, the comfort of those on board was not increased by their getting into a thick white woolly sea-fog, which had crept over the Isle of Wight from the Channel.

On their reaching the pier at Southsea again, they found the fog had got there before them; and, crossing the common, they could hardly see each other at a couple of yards distance.

Neither the barrister nor Mrs. Strong liked the appearance of things, thinking that this mist of the sea resembled one of their own 'London particulars,' and betokened a spell of bad weather.

The Captain, however, made light of it.

"Pooh, pooh!" cried he, "it's only brought up by the south easterly wind and will be cleared off by the morning, when you'll probably have a hotter day than ever."

This allayed Mrs. Strong's forebodings in reference to the weather, and she began to wonder what had become of Bob during their absence.

"He must have found the day very long, poor boy!" she said. "I wonder what he has been doing?"

"Oh, I've no doubt he's been amusing himself," replied the Captain cheerfully. "I don't think Bob would remain dull very long if even left alone"

The same thoughts were passing through the minds both of Nellie and her aunt, although they said nothing; and all were looking forward to their conjectures being solved as to how Bob had passed the time when they should arrive at 'The Moorings.'

However, on coming to the house, who should greet them but Rover, who got up languidly from the doorstep, his coat all dripping with wet.

"Poor doggie!" exclaimed Nell, patting him. "Why, you're all damp with the fog! Your master shouldn't have been so cruel as to leave you outside. Where's Bob?"

Usually on being asked this question, Rover's invariable answer would be a short, sharp, joyous bark; but now, in place of this, the retriever put up his head and uttered a plaintive whine that was almost a howl.

It struck dismay into all their hearts; and on Sarah's opening the door at the same moment, Nell's question to the dog was now put to her.

"Where's Master Bob?"

The girl started back in astonishment.

"Law, mum!" said she, addressing her mistress, Mrs. Gilmour. "Ain't he with you, mum?"

"No," she replied, much frightened at Sarah's answer, or rather counter-question; while Mrs. Strong grew as pale as death and Nellie clung to her convulsively, Rover's demeanour having roused their worst fears. " You don't mean to say you haven't seen him ? "

"No, mum, I thought he was with you," repeated the housemaid, beginning to cry as if accused of some fault. "I've never set eyes on Master Bob since he went out to bathe before you did, mum, this morning ! "

"I wonder where the young rascal is ?" sang out the Captajn in a jovial sort of way, to allay the alarm of the others and hide his own uneasiness. " You'd better get inside out of the damp all of you while I go off to the coastguard station. I wouldn't mind betting a brass farthing I'll find Master Bob there hobnobbing with Hellyer and Dick. He's very fond of going there to listen to my old coxswain's yarns when he has got a chance."

"I'll come with you," said Mr. Strong, not liking to let him go alone, besides also beginning to feel anxious, adding to his wife—" Go in, Edith ! you need not be uneasy. We'll soon bring back our young truant ! "

So saying, he and the Captain, followed by Rover with drooping tail, started for the coastguard station on the beach.

However, on getting there, their fears, instead of being dispelled, were, on the contrary, alarmingly heightened !

Hellyer told them that he had not come on duty until a late hour in the day ; and had then not seen anything of either Bob or Dick.

" The man as I relieved," continued the coastguardsman, " told me as how he seed two boys in the Cap'en's boat about midday ; and, all at once, arter his dinner, for which he goes into the cabin, you know, he misses the boat and the boys too. But, he doesn't think anythink o' this, he says, believin' they has took her into the harbour."

"Confound him !" cried the Captain excitedly. "Who was the man? He ought to have known something was wrong when he saw the two lads alone in her like that."

"He would be a stranger to you, sir," said Hellyer. "He wer' a man from the Hayling beat as just come on fresh to jine this station here to day, sir. He's a man, sir, of the name of Jones, and rayther soft, like!"

"How unfortunate!" muttered the Captain, while Mr. Strong groaned and upbraided himself for his seeming harshness to Bob in the morning. "How very unlucky!"

"Of course," went on the coastguardsman earnestly, in deep sympathy with both "the moment the man tells me of this, I knows what happens, seeing that blessed sea fog a creeping up and the wind falling; and so I goes off to the commander and tells him what I thinks as how Master Bob and that young Dick o' yourn, Cap'en, were most likely all adrift and couldn't fetch in to the land. I——"

"But what did your commander do?" cried the old sailor, interrupting. "Tell me that!"

"Why, sir, he sent word round to all our stations and down to the Dockyard, and he's telegraphed likewise to the h'Island so as how there'll be a strict look out kep' all round the coast for the poor lads."

"I am very much obliged to you, Hellyer, and to the commander as well," said the Captain as he and Mr. Strong turned away mournfully, retracing their steps back to 'The Moorings.' "I'm afraid we can do nothing more now."

No, nothing more could be done then.

The morning brought no news to gladden their hearts or brighten their hopes.

Matters, indeed, looked worse than had been expected.

For, as the day wore on, reports reached the Dockyard from the different coastguard stations along the eastern and western coast of the mainland and from the Isle of Wight, whence a strict look out had been kept on the approaches to Spithead and the adjacent waters of the Channel.

These reports were all to the same effect.

Not a trace had been seen of the missing boat; nor anything heard of Bob and Dick.

It was the same the following day, nothing likewise being then reported ; although the search had been redoubled and one of the Government tugs sent out from the harbour to scour the offing.

Hope now gave way to despair before the certainty that stared them in the face, putting possibility beyond doubt.

Everybody believed the boat had been swamped, or run down in the fog, and that Bob and Dick were drowned !

Poor boys !

CHAPTER XXIII.

"Now," said Bob to himself, when he got down to the beach after a sharp run across the common, "I must be as spry as possible with my swim, or else I shall be too late for the boat, as dad said I would be, for I really haven't got much time to spare ."

Unfortunately, however, at the very outset, poor Bob met with obstacles that prevented this praiseworthy intention being effectively carried out. In the first place, Dick, with whom he had always bathed in company since their first involuntary dip together off the castle rampart on the first evening of their arrival at Southsea, was not at their usual trysting-place. Not only that, he was nowhere to be seen in the neighbourhood of the shore.

"I wonder where he can be?" said Bob, continuing his soliloquy in a very disjointed frame of mind, after looking in every direction fruitlessly, and calling out Dick's name in vain. "I wonder where he can be? The Captain did not say he wasn't to come with us this morning!"

At last, after wasting some precious minutes thus waiting, he began undressing very slowly, instead of in the usual brisk manner in which he was in the habit of peeling off his clothes, running a race with Dick to see who would get into the water first.

Then, at length, he plunged in to take his swim in a very

half hearted fashion, going in reluctantly and coming out in the same undecided way; while, to make matters worse and further protract his loitering, just as he was beginning to dress again, a nasty spiteful bloodhound, which was prowling by the shore, made a most unprovoked attack on Rover, necessitating his going to his rescue with a big stone Master Bob hopping up to the scene of action 'with one shoe off and one shoe on,' like the celebrated 'John' the hero of the nursery rhyme!

Rover was not quite a match for the brute that assailed him; but with Bob's help, not omitting the big stone, the two routed the enemy 'with great slaughter,' the bloodhound fleeing away ignominiously with his tail between his legs, and Rover raising a pæan of victory in the shape of a defiant bark as he retreated.

Still, the episode consumed a few more minutes of valuable time; so when Bob had hopped back again to where he had left his clothes to complete his toilet, and then raced down to the pier, it was not only past the hour fixed for the Southampton steamer to start, but she was already well on her way.

In fact, she was just then rounding Gillkicker Point, which juts out from Stokes Bay, bearing away on board her, his father and mother and Nell, besides the Captain and Mrs. Gilmour; and not only that, leaving him behind!

Bob did not know how to contain himself.

He was too manly to cry; although he felt a big lump in his throat which made him take several short swallows without gulping anything down; while, strangely enough, something seemed to get in his eyes, for a moment preventing him from seeing anything seaward but a sort of hazy mist as he stood listlessly by the head of the pier, trying vainly to discern the excursion-boat, now fast disappearing in the distance!

Presently, however, after remaining there awhile, staring at nothing, the Captain's favourite maxim occurred to his mind— 'What's done can't be helped'; and coming to the conclusion that there was no use in his stopping on the pier any longer, since the steamer had left, and there was no possibility of his being able to join the others, he determined to bend his steps in the direction of the coastguard station, with the hope of finding Hellyer there to cheer his drooping spirits.

Bob's fates, though, appeared singularly unpropitious for him this morning; for on his arriving anon at the little cabin beyond the castle, which was the Captain's regular trysting-place, lo, and behold, a strange man was there, who told him that Hellyer was 'off duty,' and it would not be his turn 'on' again until late in the afternoon.

Here was another misfortune!

But there was 'balm in Gilead' in store for Bob; for, hardly had the long face that he pulled on learning the un welcome news of Hellyer's absence merged again into the ordinary round contour with which his friends were familiar, than, whom should he see coming along the beach, only a little way off, but—who should you think?

Why, Dick!

Yes, he had been into Portsmouth, he explained, to take a letter to the Dockyard for the Captain; and now, also in pursu-ance of the old sailor's orders, he was about going off to the cutter, which lay at her moorings abreast of the coastguard station, and only about a cable's length out, so as to be within easy reach, so that they could haul her up on the shingle in the event of any sudden shifting wind rendering her anchorage unsafe.

Bob at once flew to him with open arms, so to speak; and so did Rover too, the sagacious animal always reflecting his young master's moods, and having turned as woebegone as a naturally cheerful dog could be since he noticed Bob's being mopy, he had now resumed his proper tone of bark and mien, wagging his tail at the sight of Dick and thus reciprocating Bob's feelings.

"Hullo, Dick." said the latter, when the young yachtsman

had approached near enough for them to speak without getting to each other. "What are you going to do aboard?"

"To clean out the yacht ready for another trip, Master Bob. The Cap'en told me to get her done afore he come back."

"That's jolly!" exclaimed Bob, brightening up at the prospect of some sort or any sort of expedition in lieu of the one he had missed. "May I come with you?"

"Ees, sure-ly, Master Bob," returned Dick. "But how comes it you bain't a-gone wi' the Cap'en and t'others?"

Bob did not like any allusion to this delicate subject.

"I was too late," he said abruptly, changing the conversation at once. "How are you going off to the cutter, I see she has got the dinghy towing behind, eh?"

"P'r'aps I'm agoing to swim out to her," replied Dick, with a grin. "What say you to that, Master Bob, hey?"

"If you do, I will too," retorted Bob; "although I've had my dip already, and very lonesome it was. Why didn't you come down this morning?"

"I sang out to you jist now, sir, as how I had to take a letter for the Cap'en, who told me as he didn't think you'd have time to bathe afore starting for the steamer."

"I thought I had and missed it!" said Bob ruefully. "But you're not going really to swim out to the cutter now, Dick, eh?"

"No, no, Master Bob," cried Dick, his grin expanding into a laugh. "I were only a joking. There's a waterman just shoving down his wherry as will put us off to her. Hi, ahoy, there!"

"Hi, hullo!" also shouted out Bob; but the two only succeeded in ultimately attracting the attention of old Barney the boatman, who was rather deaf, and required a deal of hallooing before noticing any one, by setting on Rover with a "Hi, catch him, sir!"

This rather exasperated old Barney at first. However, after

some violent explanations they were grudgingly given a passage out to the anchored yacht, Barney grumbling at doing it for nothing !

Rover was not included in the bargain; for, he disdained adventuring his valuable person in a small row-boat, no inducement being ever strong enough to persuade him so to do. He was quite satisfied to swim out after the boys had started off in the wherry, being lugged subsequently on board the cutter by his legs and tail as soon as they fetched alongside.

For some little time after Bob and Dick got on board, both were very busy, Bob dipping overboard a bucket that had a 'becket' of rope for a handle, and a longer rope bent on to this with which he proceeded to haul the bucket up again, full of sea water, wherewith he sluiced the decks fore and aft thoroughly ; while Dick, on his part, scrubbed the planks with a piece of 'holystone,' then adroitly drying them with a mop, which he could twirl now, after a little experience, with all the dexterity of an old salt !

When the little cutter was thus presently made 'ataunto' by their mutual exertions, they sat down to rest for awhile, Dick sharing his luncheon of bread and cheese with Bob, who, of course, had long since consumed the slices of bread and butter he had brought out with him for his breakfast.

By and by, on a gentle breeze springing up from the southward and westward, Master Bob, boylike, suggested their slipping the *Zephyr's* moorings and going for a little sail out into the offing.

"We needn't run very far," he said. "Say, only to the fort there and back again, you know."

But Dick would not hear of the proposal.

"No, Master Bob, not lest the Cap'en gived orders," he remonstrated. "Why, he'd turn me off if I did it; and, he's that kind to me as I wouldn't like to vex him, no not for nothing !"

"He wouldn't mind me though," argued Bob. "Didn't he

say the other day why, you heard him tell Hellyer yourself—
that he'd back you and me to manage a boat against any two
boys in Portsmouth, aye, or any port on the south coast?"

"Ees, I heerd him," reluctantly assented the other; "but
that didn't mean fur us to go out in the boat alone."

"Well, Dick, I didn't think you were a coward!" said Bob
with great contempt, angry at being thwarted. "I really
didn't."

This cut the other to the heart.

"You doesn't mean that, Master Bob," he exclaimed re-
proachfully, hesitating to utter his scathing reply. "Ah, you
didn't say as I wer' a coward that time as I jumped into the
water arter you behind the castle."

"Forgive me, Dick," cried Bob impulsively, "I was a beast to
say such a thing! Of course, I know you are not a coward;
but, really, I'm sure the Captain would not mind a bit our
going for a sail—especially if he knew, and he does know,
about my being left behind all alone while they all have gone
off to Southampton in the steamer enjoying themselves!"

This last appeal made Dick hesitate; and, in hesitating thus,
he lost his firmness of resolution.

"Well, Master Bob, if we only goes a little ways and you
promises fur to come back afore the tide turns, I don't mind
unmooring for a bit; though, mind, Master Bob, you'll bear
all the blame if the Cap'en says anythink about it!"

"Of course I will, Dick, if he does; but I know he won't
say anything. You may make your mind easy on that score!"

With these words, Bob sprang forward on the fo'c's'le
and began loosening the jib from its fastenings; while Dick,
now that his scruples were overcome, set to work casting off
the gaskets of the mainsail, the two boys then manning
the halliards with a will, and hoisting the throat of the sail
well up.

The jib was then set, its sheet being slackened until Dick
slipped the buoy marking the yacht's moorings overboard;

when, the tack being hauled aft, and the mainsail peaked, the bows of the cutter paid off and she walked away close-hauled, standing out towards 'Noman's Fort,' on the starboard tack.

It was now past midday and the tide was making into the harbour; so that, as the wind from the south west had got rather slight, veering round to the southwards, the cutter did not gain much of an offing, losing in leeway nearly all she got in beating out to windward.

"I vote we let her run off a little towards the Nab," said Bob, seeing what little progress they made towards the fort; and he, being the steersman, put the helm up, easing off at the same time the sheet of the mainsail; Dick, who was in the bows, attending to the jib. "It's awful poor fun drifting like this!"

"Mind you turns back agen when the tide begins to run out!" premised Dick. "You promised as we wasn't to go fur!"

"All right," replied Bob, "I won't forget."

But, now, a strange thing happened.

No sooner had the cutter's bows been turned to the east-wards, than Rover, who had previously been looking very uneasy, standing up with his hind legs on one of the thwarts and his fore-paws on the taffrail astern, gazing anxiously behind at the land they were leaving, all at once gave vent to a loud unearthly howl and sprang overboard.

"Hi, Rover, come back, sir!" yelled out Bob, at the pitch of his voice—"Rover, come back!"

But, the dog, although hitherto always obedient to his young master's call, paid no attention to it now, turning a deaf ear to all his whistles and shouts and swimming steadily towards the shore.

"Poor Rover, he'll be drownded, sure-ly!" said Dick. "Don't 'ee think we'd better go arter he, poor chap?"

"Not a bit of it!" replied Bob, angry at the dog's desertion, as he thought it, putting down Rover's behaviour to some strange dislike on his part to being in the yacht, at all events when she was moving briskly through the water. "He has swum twice as far in the river in London, and I won't go after him!"

Bob, however, brought the little yacht up to the wind again, watching until Rover was seen to emerge from the sea and crawl up on the beach again; when the cutter's head was allowed to pay off again, and within a couple of hours or so, although neither of the boys took any note of how the time was going, they had not only passed the Nab but were now nearing the Ower's light ship.

Not till then did Dick become aware how far they had reached out, Portsmouth having long since disappeared and even the forts beginning to show hazy to windward; while Selsea Bill loomed up on their port hand.

"Master Bob, Master Bob!" he cried in consternation, never having been so far out before, even with the Captain. "Do 'ee know where we be now?"

"Why, out at sea, to be sure!" said Bob, his face all aglow with delight at gliding thus like Byron's corsair—

'O'er the glad waters of the deep blue sea.'

For his soul certainly was, for the moment, quite as 'bound less' and his 'thoughts as free,' from all consideration, save of the present "Isn't it jolly?"

"Well, I doesn't know about that," replied Dick, looking very glum. "I'm a-thinking of the gitting back; which, wi' the tide a setting out from the harbour, won't be so easy, I knows!"

"Nonsense, Dick!" said Bob in his usual offhand way, though bringing the cutter up to the wind, so as to go about on the other tack. "You're frightening yourself really, my boy, about nothing! The wind has got round more to the south;

so we'll be able to run back to Portsmouth in no time. The cutter is a very good boat, so the Captain says, on a wind!"

However, 'Man proposes and God disposes.'

The wind suddenly dropped, just as the tide turned, the ebb setting out from Spithead towards the east, dead against them; when, instead of running in homewards 'in no time,' the cutter, after a time, became becalmed first, and then gradually began to drift out into the open Channel again.

Dick was the first to notice this.

"Look, Master Bob!" he cried. "We aren't making no headway at all! I don't see we're getting any the nearer to the Nab!"

"We will, soon," replied Bob, all hopeful. "It's only because the breeze has dropped a bit. Before long, we'll pick it up again! I think, Dick, we'd better slacken off the sheets and let her bear away more!"

This was done; but, still the *Zephyr* would not move.

She had net way enough, indeed, to answer her helm; for, her bows pointed west, and south, and east, alternately, as the tidal eddies swayed her in this direction and that.

"I knewed we was doin' wrong," remarked Dick presently, after a long silence in which neither of the boys spoke a word. "It's a judgment on us!"

"A fiddlestick!" retorted Bob. "We'll only drift about like this for a short time; and, when the tide turns again, it will sweep us back to Spithead like one o'clock!"

"I doesn't believe that, Master Bob," said Dick disconso lately, sitting down on a thwart, and looking longingly at a faint speck in the distance which he thought was Southsea; although they were almost out of sight of land now, the swift current carrying the boat along nearly four knots an hour. "We should ha' tuk warnin', Master Bob, by Rover. He knowed what wer' a coming and so he swum ashore in time, he did!"

"Rover is a faithless creature!" cried Bob hotly. "I'll

give him a good licking when we reach the land again, you see ! "

" When'll that be, Master Bob ? "

" Oh, some time or other before night," replied he defiantly, but Dick could easily tell from his tone of voice that he did not speak quite so buoyantly as before ; and his already long face grew longer as the day wore on without the breeze springing up again or any change of circumstances.

They did not pass a single ship near, notwithstanding that they saw several with all their sails set, their loftier canvas catching a few lingering puffs of air that did not descend low enough to affect the cutter. The sight of these vessels moving, however, raised their drooping spirits, Bob and Dick thinking that the wind by and by would affect them, too.

But no breeze came ; and all the while they were being carried further and further out to sea.

" Hallo, there's a steamer ! " sang out Bob after another protracted silence between the pair. " I see her smoke easily. She's steering right for us ! "

" Where ? " asked Dick. " I doesn't see no steamer, Master Bob."

" There ! " said the other, pointing to a long white line on the horizon. " There she is, blowing off her steam, or her funnel smoking, quite plain ! "

" Lor', Master Bob ! " ejaculated the other, after peering fixedly for a moment where his companion directed him to look. " That arn't no steam or smoke as ever I seed. It be a cloud, or fog, I knows; or summut o' that sort, sure-ly, Master Bob ! "

Bob, however, would not be persuaded of this, persisting that he was right and Dick wrong.

" I don't know where your eyes can be ! " he said scornfully. " I'll bet anything it's a steamer ; or, I never saw one ! "

But ere another hour had passed over their heads, Dick was proved to be the true prophet; he, the false !

The low lying bank of vapour, which originally resembled the trail of smoke from some passing steam-vessel on her way down Channel, gradually spread itself out along the horizon.

It then rose up, like a curtain. from the sea ; and, stretching up its clammy heads towards the zenith, widened over the heavens until it shut out the western sun from their gaze, making the still early afternoon seem as night.

Creeping over the surface of the sullen water with ghostly footsteps, the mist soon shrouded the boat in its pall-like folds ; impregnating the surrounding atmosphere with moisture and making the boys believe it was raining, though never a drop fell

It was only a sea-fog, that was all.

But it was accompanied by a dampness that seemed like the hand of Death !

'IT is the last straw,' says the proverb, 'that breaks the camel's back!'

Bob's courage had been on the wane long before the white, woolly fog environed them; although, up to now he had endeavoured to brave it out in the presence of Dick, the very consciousness that he was the main cause of their being in such a perilous predicament preventing him from betraying the fears he felt.

But, when this octopus of the air clutched them in its corpse like grip, breathing its wet vapoury breath into their faces, soddening their clothes with heavy moisture and slackening their energies as it had already damped their hopes of a steam-vessel coming to the rescue, Bob, whose nerves were strained to their utmost tension, at last broke down.

"Oh, Dick!" he cried, bursting into a passion of tears, all the more vehement now from his ever having been a manly boy and in the habit of stifling all such displays of emotion, even when severely hurt, as had happened on more than one occasion in a football scrimmage at school, whence he got the name of Stoic amongst his mates. "Oh, Dick, poor Dick! I'm sorry I made you come with me to your death! I wonder what my mother and dad will say, and Nell too, when they come to learn that we are lost?"

"Don't 'ee now, Master Bob, give way like that!" said

Dick, the brave lad, forgetting his own sad plight on seeing his unhappy comrade's alarm and grief. "Cheer up, Master Bob, like a good sort! We bean't lost yet, ye knows!"

"I'm afraid we are, Dick! I'm afraid we are!" sobbed Bob, as the pair of unfortunates got gradually wetter and more miserable, if that were possible; the density of the atmosphere around them increasing so that it seemed as if they were enveloped in a drenching cloud, this mist of the sea being the offspring of the waters, and consequently taking after its humid parent. "Why, we're miles and miles away from land, and drifting further and further off every moment! Oh, Dick, we're lost—we're lost!"

"Now, don't 'ee, Master Bob, don't 'ee!" cried Dick, folding one of his arms, like a mother, round the other's neck and drawing him towards him to comfort him. "We ain't a bit lost yet, I tell 'ee, sure ly. Why, we ain't at sea as you says at all. We be ounly in the h'offin' hereabouts."

This woke up Bob to argument.

"Only the offing, you say, Dick?" he replied, with some of his old dogmatism as they drifted on and on, the ebb tide that was bearing them away on its bosom lapping against the sides of the boat with a melancholy sound, though almost deadened by the oppressiveness of the damp sea fog. "Do you know how wide the Channel is 'hereabouts,' as you say?"

"No, Master Bob," said the other lad humbly. "I doesn't. I ain't no scholard, as you knows."

"Then, I'll tell you," rejoined Bob triumphantly. "It must be nearly a hundred miles wide here between the French and English coasts!"

Dick, however, was not abashed by this broad statement.

"That mebbe, Master Bob," he replied modestly, scratching the back of his neck where one of his damp locks of hair tickled him at the moment. "But, I heard the Cap'en say ounly t'other day as how there was so many ships a passing up and down as a boat adrift wer' bound to be sighted!"

"But, suppose a hundred ships passed us," said Bob, who would not be comforted, in spite of all Dick's efforts. "Why, old chap, they couldn't see us! The fog would prevent them!"

"Lor', so her would!" assented Dick, unable to gainsay this argument. "I forgets that, I did, sure ly!"

After a time, Bob's sobs ceased and he began to think of something else; something that affected him, for the moment, even more strongly than his fears.

"I'm awfully hungry, Dick," he said. "Have you got any more bread and cheese left?"

"No, not a scrap," was the melancholy answer. "I giv' yer half, share and share alike; and I've ate every crumb o' mine!"

"Isn't there anything in the locker?"

"Nothing, but the Cap'en's hatchet. Don't you bear in mind as how I scrubbed her out afore we started?"

"Yes, so you did, I recollect," replied Bob moodily, his appetite being well nigh unbearable from its insatiable gnawing. "How do you feel, Dick?"

"I feels as if I could eat the h'elephant we seed in the circus."

This made Bob laugh hysterically.

"I think I could, too," he said, between his paroxysms of laughter and sobs. "I never felt so hungry in my life before!"

Another interval of silence followed this confession.

"I'll tell 'ee what, Master Bob," observed Dick, on their comparing notes again presently, when both acknowledged to being cold and wet and miserable. "Let us crawl into the cabin and lie down, hey? It'll be warmer than here, sure ly!"

"So it will," cried Bob, getting up and stretching his limbs, which were stiff with cramp from sitting so long in the damp air; the fog around them appearing to get all the thicker as the time passed. "I wonder neither of us thought of that before?"

The two then crept in under the half deck; and, covering themselves up with the cutter's gaff-topsail, which had been placed within the cabin along with some spare canvas, dropped off into a sound slumber, forgetting their sad plight and their hunger alike, in sleep, the yacht meanwhile still floating along, down Channel, in a west-by north direction with the ebb

Their rest did not last long.

Bob was suddenly awakened from a dream of a wonderful banquet, which he was enjoying, by a sort of rushing gurgling sound ; while the boat rocked to and fro at the same time uneasily.

Rubbing his eyes, he started up and listened for a moment.

Then, he shook Dick to arouse him.

" Hullo ! Wake up ! " he cried. " The wind has sprung up again ; and, I think, we're moving through the water ! "

" I'll soon find out," said Dick, going outside and putting his hand over the gunwale, calling out the instant afterwards, " You're right, Master Bob ! We be moving, right enough. Aye, so we be, sure-ly ."

" I wonder where Portsmouth is ? " remarked Bob, as the two cogitated what was best to be done, their hopes rising with the welcome breeze ; although this was only very feeble as yet, not being sufficient, indeed, to blow away the fog that still hung over the sea.

" If we only knew whereabouts we was we'd know where to steer ; but we've turned about sich a lot, that I'd be puzzled to tell."

" So would I," agreed Bob. " But, I tell you what I think. Let us run before the wind. It'll be sure to bring us some where, at all events, in the end ."

" Aye, that it would, sure ly, Master Bob," cried Dick, surprised at the other's cleverness. " I declare I never as much as thought o' that ! "

Thereupon, they wore the little cutter round, she having been previously going like a crab sideways, which fully accounted for the lively motion that had aroused them ; and, Bob having stationed himself at the helm, which he had put hard over, Dick mounted up on the fo'c's'le to act as look-out, in case they should run against anything in the semi darkness around them, or, more happily still, come in sight of land.

They had not long occupied their respective positions, when Bob's attention was attracted by a cry of alarm from his companion in the bows.

"Lawks a mussy!" yelled out Dick in accents of unfeigned terror. "I sees a white ghostess a flying down on us, with big wings like a h'angel!"

"Nonsense, Dick!" cried Bob from aft, trying to peer ahead under the belly of the sail as he was sitting to leeward. "There are no such things as ghosts; and, besides, I don't see anything at all but the fog and the water!"

"Oh, lawks, Master Bob!" screamed the frightened Dick in answer to this. "Look t'other side and then you'll p'r'aps believe me. Look t'other side . Look t'other side! I bees afeered! I bees afeered!"

Bob shifted his seat to windward, so as to get a better view forwards and see what had alarmed Dick.

"Why, Dick, it's a ship!" he exclaimed in an ecstasy of delight the next instant. "What you thought are angel's wings are the vessel's sails, though they are angel's wings to us."

"Be her a real ship, Master Bob?" asked Dick, having another peep at the suspicious object and still not quite convinced as yet. "Sure ly?"

"Of course she is, I tell you," cried Bob. "Look out now and let go the jib sheet as I luff up. I'm going to lay to, for the ship is coming up with us rapidly and will run us down if we don't take care!"

She was diminishing the distance between them quickly enough.

A big ship she looked, too, appearing all the larger from the intervening veil of mist, which magnified her proportions wonderfully, in similar fashion to the 'Fata Morgana' seen sometimes in Italian waters.

Like as in the same spectral phenomenon, too, this vessel seemed to be gliding towards them without sound or apparent motion.

She was a veritable phantom of the deep!

There were no lights visible on her, nor did it look as if any one was on the watch.

So far as the boys could judge from the ocular evidence before them, there might really not have been a single soul on board.

But, whether that was the case or no, on she came steadily towards them bow on, emerging bigger and bigger from the ghostly mist, each movement sensibly affecting her and increasing her size; so that, presently, she became a monster ship.

She came too near to be pleasant, however, without sheering either to right or aft.

It looked as if she were going to run them down!

Bob and Dick's hopes of a rescue paled before the imminent dread of a collision that now stared them in the face—nay, was close at hand.

"Shout, Dick! Shout out with me as loud as you can so as to wake them up on board and make them see us!" cried Bob, letting go the tiller and standing up on top of the stern locker. "Now, all together, Dick! Ship, ahoy! Ship, ahoy!"

CHAPTER XXV

DRIFTING.

"HELP, ahoy, look out !" sang out Bob and Dick in chorus, well nigh paralyzed with fright. "Ahoy there, look out ahead ! "

But, in spite of their cries, the phantom ship, whose pro portions became all the more magnified the nearer she approached, rose upon them steadily out of the mist, growing into a gruesome reality each second, her hull towering over the little cutter as she bore down upon her, like a giant above a pigmy !

"Help, ahoy, look out there !" they once more shouted frantically. "Help ahoy ! "

It was all in vain, though, their shouts and cries being unnoticed.

The next moment the on coming vessel struck them, fortunately not end on or amidships, but in a slanting fashion, her cutwater sliding by the gunwale of the cutter, from bow to stern, with a harsh, grating sound and a rasping movement that shook their very vitals the little yacht heeling over the while until she was almost on her beam ends.

Had the vessel caught her midships, she would have at once crushed her like an eggshell ; as it was, the fluke of one of her anchors, which was hanging from her bows ready for letting go in case of emergency, the barque being not yet clear of soundings, got foul of the cutter's rigging, sweeping her mast and boom away, the stays snapping under the strain as if they were packthread.

Poor little cutter! She was left a complete wreck and nearly full of water; still rocking to and fro from the violence of the collision, even after the craft that had done all the mischief had again, seemingly, re-transformed herself into a phantom ship and faded away in the mist that hung over the sea, like the creation of a dream!

It was a very bad dream, though; and Bob and Dick gave themselves up for lost altogether.

Their fate, drifting helplessly about, an hour or so before, hungry and miserable, had seemed desperate enough; but their slight sleep, with the subsequent awakening to the know ledge that the wind had sprung up again and was bearing them once more in some certain direction, had restored their courage and revived their hopes.

This courage, too, had became more courageous, this hope more hopeful on the approach of the barque; for, they believed she would take them on board and restore them by and by to their friends, advancing so gallantly as she did towards them, like an angel, so Dick thought.

But, now!

What were the calamities which they so recently bewailed in comparison with the present?

Then, the yacht might have been at the mercy of the mist and tide; but she was still staunch and sound, capable when a breeze blew once more of wafting them home— whereas, now, the little cutter was dismasted and water logged, nay, even sinking for all they knew!

Thus, their present position was a thousandfold more terrible than the one before.

But, still, only boys though they were, hope did not yet quite desert them.

The indomitable courage of youth triumphed over disaster.

For a few seconds neither could speak.

However, when the ship had disappeared, going away as silently as she had approached them, they bestirred themselves to see what damage the cutter had sustained.

Bob was the first to recall his scattered wits.

"Well, they haven't sunk us, as I was afraid they would, Dick!" said he. "I wonder if any of the planks are really started?"

"How can we see, Master Bob?" asked Dick anxiously. "So as to know if she be all right?"

"Why, by baling her out," he answered. "If we lessen the water in her, then we'll know she's all right."

"But if the water don't go down?"

"Then, *we* will!" replied Bob rather curtly. "Have you got anything to bale her out with?"

"Well, Master Bob," observed Dick, grinning, "fur a young gen'leman as is so sharp, you've got a orful bad mem'ry! Don't 'ee recollect the booket as ye helped me fur to wash down the decks wi' this very marnin'?"

"Dear me, Dick, I declare I quite forgot that!" said Bob, with a laugh, seeing Dick's grin; for, it was not so dark now in their immediate vicinity, the breeze having lifted the fog slightly from the surface of the water. "Where is the bucket stored?"

"In the locker, joost by 'ee,' was Dick's response, as he waded through the water and came up to his companion. "Stop, I'll get 'im for 'ee! I'll have to make a dive fur he, though!"

"Have you got it?" inquired Bob, after Dick had groped about for some time, popping his head under water and coming up at intervals for breath. "Have you got it?"

"'Ees," said he at length, lugging out the bucket, "I've got un!"

Then, they set to work, each using it alternately.

The exertion did them both good, too, standing up as they were to their middles in water; for, it prevented them shivering with cold as they had before done.

Bucketful after bucketful they emptied over the side; and, still they did not appear to decrease the quantity the cutter contained to any appreciable extent, bale they, as they baled, their hardest!

Gradually, however, the after thwart became clear.

"Hooray!" exclaimed Bob. "We're gaining on it."

This inspired them with renewed strength; and, after nearly an hour's hard work, they had so lessened the water that only a small portion now remained washing about under the bottom boards of the boat, which, recovering all her old buoyancy, floated again with a high freeboard, light as a cork, above the surface of the sea, instead of being level with it as before.

"That's a good job done!" said Dick. "I wish that theer murderin' shep hadn't a bruk our mast; fur, we'd soon been all right!"

"While you're about it, Dick," said Bob, "you might, just as well, wish she hadn't carried the mast and boom away with her. I don't believe they've left us anything!"

No, the colliding ship had made a 'clean sweep' of all their spars and rigging and everything; hardly a rope's end remaining attached to the cutter, beyond a part of the mainsheet and a bit of the forestay, which latter was hanging down from the bowsprit, the only spar the yacht had left.

Not a single thing of all her deck-fittings, either, had the little vessel to the good; even her tiller had been wrenched off and the rudder smashed.

Nor were there any oars left in the little craft; though, even if there had been, the yacht was too heavy for boys like Bob and Dick to have made her move at the most infinitesimal rate of speed.

It is true, there was the old gaff-topsail still in the forepeak, as well as a spare jib; but they had nothing to spread them out to the wind with, or affix them to.

They were, in fact, oarless, sailless, helpless!

"I don't see what we can do," said Bob, when they had

looked over all the boat, in case something perchance might have escaped their notice. "We can only hope and pray!"

"Aye, do 'ee pray, Master Bob," replied Dick eagerly. "P'r'aps God 'll hear us and send us help!"

So, then and there the two boys knelt down together side by side in the battered boat, that drifted about at the mercy of the wind and sea, imploring the aid of Him who heeds those who call upon Him for succour, in no wise refusing them or turning a deaf ear to their prayers!

By and by, as if in answer to their earnest supplications, the day dawned; when, the mist, which yet lingered over the water, hanging about here and there in little patches, like so many floating islands, was either swallowed up by the sea or absorbed into the air, as if by magic.

Bob and Dick now got some idea as to the points of the compass, even if they were not able to tell precisely where they were; for, as the day advanced, a rosy tinge crept upwards over a far off quarter of the horizon which they knew instinctively to be the east, the birthplace of all light!

This tint, almost like a blush, spread quickly over the sky, reaching away to the north and again south, coming full in both their faces and making them glow.

The bright hue then gradually melted into a ruddier tone, which first darkened into purple and red and then rapidly changed to a greenish sort of neutral tone that, after an interval, finally became merged into the pure ultramarine of the zenith; for, the heavens were now as clear as a bell, no mist or fog or cloud obscuring the expanse of the empyrean.

A sort of golden vapour then, all of a sudden, flooded the east, which in another second gave place to the red rays of the crimson sun; though the latter did not seem so much to rise, but rather appeared to Bob, who was watching intently the various changes that occurred, to jump in an instant above the sea, glorifying it far and near with its presence and warming it into life.

R

This warmth soon cheered the boys, as the light banished the despondent feelings inseparable, as a rule, from darkness; and, beyond that, the death like stillness around, which had previously added to their fears, was banished by the new stir and movement observable in everything.

Previously, the sea had risen and fallen tumidly, as if Father Neptune had been asleep and its monotonous pulsation was caused by his deep, long-drawn breathing; but, now, it crisped and sparkled in the sunshine, whilst its surface was broken by innumerable little wavelets, like curls, that grew into swell-crested billows anon, and, later on still, into great rolling waves as the wind got up   this blowing steadily from the eastwards first and then veering round south, following the course of the orb whose heat gave it being.

Nor was inanimate nature only stirring.

Grey and silver sea gulls hovered over the little cutter, all sweeping down curiously every now and then to see what the boys were doing there in that mastless and oarless boat out on the wide waters; and, presently, a shoal of mackerel rose round about them, so thickly that Dick thought he could scoop up some in the buckets, only the fish were too wary and dived down below the surface the moment he stretched his arm out over the side beyond his reach.

A couple of porpoises, too, swam by, playing leap-frog again; and, after these, a much larger monster, which might possibly have been a grampus, though Bob could tell nothing about it, not knowing what it was.   The movements of all these, with the constantly-changing appearance of the sea, now blue, now green, now brown, as some cloud shadow passed over it, made up a varied panorama such as neither of the two lads ever saw or thought of before!

Ships, also, hove in sight and disappeared on the horizon, their white sails gleaming out in the far off distance; one moment high in the air as if bound skywards, the next sinking into the curving depths of the sea.

Now and again, too, the smoke-wreath of some passing steamer, coasting along more speedily than the sailing craft, would sacrilegiously blot the blue of the heavens!

But, all the while, though the distant ships might sail along to their haven, and the steamers shape shorter courses to their port independent of wind and tide alike, the poor dismasted, dismantled little yacht was the sport of all alike; first setting down Channel with the ebb, as if going out on a cruise into the wide Atlantic, and then again up Channel with the flood towards Dover.

The boat was ever drifting and tossed about ever, like a battered shuttlecock, by the battledore currents, some four of which contend for the mastery throughout the livelong day in that wonderful waterway, the English Channel; two always setting east, relieving each other in turn, and two west, with a cross tide coming atop of them, twice in every twenty-four hours, trying fruitlessly to soothe the differences of the quarrelsome quartette!

CHAPTER XXVI.

DESPAIR!

"How hot it be, Master Bob!" said Dick, when the sun had climbed so high that he seemed right overhead, sending down his rays vertically and making it so warm that the boys began to perspire, while they were tormented with thirst. "I be parched wi' drout and could swaller a gallon o' spring wutter if I hed the chance!"

"I say, let us have a swim," suggested Bob. "I've heard it will relieve a person suffering from thirst; and, besides, I believe it will do us both good and freshen us up."

"All right, Master Bob," said Dick somewhat hesitatingly, in reply to this proposition. "But, ain't it deep here?"

"Deep! What does that matter?" replied Bob lightly. "Why, Dick, you silly fellow, you forget we always used to swim out every morning into deep water. Ah, I forget, I forget! Oh, mother, my mother!"

The poor boy broke down utterly again at this point, it having suddenly flashed across his memory that his former swims from the beach were things of the past; and that he might never see his mother or any of the home folk again.

No, never, ah, never again!

Dick, however, once more comforted him, ceasing to dwell on his own pangs of thirst; although the lad's tongue had swollen to such a size that it seemed too big for his mouth, and his lips were all parched and cracked.

A little later, when Bob had become more composed again, his idea of a bathe was carried out, the boys making use of their solitary rope, the end of the broken forestay that was hanging from the bowsprit, to climb back into the boat after they had had a dip alongside.

They were not able to swim far, being incapable of much exertion ; but the plunge alone and the immersion in the water while holding to the rope's end refreshed them greatly, making them feel stronger, in addition to allaying their burning thirst.

Still, when this great longing was quenched, they were tortured with hunger, Dick actually tearing off one of the soles of his boots and setting to work gnawing it.

Bob kept up his spirits so far as to make fun of this, chaffing his companion and saying that he preferred the way in which the Captain served up his soles to Dick's !

"Ah," said the other in reply, "I wonder what the good Cap'en 'ud think if he seed us now ? "

"Why, that we were two unfortunate fellows !" replied Bob, becoming grave again in an instant. "I'm sure he would pity us from the bottom of his heart ! "

Thus the long day wore on ; although, it seemed as if it would never end !

However, when night came round again, they wished they had yet the day ; it was so dark, so dreary, so eerie, pitching and rolling about there, carried hither and thither as the tide listed, with never a vista of the wished for land, with never a sound but the sobbing sea.

Yet, it was wonderful how the boys encouraged each other to bear up and be hopeful, in spite of everything.

Whenever, in the early morning previously and during the day in their respective sufferings, one or the other grew despondent Dick cheered Bob and Bob cheered Dick, as the case might be.

Then, somehow or other, the principal portion of the cheering-up work was borne by Dick ; the very brightness and look of everything, even while he noticed them, seeming to have the effect of depressing Bob's spirits by some unknown association or connection with those at home.

At night, however, it was Bob's turn to sustain the drooping courage of Dick, who, like most country bred lads, was intensely superstitious, fancying the darkness to swarm with ghosts and goblins, who were on the watch to devour him; the boy, while bearing up bravely against palpable privations and open dangers, staring them in the face, from which grown men would have quailed, was now affected by silly fears which a baby would have blushed to own!

All through the wearisome hours of the dragging night, whose minutes were as iron and hours like lead, he was constantly starting up in nervous terror; the moan of the sea, the cry of some belated sea-gull, the plunge of a fish in the water, nay even the creaking of the boat's own timbers, with each and all of which Dick was perfectly familiar, alike arousing his frenzied alarm.

It was, "Lawks, Master Bob! what be this now?" throughout the terrible interval that elapsed between the fading of the twilight on the one day and sunrise on the next. "Lor', what's that?"

And, that next day!

The boys were weaker then, for very nearly eight-and forty hours had elapsed since they had been on board the cutter; forty-eight hours without food, without any regular sleep, without any real rest even, as their attention was always kept on the alert, while, all the time, the peril they were in was sufficient alone to have crushed their every energy!

Hope, undying hope that had kept them up so long, now left them at last. Who could hope against such continual disappointment, with ships all around them sometimes and yet never a one to come near where they floated and drifted and gave way to their despair?

Towards the evening of this day Dick got very weak.

Strange to say, although brought up in the country and
accustomed, probably, all his early life, at any rate, to exposure
and hard living, Dick was not able to bear up against their
present sufferings by any means so well as Bob, who, on this
third night of their being adrift, was yet full of vitality!

It was in vain for him, though, to try and reanimate Dick,
who, hopeless, and almost helpless, lay down in the bottom of
the boat, only asking to be left alone to die.

"I'm a-dying, Master Bob," he gasped out faintly, when
Bob tried to raise him up. "Let me be; let me be!"

"Dying, nonsense," repeated Bob, pretending to joke about
it; though, truth to say, he felt in little joking mood then,
being almost as weak as his companion. "You are worth
twenty dead men yet, as the old Captain would say!"

But, in spite of all his encouraging words, Dick grew
gradually weaker and weaker; until, towards midnight, his
breathing became so very faint that Bob could hardly feel it,
though kneeling down close beside him and with his face
touching that of poor Dick.

"I'm a—dying Master Bob,' he whispered, in such low
accents that Bob had to bend down his ear close to his mouth
to hear what he said. "I bees a dying—Mas ter Bob.
I knows—I—be! I—hears—the—h'angels a flapping on
their wings! I knows they be a coming for—me! God—
bless—'ee, Mas ter—Bob! Ah if—'ee ever get 'shore—
'gain tell—Cap'—I didn't—mean—no—'arm!"

Soon after faltering out these broken words, Dick fell back
insensible in the bottom of the boat.

"Oh, Dick, poor Dick, good Dick!" sobbed out Bob,
throwing himself down beside him on the floor of the boat's
little cabin and bursting into an agony of tears. "It is I who
have killed you. But for me, you would never have been
here at all! Poor, brave Dick, you saved my life, and in
return I've killed you!"

The torture of mind in which he now was on seeing, as

he thought, Dick dead before him, coupled with all he had already gone through, but of which he had taken little heed while he had his comrade to console, now coming together affected Bob's mind.

He began to wander in delirium, imagining himself not only safe ashore, but in his London home, amid all the surroundings to which he had been accustomed before coming to Southsea and to this sad extremity.

He thought it was Sunday and that he was going to church with his mother and Nell; and that he was late, as usual, and they were calling him to hurry.

"I'm coming, I'm coming!" he screamed out in such a shrill voice, attenuated by famine, as hardly to be recognized as human, so shrill that it startled the sea gulls hovering over the boat. "I'm coming! There's lots of time, the bells are ringing still! The bells are ringing, I hear them! Ring—ring—ring—I hear—I hear——I "

Then he, too, lost consciousness and fell, like a log, insensible, across the body of poor Dick; the far off bell which he had fancied to be ringing miles and miles distant from where the boat was floating in the Channel, being the last echo that sounded in his ears as he fainted away.

But, there was reason in his madness.

A bell was ringing; and ringing too realistically not to be real!

CHAPTER XXVII.

ON THE CASQUETTES.

Bob's hearing was not at fault, this sense of his remaining perfect though his mind was wandering; and so, the unwonted sound that fell upon his ear had got woven amongst his delirious fancies.

It was, without doubt, a real bell, which if it might not summon pious folk to prayer, yet fulfilled almost as sacred a duty, warning, as it did, poor mariners of impending peril and so answering the petition oft put up 'for those travelling by sea.'

This bell belonged to the lighthouse tower erected on the highest peak of the Casquettes, a terrible group of rocks jutting out into the Channel, just off the French coast hard by Alderney, some six miles to the north-west of which island they lie. Rocks that are cruel and relentless as the surges that sweep over them in stormy weather, and which are so quaintly named from their helmet, or 'casque'-like resemblance — rocks, concerning which the poet Swinburne has sung in his eloquent verse, that breathes the very spirit of the sea in depicting the strife of the elements :—

> " From the depths of the waters that lighten and darken,
> With change everlasting of life and of death,
> Where hardly by morn if the lulled ear hearken
> It hears the sea's as a tired child's breath,

Where hardly by night, if an eye dare scan it,
   The storm lets shipwreck be seen or heard,
As the reefs to the waves and the foam to the granite
   Respond one merciless word,

Sheer seen and far, in the sea's life heaven,
   A sea mew's flight from the wild sweet land,
White plumed with foam, if the wind wake, seven
   Black helms, as of warriors that stir, not stand,
From the depths that abide and the waves that environ
   Seven rocks rear heads that the midnight masks ;
And the strokes of the swords of the storm are as iron
   On the steel of the wave worn casques.

Be night's dark word as the word of a wizard,
   Be the word of dawn as a god's glad word,
Like heads of the spirits of darkness visored
   That see not for ever, nor ever have heard,
These bashets, plumed as for fight or plumeless,
   Crowned by the storm and by storm discrowned,
Keep word of the lists where the dead lie tombless
   And the tale of them is not found ! "

Hither the boat had drifted in the course of the three days
that had elapsed since she had been first becalmed off Spit
head, or rather between the Nab and Warner lights ; for, it was
then that the wind had dropped, leaving her at the mercy of
the stream, going whither the current willed.

She had pursued a most erratic course, however, to reach
this point.

To commence with, she had floated on the ebb tide, which
for two hours after high water runs south by west, out into
the Channel past the Isle of Wight ; the wind, slight as it was,
that subsequently sprung up from the eastward, to which point
it had veered after the sea-fog had risen, combined with the
westward action of the tideway, making the little vessel take
almost a straight course across the stream of the current
towards the French coast.

When about midway, however, she got into a second channel
current, which swept her nearer and nearer to Cape La Hogue.

Then, again, when still some miles out from the land, yet another current took charge of her, bringing her within the influence of the strong indraught which runs into the Gulf of St Malo; by which, finally, she was wafted, in a circular way, up to 'the Caskets,' or 'Casquettes,' to adopt the proper French version.

Here she had arrived at the time of Bob's delirium, drifting in closer and closer to the rocks, on which the cutter would probably have been dashed to pieces and her fragments possibly picked up anon on the opposite side of the Atlantic, had not fate intervened.

It was in this wise.

The little cutter drifted in near the rocks while it was still early morning; and the reason for the bell on the lighthouse ringing was because some of the mist, or fog, that had been blown across the Channel, yet lingered in the vicinity, as if loth to leave altogether the waters over which it loved to brood.

When, however, the rays of the bright morning sun sent this nightmare of a mist to the right-about, a small French fishing lugger might have been seen working out towards the offing from St. Malo, giving the 'Casquettes' a pretty wide berth you may be sure; those who have to do with seafaring matters across Channel knowing full well of the dangerous race that runs by the fatal rocks, ever seeking in its malice to engulph passing crafts and bear them away to destruction!

Two men were in the lugger; one, as usual, attending to the helm, the other minding the sheets and sitting midway between the bows and stern of the vessel, so as to be handy when required and thus save unnecessary locomotion.

Sailors, it may here be mentioned in confidence, especially those hailing from la belle France, never give themselves more trouble than they can help; which philosophic way of going through life might be studied to advantage, perhaps, by some shore folk!

These mariners, consequently, were taking it very easy, the
one forward sitting on the break of the 'fo'c's'le' and smoking
a pipe, there not being much to do in the rope hauling or
letting go, as the lugger was only creeping lazily along through
the almost still water with the aid of the light breeze then
blowing.

Presently, this latter gentleman, casting a casual eye around,
spied the poor mastless, derelict looking little yacht, rolling
about in the heavy tide race that was taking her on to the rocks.

Instantly, sailor like, he became all animation; taking his
pipe out of his mouth and shouting out to his fellow voyager
astern with much gesticulation.

"Tiens, Jacques!" he cried, "voila un bâteau qui courre
sur les brisants!"

"Quoi?" carelessly asked the other. "Vous moquez
vous!"

But the one who had first spoken repeated what he'd said,
to the effect that there was 'a boat drifting on the rocks, and
likely to be wrecked.'

'Jacques,' however, as his comrade had called him, did not
seem much interested in the matter, merely shrugging his
shoulders, implying that it was 'none of his concern.'

"C'est bien," said he. "Pas mon affaire."

The other, though, seemed more taken with the little craft,
climbing up a couple of steps into the rigging in order to have
a better look at her.

He had not gazed a moment when his excitement became
intensified.

"Mon Dieu, Jacques!" he sang out. "Il y a quelqu'un à
bord! Deux personnes, et des garçons je crois; mais, ils sont
morts!"

"Pas possible," cried the helmsman, showing a little more
interest. "Really?"

"Parbleu, c'est vrai! Vire que nous nous en approchions."

"C'est fait," exclaimed Jacques, now quite as much excited

as the other, and eager to rescue any one in peril or distress, as every sailor of every nationality always is—that is, a true sailor. "Starboard it is!"

"Babord!" cried out Antoine, as the helmsman called him, telling the latter he was to put the tiller over. "Port."

Jacques replied by a counter order.

"Toi, Antoine," shouted he, "lâche la grande voile!" meaning him to 'slacken off the mainsheets;' whereupon the lugger was brought alongside the wreck of the cutter.

Our friend Antoine, without wasting a moment, at once stepped on board, exclaiming, "Tenez bon dessus Hold on."

The man was shocked at what he saw, the dead bodies, as he thought, of Bob and Dick lying across each other on the floor of the little cabin, half in and half out of which the boys were exposed to his view at the first glance.

"Pauvres garçons!" he cried in a husky voice, wiping away a tear that sprang unbidden to his eye, with the characteristic ready emotional sympathy of his countrymen. "Pauvres garçons."

Jacques, who was a little longer in coming to inspect the derelict, hearing what his companion said, called out for further information.

"De quel pays sont ils?" he asked. "Can you tell their nationality?"

"Anglais, sans doute!" was his reply. "Je le crois par leur air."

This made Jacques prick up his ears.

"Comment?" said he; and, without waiting to hear anything else he, too, jumped down into the boat. "Anglais? Mon Dieu!"

Jacques was a man of common-sense; so, instead of contenting himself with staring at the apparently lifeless boys, as Antoine did, he bent down to see whether they yet breathed.

"Bête! Quant aux enfants, ils ne sont pas plus morts que

toi ou moi !" he sang out indignantly. "You fool! The
boys are no more dead than you or me."

But Jacques was a kind hearted man as well as one
possessed of common sense

So, under his directions, he and Antoine between them
transshipped the apparently lifeless but still animate forms of
Bob and Dick from the wrecked cutter into the fo'c's'le of the
lugger, where a charcoal fire was smouldering in a small stove
on which simmered a saucepan containing something savoury,
judging by its smell.

Here Jacques proceeded to rub the bodies of the boys
alternately with a piece of flannel dipped in spirit, which he
first held in front of the stove to warm ; Maître Antoine,
meanwhile, attending to the navigation of the lugger and
guarding lest she should run upon the Casquettes, or get led
astray out of her course by Alderney Race, a current of these
regions which, like the St. Malo stream, is not to be played
with when the wind's on shore !

Not content with merely rubbing them down with the spirit,
Jacques presently varied his external application of some
brandy, a remedy with him for most complaints to which flesh
is heir, by administering to each boy in turn a few drops in-
ternally of the spirit, forcing it dextrously between their lips as
soon as respiration was restored and they began to breathe with
some regularity ; Bob, however, progressing much more rapidly
than Dick, whose pulse obstinately remained feeble and barely
perceptible, while the author of all the mischief was nearly
all right.

Bob opened his eyes almost as soon as he tasted the
brandy.

"Where am I ?" he stammered out, gazing round the little
fo'c's'le of the lugger in wonder. " Where am I ?"

CHAPTER XXVIII

JIM CRADDOCK.

"Ah, le petit bon homme vit encore!" cried Antoine, hearing the voice and bending over from his seat on the after-thwart, being anxious as to the condition of the patients to whom Jacques was ministering. "Donnez lui encore d'eau de vie, mon ami!"

Jacques thereupon repeated the dose of brandy to Bob, who closed his eyes again and leant back, the spirit and the sound of the strange language, with the queer surroundings that had met his gaze on looking round the fo'c's'le of the lugger, making him believe he was still in a dream.

"Where am I?" he presently repeated, rousing up again. "Where am I?"

"In France," replied Jacques in English as good as his own, smiling as he spoke. "At least, you're aboard a French vessel; and, that's as good as being in France!"

"But, you are English," replied Bob freely. "You are English, eh?"

"Yes, I'm English," answered the other. "But, you had better not talk now. Wait till after you've taken some nice soup which I've got cooking here that will put new strength into you, and then we'll tell each other all about ourselves."

He then left Bob to attend to Dick, whom it took con-siderably longer to bring round; although by administering a few drops of brandy at intervals, varied by an occasional

spoonful every now and then of the savoury soup from the
saucepan on the fire, which was really a regular French stew,
Dick became ultimately, as Bob already was through the same
regimen, much better the poor boy now recovering his
consciousness and being able to speak.

The two invalids were then put to bed comfortably in a
couple of bunks on either side of the fo'c's'le; while the
lugger, whose name, by the way, was the *Jeanne d'Arc*, reached
over towards the English coast, to see what fishing she could
get in those prohibited waters.

Late in the afternoon, Bob and Dick both woke up
refreshed; when, each had another jorum of the savoury
soup, which Bob said subsequently was the nicest thing, he
believed, he had ever tasted in his life !

The boys then, feeling quite well, so to speak, went on to
tell the kind sailors all about their adventures, Bob, of course,
being the principal spokesman.

"Ah !" observed Jacques. "You are living at Portsmouth,
then ? "

"No, I've only been stopping there for the season," replied
Bob. "But, I like it very much !"

"It's my native place, sir. I was born there !" cried
Jacques. "My father was in the English navy; and my
old mother, who is yet alive, has a house of her own in the
town ! It's only through my having married a French wife
that has took me over here along with the Parlyvoos !"

"How strange !" exclaimed Bob. "Why, we went to see
only the other day a Mrs. Craddock, who has a daughter who's
very ill, that my aunt Polly goes to see ; and she told us she
had a son married to a French girl and he was living at St.
Malo !"

"Why, that's me !" cried Jacques; although 'Jacques'
no longer to us. "I'm Jim Craddock, and the old lady that
you saw is my mother ! My word ! this is a rum start !"

After the curious coincidence of Bob and Dick being

rescued by the son of 'the old egg woman,' as they always called her, between whom and themselves Rover had in the original instance scraped an acquaintance, nothing would content Jim Craddock but that he must bear up at once for Portsmouth, and restore Bob and Dick to those who bewailed them as lost, as well as return the battered little yacht, which the lugger had in tow astern, to her proper owner.

The meeting between Bob and his parents is too sacred a matter to touch upon here; but, it is easy enough to imagine the delight of those welcoming one coming back to them as it were from the dead; Dick, too, being received like another son.

As for Nellie, her joy was so great at beholding again her brother Bob, whom she loved so dearly, that she laughed till she cried and then fainted; while, on her recovery, she laughed and cried again, though she did not faint a second time !

But, you should only have seen Rover when he saw his young master.

Sarah, 'the good Sarah,' said that she would never forget "the way in which that there dog went on as long as she lived !"

Of course, it can be well understood that there were no ill feelings between Bob and the retriever anent the desertion of the latter from the cutter on the day of the boys' terribly punished escapade; though, the mystery of the dog's swimming ashore so strangely on that memorable occasion, it may be mentioned here, was never cleared up !

The Captain, it must be said, behaved much more unconcernedly than Rover.

"By Jove ! I told you they'd turn up all right !" said he, chuckling away at such a rate that he could hardly stop to get out the next words. "I always told you so, didn't I, ma'am now, didn't I ?"

"My gracious goodness, Cap'en Dresser, why you were the first to give them up!" cried Mrs. Gilmour laughing. "Sure, I never did see such a man!"

At this the Captain chuckled still more; and he then told Dick, whom every one was as glad almost to see amongst them again as they were to see Bob, that he intended, when he got strong enough, to send him into the navy so as to prevent him from going to sea again!

After a few days' rest, in order to recuperate from the effects of the strain on all their nerves, Bob's father said they must all go back to town, their holiday limit being at length reached.

Bob and Nellie, on this intimation, began a round of leave-taking which would well-nigh have consumed another long holiday, to have been carried out in accordance with their intention; for they wanted to say 'good-bye!' to all their favourite haunts and many acquaintances of the animate and inanimate world in turn.

Yes, they must see once more the halcyon spot where they caught the Pandalus, that gem of their aquarium; they had to bid adieu to Mrs. Craddock's cottage, and the old lady herself and daughter; and again inspect the place where the unfortunate *Bembridge Belle* was wrecked.

They had to give a handshake, too, to their friend Hellyer and all his fellow coastguardsmen; besides having to go over the Captain's yacht, which had been sparred and rigged anew, the little *Zephyr* looking now 'as fresh as paint again' after her eventful vicissitudes adrift in the Channel.

Aye, they paid farewell visits to every one and everything, and then wanted to begin over again, it was so hard to part with them all!

At last, however, the ordeal was accomplished; and all their goods and chattels and new acquisitions, especially the aquarium and its various occupants, that terrible Mesembryanthemum included, being properly packed up and labelled, behold the party one fine morning at the railway-station on their way to London as soon as the train should start!

Here Rover, despite his frantic howls on escaping his former prison, was snugly incarcerated in the guard's van; when the others, after exchanging last words with Mrs. Gilmour and the Captain, entered a saloon-carriage which had been reserved for them for the journey, Bob and Nell, it may be taken for granted, being the last to get in, loth to leave 'aunt Polly' and 'that dear old sailor' who had won their hearts, as well as say 'good-bye' to Dick, the whilom uninvited guest of their first eventful journey 'Down the line,' and subsequent faithful companion of Bob in his wonderful adventures by sea and land.

CHAPTER XXIX.

THERE was a warning shriek from the engine's steam whistle, as if it were impatient to be off, and angrily wanting to know why it was kept thus unnecessarily waiting.

Following up the scream of the whistle came the last cling! clang! of the railway porter's bell, telling belated passengers that 't'me' was 'up.'

Next ensued the scrambling and scurrying of the aforesaid belated passengers, who always appear to put off making up their minds as to whether they shall start or not until the last moment of grace has expired.

Then, finally, after much clanging of doors upon the backs of those thus nearly left behind, with a snort of indignation and defiance of things in general, and late passengers in particular, the panting, puffing, fuming iron horse metaphorically and practically 'put his shoulder to the wheel,' lugging the rolling, rumbling, heavy train out of the station Londonwards, with a 'puff puff, pant pant!' from his hoarse throat, answered by the groans and creaks of sympathy from the laden carriages and the clinking rattle of the coupling-chains, as they drew taut from the tension, lending a sort of cymbal like accompaniment to the noisy chorus.

Bob and Nellie watched their aunt and the Captain standing on the platform, waving their handkerchiefs from the window of their compartment, which they found it a hard matter to shove their heads through two at a time, until a bend in the line swept aunt Polly, Captain Dresser, platform and all out of sight.

Then, sitting down disconsolately in their seats, Bob, who, of course, thought it unmanly to cry, screwed himself up in a corner in default of that alleviation of his misery, looking the very picture of woe; while poor Nell, being a girl and freed from such Spartan obligations, sought refuge from her sorrow in silent tears.

"Now, Nellie dear," said her mother reprovingly, "you mustn't be so foolish! Of course, I can make allowance for your sorrow at leaving Southsea, where you have been so happy; but these partings, dearie, will come some time or other, and, besides, you know, both aunt Polly and Captain Dresser have promised to come up to us at Christmas, so you'll see them again soon."

This made poor Nell try to compose herself; and presently she smiled through her tears, exchanging reminiscences of the past few weeks of their enjoyment by the sea with Bob, who also, after a time, shook off his grumpiness the feeling that they were going 'home' again, by and by overcoming their depression at leaving, perhaps for ever, the scene of so many delights and such a terrible ordeal at the last!

"I wonder how old Blinkie will look?" said Bob, trying to picture the jackdaw as he would appear when conscious of his owner's return; and then, deciding in his own mind that the only tribute of affection which he might expect would, most probably, be a sharp peck from Blinkie's beak, he added, "I dare say he won't remember me at all!"

Nellie's thoughts were directed to Snuffles the asthmatic cat, her great pet; and she believed that highly trained animal would not only know her again after her long absence, but would certainly express her satisfaction in a much more endearing manner, if not quite so touching or pointed!

Thus the two beguiled the tedium of their journey; and, such was their joy on the train's arrival in town at last, that no one would have believed them to be the same Bob and Nell who had given way so greatly to their grief on leaving the seaside!

Naturally, Rover's pleasure at being released from his temporary imprisonment in the guard's van could be easily accounted for ; but, the way in which, when he got back to his old home, he walked deliberately to the bottom of the garden in perfect remembrance of the spot where he had buried his last bone before going away, showed that he, at least, did not forget so easily.

The dog's memory, too, was equally green concerning his old friends Snuffles and Blinkie, as that of his young master and mistress ; for he so sniffed and snuffed Snuffles in his exuberance at seeing her again, that he seriously disarranged her fur, while he allowed the jackdaw to peck at his legs and even his nose, without the slightest attempt at retaliation !

Not long after their getting back, Bob and Nell had a great joke all to themselves.

Their father and mother were sending down an invalid chair for Mrs. Craddock's daughter, one in which she could be taken out into the open air it was a thing for which the poor girl had always been longing, as aunt Polly managed to find out for them when they were thinking of what sort of return they could make for the kind way in which the old lady's son had rescued Bob, Jim himself refusing any recompense whatever, despite all the barrister's and Captain Dresser's efforts.

So, this parcel being about to be dispatched 'Down the line,' Master Bob and Miss Nell bethought them that they would send a present too ; not only to Dick, who was always in their minds, but one also for whom do you think ?

Why, for Sarah, 'the good Sarah !'

And, what do you think the present was, eh ?

You would never guess.

Well, a nice little loaf of bread and an ounce packet of the best black tea, both packed up in a very pretty box that also contained a remarkably smart cap, with ribbons of a colour such as the soul of Sarah loved.

Nor was this all,

On the lid of the box was an elaborate device in hieroglyphic characters, which could be readily understood when properly explained by the young designers, detailing the leading incidents of a celebrated picnic in the woods which once occurred; although, possibly the uninitiated might experience some little difficulty at first in discriminating between what were meant for the figures of the principal personages of the story and the objects of still life depicted in the drawing, though otherwise it was an admirable work of art.

Regarding the copy of verses also pinned on to the box, which the device in question was intended to illustrate, there could be no mistake; the verses, indeed, being a replica of an original poem, preserved in the Bobo Nellonian archives and entitled, 'Sarah's forget me nots,' wherewith the reader has been already made acquainted.

The parcel was duly dispatched down to Southsea; but, though Nellie subsequently wrote a nice little letter to the Captain in her own nice handwriting, large and legible, such as the old sailor could read comfortably without spectacles, wherein she mentioned all the latest news of her aquarium tenants, telling how the hermit crab had distrained for his rent on a young lobster who had cast off his shell, and that a small skate objected to the ice, she could learn nothing of how 'the good Sarah' received her present.

Nor could Bob gain any information on the subject from aunt Polly, to whom he sent a long epistle bearing on the same momentous theme.

Both had to wait to have their curiosity satisfied until their aunt Polly and Captain Dresser came up to London at Christmastide; when at length the two of them managed to worm the secret out of the Captain.

The old sailor had been giving them all the news about those they had known down at Southsea; how Dick had at last been accepted for the navy and entered as a second class boy on board the *St. Vincent*, being bound to make a full able bodied sailor in time; and how Hellyer had got a little pension in addition to his pay, as he was now 'chief officer' of the coastguard; after which, the Captain at last referred to Sarah, 'the good Sarah!'

"By Jove!" said he, "I shall never forget that night your box came! I was playing cribbage with your aunt Polly— and she cheated me, too, by the same token, in the fuss that occurred on opening the parcel, by scoring 'two for his heels,' when it only should have been 'one for his nob.' You never saw such a disgraceful thing done in your life, really a most barefaced piece of cheating!"

"Oh!" exclaimed Mrs. Gilmour. "Sure, I'm listening to all those stories you are telling! Won't I pay you out, too, by and by, when you come round to 'The Moorings' again. You just wait and see!"

"I assure you, ma'am, it's a fact," persisted the Captain unblushingly, his little eyes blinking with fun under his bushy eyebrows, which were going up and down at a fine rate, I can tell you. "I saw you move the pegs, ma'am, when you thought I wasn't looking!"

"But, what did Sarah say?" asked Nellie, clinging to the old sailor and trying to attract his attention to the point at issue, from which he seemed sadly inclined to stray. "What did the good Sarah say?"

"Eh?" said he, cocking his head on one side in his most bird-like fashion and pretending not to understand his questioner. "Eh?"

"Oh, do tell us!" cried Bob, catching hold of him by the other arm. "How did 'the good Sarah' look?"

"Why," chuckled the Captain, bringing down his old malacca cane with a thump on the floor. "Jolly, my boy, jolly!"

THE END.